BLACK CURTAIN (Book #16)

BOOKS IN THE BRIDGE & SWORD SERIES - COMPLETE
(RECOMMENDED READING ORDER)

To the city of San Francisco, which will probably always feel like home, whether I'm there or not.

PROLOGUE
PARTNERS

"Y ou know where he is right now?" she demanded.

Lara St. Maarten, CEO and majority shareholder of Archangel Enterprises, didn't look back as she spoke the question out loud.

Her eyes remained forward, out of focus. She gazed over a pristine, Central Park view, but her companion doubted she was seeing it. From the direction of her eyes, she watched a procession of newly-reintroduced, genetically-designed, white tail deer.

Brick watched a few of those deer stop and look around.

He saw them blink at the lights rising out of the darkness in the surrounding city.

A few paused to drink at a nearby pond. One rubbed its head and back against one of the park's elm trees. Most lowered their heads, placidly grazing on the genetically-designed grass.

The scene was idyllic, picturesque.

Everything about it was man-made.

Utterly fake, in the old parlance.

"Right now?" St. Maarten repeated. "Do you know where he is right now?"

At Brick's continued silence, she turned to stare at the

vampire. He perched easily in a white leather chair just behind her, gripping the end of an ivory-tipped cane.

"Do you know where he is *right now,* vampire?" she asked a third time, clearly expecting her repeated attempts to eventually elicit an answer. "Were you told where he's gone? Did they inform you prior to his leaving?"

"I follow the boxing trades, yes."

"Why was this allowed?" she demanded. "Don't you have pull with Farlucci? With the other big promoters in the underground boxing circuit?"

Brick arched a dark eyebrow.

He stared up at her unflinchingly.

"Don't you have pull with the NYPD?" he asked drily.

Another silence fell between them.

Nothing in Lara St. Maarten's expression changed.

She continued to look agitated, even as she remained standing in front of the long window of her penthouse apartment. She shifted her weight on her high-heeled shoes, her arms crossed over her chest. Her fingers gripped her biceps tightly as she watched the light fail, as the virtual advertisements gradually lit up the skyline behind the darker swath of park.

"I thought they had to go through you," she muttered, seemingly as much to herself as to him. "I thought they more or less needed your approval to do any of it—"

"Were you expecting me to 'forbid' this tournament?"

"Of course I was!" She turned her head to glare at him a second time. "Why wouldn't you? Don't you realize how risky it is, him going back there?"

When Brick didn't visibly react that time, either, she scowled back at the window.

"I don't understand why you have let this charade go on for as long as it has." She fingered her severe bangs to arrange their line, her lipsticked mouth firm. "It's ludicrous. You should have told him years ago…"

Brick didn't respond to that, either.

Clearly, she'd meant for him to answer her implied question, however.

When he didn't, she again sharpened her voice.

"*Why* didn't you tell him?" She re-folded her arms, looking away from the transparent, curved wall encircling most of her living room. "Just how long do you think you can keep this up? How long do we expect to hide the truth from him?"

"We?" he asked mildly.

"Do not pretend this doesn't concern me!" she snapped. "Do you really want to have to kill him? Or worse? Do you want him out there on his own somewhere... going rogue in some way... maybe even figuring out his own way through the portals?"

She gestured sharply towards the window.

Brick wasn't sure what she was gesturing *towards* exactly.

But he got the general idea.

"You heard that old seer... the telekinetic. Clearly they'd be on *his* side, if they ever came back here. Do you really want to go to war with *that?*"

Brick watched her warily.

Was it possible the human was afraid?

It wasn't an emotion he normally associated with Lara St. Maarten.

Whatever her other... eccentricities... fear was not one he had yet encountered.

"It would never come to that," Brick assured her carefully.

"The old telekinetic already *said* he would pass on the message to the Blacks. He already *said* they would visit." She faced him directly for the first time. "We're damned lucky he didn't tell the two of them anything specific in the short time they spoke—"

"I'm aware of that," Brick warned.

She opened her mouth.

Seeing to think better of whatever she'd been about to say, she closed it again.

She stood there, shaking her head, her lips firm.

3

Brick watched her from that obscenely expensive, real-leather chair.

One of his hands continued to rest on his even more expensive ivory-tipped cane, an accessory he'd now brought with him through several lifetimes, so to speak—several different incarnations in this odd mélange of opening and closing doors.

A small smile played at his lips, but it did not reach his eyes.

He studied her profile carefully. He noted the way her severe, auburn bob framed her nearly vampire-pale face.

She truly had riveting eyes—green, emerald-stone eyes, which stood out even more over a hard, dark-painted red mouth.

She would make a glorious vampire.

He had offered the change to her once.

She had, sadly, declined.

Brick had mixed feelings about her decision still.

"Which truth would that be, dear friend?" he asked mildly. "What has got your sexy, deliciously silky, handmade designer panties in such a twist, my darling pet?"

Her green eyes glimmered faintly in the near-sunset light.

As he watched, they grew stone-like, losing any pretense of the mask she wore for most people, most of the time. Even him. She wore it for him most of the time, too.

Now, seeing past it, his predator grew aroused.

He liked this in her.

He had always liked it.

"Don't play games with me vampire," she warned.

Brick let the smile play out wider on his mouth.

"I don't know why you'd assume my query to be in bad faith." Flipping his fingers up off the cane's end, he shrugged. "We are, after all, keeping so many things from so *many* people, pet. It is immensely difficult to keep track of them all."

Lifting his eyebrows expressively, he pursed his lips, imitating an exaggerated human affectation for thought.

"I could just as easily ask you *who* you mean, my dear... as in, which of the many people in either of our employ we are lying to *presently*. The question would be just as legit. Further, if we traced that down the appropriate rabbit hole, trying to pull all of those lies apart may prove to be infinitely educational..."

She turned, staring at him incredulously.

Anger rose in those emerald eyes.

He let his smile fade.

That time, it was he who showed her more of himself through his eyes.

"However," he warned coolly. "Given the precise quantity and make-up of the emotions I hear behind your query, my pet, I'm going to go out on a limb and assume you mean my darling boy, Naoko. And likely, his very lovely wife."

St. Maarten dropped her last pretense of caution with him.

Even of politeness.

She dropped her arms from where they'd been folded over the suit.

Walking over to the leather chair across from his, she sat tidily, crossing her slim legs inside the blood-red, retro-styled business suit.

She stared at him, her predatory eyes cold.

"You know he will learn it eventually." She frowned when Brick didn't speak. "You must know it. And you heard *him*. That old seer. The telekinetic. Black could really come here... him and his mate. And if they do, the two of them will tell him everything. And you know Nick. You know how he will react."

"They cannot come here." He shook his head. "It is impossible. They lost those abilities years ago. Centuries now."

Briefly, her eyes turned confused.

"What? What are you talking about?"

"Quentin Black. And Miriam Fox." Brick made a dismissive gesture with his fingers. "They will never come here. They cannot."

"The old seer seemed to think it was possible," Lara remarked drily. "More than possible. Likely. He as much as told them to expect the Blacks here. Pardon me if I trust him over you on that point, since he seemed to have the ability to conjure wormholes out of *thin air…*"

Brick shrugged eloquently.

He made his face noncommittal.

He had said what needed to be said.

He had never enjoyed repeating himself.

Lara St. Maarten seemed to sense he would not defend his own words. After a pause where she waited anyway, she leaned back in the chair across from his.

She adjusted her spine and re-folded her arms.

"That old seer seemed to think it was *very* possible," she repeated, still looking for more of an answer. "And you are forgetting something else, vampire king… he could bring them here himself. So even if the Blacks lost that ability, presumably they now have another way to break through to the different worlds."

"That is an assumption," Brick asked coolly.

Again, her green eyes turned bewildered. "How so?"

"In the sense that we have no idea how he got here the last time. Or whether he could do it again. Perhaps this ability isn't as repeatable as you seem to think. He did, after all, come here to retrieve his son. Presumably he would have done so earlier, if he could conjure inter-dimensional portals on command."

"You're kidding, right?"

"Not at all."

"So how *did* he get here?" she asked. "What is this 'once-only' way that would allow him to cross over to retrieve his son?"

"You are the scientist." Brick gave another eloquent shrug. "You no doubt have a theory. As for me, I am only a lowly vampire. One from the early Twentieth Century, no less."

She shook her head, staring at him incredulously.

"What a load of shit you speak."

"Yet I am being completely serious." His eyes leveled on hers. "I think there is absolutely no reason to assume Yi's father, the telekinetic seer who so dramatically popped in, can open portals on his own. He definitely struck me as someone on a limited timeframe. Like he had a short window to grab his son and bring him back. While I didn't exactly *see* him checking his watch, he struck me as a man constantly counting seconds backward in his mind."

She stared at him. "Meaning what?"

"Well, to me this suggests he was not in control of the jump," Brick said, matter-of-fact. He tapped his cane lightly on the ground. "To me, that suggests he does *not* have this ability on his own. That he was sent here by some other person or means. Which means he did not do it the way Miriam Black did."

"Gee. How can that be?" Sarcasm bled into her voice. "It's not like any other beings have breached the dimensional walls before... have they, vampire?"

"You have a theory?"

"I have several," she retorted. "The most obvious being that he may have gotten here the same way our *last* visitors arrived, perhaps?"

"No." Brick shook one finger at her. "Absolutely no."

"Why not?"

"Because that door, too, was destroyed, dearest Lara."

There was another silence.

Brick did not have to ask her whether she was convinced by his words.

From her face, it was absolutely clear that she was not.

Moreover, he could practically feel the frustration emanating off her.

"You need to tell him," she insisted.

"No."

"If you do not, then *I* will," she threatened. "I'll tell his wife."

For the first time in the conversation, Brick's amusement and affection for his human business partner evaporated.

He dropped the last shield of courtesy from his vampire eyes.

He stared at her flatly.

He let her see the hunter, the animal, that lived in his soul.

"No, my dear Lara," he said coldly. "You will not."

For the barest instant, for what may have been the first time…

…he saw fear of *him* reflect back at him in those emerald eyes.

He liked that fear.

Emotion flowed through him at the thought: sensually, warmly, like a hidden caress. A more animal, predatory, sexual side of him rose, savoring it.

Yes, he liked to see her afraid of him.

Gods of the Underworld… he liked it a lot.

CHAPTER 1

EX-PARTNERS

"Hey!" A lean, muscled, shockingly white arm waved in his face, a muscular body pushing its way through the crowd. "HEY! Nick! Detective Nick! Detective Nick Midnight!"

Nick scarcely heard him at first.

There were a lot of reasons for that.

It was loud where he was.

It was really damned loud where he was.

Nick was also tired.

He'd been fighting all night.

Three bouts, pretty much one right after the other, tightly in a row, after traveling across country for two days straight to reach the underground arena on the west coast.

His wife wasn't there, and that felt weird as hell.

Three days without her was already starting to hurt.

Weirder still, for the first time in more years than he could count, Nick was back in his hometown, in the city they still called San Francisco, in what used to be called the United States of America. San Francisco now formed the focal point of the Bay Area Protected Region, a multi-domed and connected population zone that began in Marin County and stretched all the way down to the southernmost tip of San Jose.

It was strange as hell to be here.

After literal decades... possibly even centuries... Nick was back home.

It had been so long since Nick let himself venture to this part of the world, it felt like returning to his own grave.

Pressing in on all sides, red-faced humans and much paler vampires waved things at him to sign or mark personally in some way.

Nick signed pretty much whatever people thrust into his hands.

Virtual fight programs. Posters. Printed photos of him. Portraits on tablets.

Special autograph-authenticated contact plates.

Articles of clothing.

Headsets.

He even signed a few body parts, and for the first time since he got on the train, he was almost glad Wynter wasn't with him.

Almost.

Almost, and that feeling went away pretty much the instant he felt it.

He scarcely looked at any of the faces eagerly gaping and grinning at him.

His mind remained focused on other priorities.

Priorities he couldn't program out of himself, even if he tried.

Like, for example, he remained painfully aware, with razor-sharp precision, of where the exits were behind him. He calculated distances, estimating his likely relative speed, both in terms of the crowd and his own tiredness. He never stopped being conscious of the fact that he remained more or less behind the line of bodyguards employed by his fight promoter, Farlucci Enterprises, or where each of those bodyguards stood in relation to him.

He knew what each bodyguard came armed with, in terms of weapons.

He knew their individual strengths, speeds, and fighting ability.

He also more or less knew their individual level of personal motivation to actually keep Nick alive… because that sure as fuck varied, too, depending on which guard it was.

Luckily, the two standing closest to him would try their damnedest not to let Nick get killed. They might do it for Farlucci more than him, Nick, but they took their responsibilities seriously. Nick suspected they would sooner mow down every person in this crowd than let them take out the boss's cash cow while he was on a serious winning streak.

Farlucci liked to gamble.

Like most gamblers, he also liked a sure thing.

So yeah, that's where Nick's head was.

For the same reason, he didn't really see or notice the large male's body or face until it was pretty much right in his.

The enormous vampire shoved past a human fan.

Then another.

Then a few more.

When Nick finally noticed and looked up, a mouthful of white teeth and pointed fangs grinned at him from only a few inches away.

"Nick!" He grinned wider, shouting. "Nick Midnight! Remember me? Corey Scotsman?"

Nick barely gave him a glance.

"No, man."

Nick let his California accent slip out, maybe because of where he was. Regardless of his location on the map, it was an accent and collection of words from a different city, a different time, a different era, a different world.

He corrected his words, and his accent.

"No, I don't remember you," he said more politely. "Sorry."

"It's me! Corey! I know it's been a long time, but you *got to* remember me! We knew each other for *years,* man! We were buds!"

Nick looked up at that, frowning.

This vampire had the same California accent he did.

More or less.

He finished signing the contact plate he was in the middle of signing, scanning the vampire's face. Vampires had good memories—better than humans. Not quite as good as seer memories, but still more than decent.

"No," Nick said, blunt. "I really *don't* remember you. I don't know you. I don't remember knowing anyone with that name. I really think you've got the wrong guy, pal."

"Come *on,* man! I mean, what's a few hundred years between friends..." He let out a laugh. "We were human together. Remember?"

Nick stared.

"No," he said, more dismissively that time. "You have the wrong person. I haven't been human since before—"

"The war," the vampire said promptly. "Yeah. I figured that... since I knew you right up until the damned thing started. Is that how they got you? As a part of those recruitment purges? I got hit when they first took San Francisco..."

Nick frowned.

He looked around, looking for some indication that this was a joke.

Then he stared straight ahead, at the human across from him.

He still didn't recognize him.

He had never seen the other vamp before in his life.

The vampire grinned wider, oblivious to Nick's piercing stare.

"Damn you look young! When *did* you get changed, man?" the vamp asked, grinning wider as he looked Nick up and down. "They got me in 2042. Just a few years younger than you were, back when I knew you. Remember? That was back when I first got my detective's badge. In the SFPD. Homicide. You were, what? Fifty? Fifty-two?"

Nick stared at him.

"I never had a human partner when I went back as a vamp."

"What? No." The guy looked confused. "You weren't a vamp. You were human!"

Nick stared harder.

"Seriously?" The vamp frowned. "We were partners for *four years*, man. Corey Scotsman." He enunciated the name, like he was sure Nick hadn't heard him right. "We ran *Bay-to-Breakers* together, like five times. We went surfing almost every weekend together for years. Hell, we went to Hawaii together... and on at least three cruises. Our *wives* were friends. You can't possibly have forgotten *all* of that?"

Nick stared openly at the strange vamp.

He wanted to believe this was a lie, a prank, a case of mistaken identity.

He wanted to believe the other vamp was fucking with him.

But looking at him, that's not what he saw.

That's not what he saw at all.

"You really don't remember me?" the vamp asked, now sounding hurt. "Shit, man. I was so psyched to talk to you! I *completely* recognized you, and you look, like..."

The vamp motioned up and down Nick's body expressively.

"...Well, you look a *lot* different, man. Thirty years younger than when I last saw you. No gray hair. No wrinkles. When I first saw you on the fight circuit, though, I totally *knew* it was you... even before I did some research and dug up your real name. I couldn't fucking believe it! You turned me into a major fight fan, man! You're absolutely *unbelievable* in there! It was a little scary the first time I saw you fight, to be honest..."

Nick continued to stare at the other male.

His mind kept trying to contextualize this in some way.

To categorize it, so he could dismiss it.

It still didn't feel like a joke, even a really twisted one in poor taste.

If it was, what was the damned punchline?

Nick struggled to see anything approaching humor in it.

Instead, it made him feel angry, and vaguely sick. Something about the emotion in the other male's voice hit at him, harder than maybe it should have. The guy managed to sound sincere, like he really cared about him.

"What do you want?" Nick said.

"Want?" The vamp looked confused. "What do you mean? I wanted to say hi. I wanted to maybe grab a beer while you were in town, talk about—"

"I was turned when I was forty-four years old," Nick said coldly. "In 2018."

The vamp blinked.

Then he frowned. "That's not possible."

"So you can imagine how you sound to me," Nick said.

"That's not fucking *possible,* man." The vampire looked angry now. "I'm telling you... you got your dates wrong, Naoko. Jesus, do you have amnesia or something?"

Nick flinched when the vamp said his name.

Then he bristled. "My turn date is a matter of record—"

"I figured that was a damned typo!"

"A *typo?*" Nick stared at him. "You really think the Human Racial Authority makes those kinds of mistakes? With someone like me? A vampire who's regularly in the spotlight, who works for the damned *police?*"

If he'd still had a functioning, human heart, it would have been slamming into his ribs inside his chest. As it was, Nick looked at the other vamp through a sheen of scarlet. He felt his fangs growing in his mouth.

"You've got the wrong guy."

"That's not possible!" the vamp growled. "You lived in Potrero Hill. With your wife, Claire, and your four kids—"

Nick let out a disbelieving laugh. "With my *what?* My fucking *what?*"

The other vampire plowed on.

"...You told me it used to be your *parents'* house," he snapped. "Hiroto and Yumi. You bought it for them in the 1990s. You took

14

it back over when they died, since your name was still on the deed, and your kids wanted to live there. You had three sisters. Numi, Maya, and Naomi. You had an old police dog you adopted. You named him Victor, after a friend of yours you lost in Afghanistan..."

Nick felt like world eclipsing in on him.

He stared at the vampire but couldn't see him anymore.

His parents' names.

His sisters' names.

Even the fucking dog. Victor.

He'd *joked* about adopting that dog.

He and that dog bonded the first time he saw him, not long after he returned to the force as a vampire. The dog was barely older than an overgrown puppy at the time.

Victor.

Gods. He hadn't thought about Victor in about a million fucking years.

The timeline even lined up.

It was all wrong, but it lined up.

What the hell was this?

"Sir?" Mickey, a freckled, red-haired guard standing next to Nick leaned closer. He stood up on his tip-toes to speak in Nick's ear. "Sir, the line. There are a lot of people waiting. Maybe you could speak to your friend later?"

Nick glanced at Mickey.

He turned, staring around at the rest of his security detail.

Only then did he remember where he was.

He wondered why they hadn't scuttled this guy out of there yet.

He was about to tell the deeply unnerving vampire to back off, to make room for the other fight fans to get their autographs and image-captures, when he met the male's gaze.

He flinched.

This guy wasn't screwing with him.

Nick couldn't have said how he knew. He just did.

This vampire, Corey-whoever, really thought he knew him.

Nick saw the intense vampire emotions there, even before the other male wiped his eyes.

"Well," the other vamp said, looking around at the crowd. "I won't hold you up…"

He looked embarrassed now.

Mostly though, he looked sad.

Sad enough that it hit at Nick's heart, even though he told himself the whole thing was completely ridiculous, that he had no reason to feel anything at all about this guy.

"…I know you got your job and all," the vamp said. "I just wanted to say hello. It was so good to see you, man. I was a little sad to see that you'd been turned. You were such a family guy in those years, and we both know what that means, becoming a vamp…"

The other vampire shrugged a little lamely, like he wasn't sure if he should be saying what he was saying, like he'd just remembered Nick said he didn't know him.

"But yeah," the vampire added, just as lamely. "Things were rough back then. Maybe, if you ever want to talk about it, you could look me up…"

Nick stared at him.

He still didn't know the vampire at all, but the sheer amount of emotion he saw in those eyes continued to hit at him, in a way that made him feel a lot of things: grief, sadness, guilt for some crazy reason, maybe that he didn't recognize the guy, or maybe just that he was brushing him off when the guy so obviously wanted to engage.

But it was crazy.

Everything the male vampire said was totally nuts.

Nick felt really weird about letting him walk away, though.

The vampire was starting to back off, when Nick blurted out words, speaking before he knew he meant to.

"What's your name again?" he said. "How would I reach you?"

The vampire stopped.

He seemed bewildered by the question, like he couldn't believe Nick was serious.

Nick watched him tug back and forth on whether to even answer.

Then he blurted out the answer, just as compulsively as Nick.

"Scotsman," he said. "Corey Scotsman. I grew up here. In San Francisco. I still live here, if you decide to look me up. I've got a place in what used to be called the Presidio. They call it 'The Coffin' now, because it's like eighty percent our kind. It's the main vamp district... at least until you get down to San Mateo."

Nick stared at him.

It hit him suddenly, that the crowd around him had gone silent.

Well, not the *whole* crowd.

The underground fight arena was even bigger than the one in Queens, New York. Like the one in New York, it encompassed at least five different fighting rings. Nick had seen all of them when they first showed up and he had some time to wander around.

He even got a little bit of a tour from the fight sponsors.

The arena also contained multiple levels, forming a steep amphitheater for fans to watch from different heights. Since the last match of the night had just finished, the arena was slowly emptying out. That last fight had been Nick's biggest one for the evening, against a local vamp with the fighting name of "Death Spider."

It had also been the headlining show.

Now, everyone was going home until the championship match tomorrow.

Sound echoed up the walls of the enormous space, from people's shuffling feet and their voices as they talked and laughed on their way out. The whole arena lived a few hundred yards underneath what had been, and still was, Union Square.

While many would take the elevators up to higher levels to retrieve their cars, a large number of locals attending the fight, not to mention people staying in hotels near Union Square, would go all the way up to the street.

Most of those people hadn't opted to stick around and wait in line for an autograph.

They likely hadn't wanted to pay the however-many hundreds of credits Farlucci charged for each of Nick's scrawls, unintelligible marks, fingerprints, and handprints.

But the immediate group around Nick had fallen silent.

Everyone standing around him had stopped talking.

They turned their heads, staring at the strange vamp.

They turned their heads again, staring at Nick.

Nick knew he should get back to signing things.

He should look away from the strange vamp with the streaked blond hair, the handsome, surfer-type face, the broad shoulders and easy smile. For a vamp, he had a kind face.

Hell, he *looked* like someone Nick would want to be friends with.

Nick wondered if maybe he *did* want to be friends with the guy, even now.

He felt paralyzed, lost somehow in those glass-like vampire eyes.

The segment of floor where Nick stood was cordoned off, crammed wall-to-wall with fans, with a thick line snaking out to the main aisle below the stadium-style benches. The cordoned-off segment consisted of a roughly ten-by-fifteen carpeted area, maybe six yards from the outer gate protecting the main ring.

Nick stood on the furthest edge, closest to the stairs leading down to the fight pit.

He was still surrounded by Farlucci's guys. At least ten more of Farlucci's people guarded the velvet ropes around the carpet itself. Nick saw a handful of venue security guys, as well, mixed in with Farlucci's protective detail.

Everybody had a vested interest in making sure their cash cow remained safe.

Even as he thought it, Nick realized they'd collectively made a decision about the vampire with the emotion-filled face and the kind eyes.

Nick looked around at his protection, feeling a little sick when they started to move towards Corey Scotsman.

"Hey," Nick said. "Don't hurt the guy. He's fine."

None of Farlucci's guys even glanced at him.

"Hey!" Nick said, louder. "I said he's fine. Look... he's already leaving..."

What Nick said was true.

The strange vampire was already backing away, his hands up. He'd obviously noticed security moving on him and tried to make it clear he wasn't a threat. Nick watched him motion with his hands for Farlucci's guys to turn around, to go back where they came from. It wasn't an aggressive posture. It also wasn't in any way a surrender.

It was more like "okay, okay, I get the message," mixed with a lot of frustration, and possibly annoyance.

A cheer went up from the closest fans.

Clearly they'd decided this Corey Scotsman guy had been hassling Nick.

A few even booed the strange vampire, telling him to get out of the way.

But that was only a small fraction of the humans and vamps standing there.

Most continued to stare, looking between Nick and the cracked-crystal eyes of the strange vampire who cried when Nick said he didn't know him. Maybe they saw something there. Or maybe they were perceptive enough to see that Nick wasn't entirely sure how he felt about Corey Scotsman, either. Maybe, like Nick, they felt sorry for the guy.

Maybe they thought something interesting just happened here.

Something worth gossiping about, or even recording to share with others.

Maybe they thought Nick and the strange vampire were involved in some way.

Or maybe they just saw *something* in all of this, even in the energy between them, and were trying to figure out what it was… what it meant.

Most of them probably didn't even hear what Nick or the strange vampire said.

The only people who didn't seem at all confused, particularly about what should happen next, were Farlucci's guys.

Stepping forward, Bonzo, the burly blond guy who ran the team, motioned for two of the other guards, both of them vampires, to escort Scotsman out.

Or maybe just to make sure he wasn't waiting for Nick outside.

They grabbed hold of his arms on either side.

Nick looked away, conscious of the cameras now on him.

He pretended not to watch.

He went back to signing things that were thrust into his hands, but some part of his attention remained on the kind-faced vampire as they dragged him away.

Some part of him kept trying to ID the guy, to remember him.

Because, unless he was going completely bonkers…

…there *was* something familiar there.

Nick had no idea if that feeling was real.

In some sense, it felt more like a dream of a dream.

He certainly didn't remember anything the vampire described.

There's no way he could have been partners with him on the force, not for four years, not without remembering him well. Nick doubted even a memory wipe would do that. Of course, he had no way of knowing that for certain, what a memory wipe could or couldn't do.

Anyway, all the dates were wrong.

Nick was sure about those.

Those, Nick remembered.

Would it be worth asking Brick about?

Of course, Brick had done nothing but lie to Nick about various elements of his vampire life since he'd been turned, not to mention elements about being a vampire in general. He'd been doing that to Nick pretty much from day one.

Going to Brick seeking real information would be a crap-shoot, at best.

Nick watched out of the corner of his eye as the two vampire guards dragged the ex-homicide detective vampire away. Some part of him wished he could just forget he'd ever seen the guy, forget the question had ever risen in his mind.

He wished he hadn't looked into those eyes and seen the man stare at him like they were brothers.

He couldn't, though.

He couldn't forget.

He also couldn't remember, and that was pretty fucked up.

CHAPTER 2

NO SLEEP TONIGHT

"Are you at home?"

She sounded busy, distracted.

She sounded like she might even be working still.

It didn't make much difference, not to what his friend Miri used to call "the lizard part" of Nick's brain. Just hearing Wynter's voice sent a shiver of heat under his vampire skin. The sensation briefly closed his eyes, darkening his vision longer than a blink.

It also made him hyper-attuned to every inflection, every subtle detail of her voice and breath… and even the heartbeat he could hear faintly across the line.

He could hear and feel tiredness on her, a mental fatigue as well as physical. He knew she'd been working a lot of hours lately, well beyond her duties as principal of Kellerman Preparatory School in the Northeastern Protected Area.

She'd been working nights, too.

She'd been working for Archangel.

Mostly, she'd been working for Lara St. Maarten personally.

Nick hadn't let himself ask her on what, precisely.

He wasn't entirely sure he wanted to know what Lara had her working on.

But tiredness and work weren't the only things Nick felt and heard on his seer wife. He thought he caught some worry there, too, in the subtler tenors of her voice.

She felt worried about him.

That part, he'd almost expected.

He knew she would have been watching his fights.

Even if she'd been working, she'd have them on in the background.

She told him once it soothed her a little, to be able to watch him there. To see him get up when he got hit. To be able to know he was okay. To watch him outfight the other vampires.

To see him win.

Luckily for both of them, Nick had been winning a lot lately.

"Nick?" Her voice grew a bit more stressed. "Are you at home yet?"

Thinking about her question, he let out an exhale.

It wasn't a real exhale; he was a vampire.

He did it more to convey emotion.

"No." He smiled wryly. "I'm *not* at home, baby. And it's weird as fuck, being here."

"I mean the hotel. Are you at the hotel?" Her voice sharpened. "You're not still at the arena, are you? Farlucci can't possibly still have you there this late?"

"It's a lot later where you are," he pointed out.

"Nick. Are you going to tell me? Where are you?"

He stared out over the city in front of him, from a high balcony in a downtown hotel overlooking the bay. He gripped the balcony railing, looking out over the city.

"I'm back," he said. "I'm at the hotel." He glanced around the luxurious suite. "It's beautiful. Top of the line. They might even be trying to bribe me to stay indoors, to not go out into the city at all. But I might head out for a bit, anyway."

"What? Why?"

He made the exhale sound again.

"I think you forget what I am sometimes," he teased.

"What is that supposed to mean?"

Hearing the anger creeping into her worry, he reminded himself that both of them were on edge. They both tended to be hyper-sensitive when they were apart. They didn't do all that well, truthfully, being apart.

Basically, it wasn't a good time to be a flippant dick.

"I just meant I don't sleep," he clarified. He subdued his voice. "I'm also more of what you'd call a *night* person."

"You sleep." Her voice held a near-accusation. "You always say vampires don't sleep, but *you* do. You sleep all the time. You even dream."

"I only sleep when I'm with you—" he began.

"That's not true either," she accused.

"—Otherwise, I generally wander around and do vampire-y things at night. Usually, I'm working, but since I'm off the clock with the NYPD right now, I might as well get my nostalgia fix over with, or I'm just going to feel like a coward."

Listening to her silence, he sighed again.

"Wynter, I want to look around. I haven't been here in decades. I grew up here. If I'm going to do that, I should do it at night. When I don't have to deal with the dome's artificial sunlight. I'll hang out at the fancy-schmancy hotel tomorrow. Maybe I'll even check to see if they have vampire massages... or at least a decent physical therapist... so I'm feeling a little less creaky and old tomorrow..."

But she wasn't in the mood to be joked out of her worry.

"There are a lot of other things you can do during the day," she said, sounding faintly accusatory. "We do things all the time in New York during the day. Museums. There are tours you can take that have vampire-safe glass—"

"Sure, yes. There are things I can do during the day. I can go to museums tomorrow. I can check out the tourist areas tomorrow. I can see all the shiny, new, vampire-safe malls. I can even go to the park tomorrow, since a lot of that is accessible to vamps, too."

Hesitating for a beat, he shrugged.

"But there are things I really *can't* do during the day, honey," he added apologetically. "Like, if I want to walk around, if I want to explore the streets on foot, to see some of the old neighborhoods, places tourists *don't* go, I need to go now. Basically, if I want to do most of the things I actually *did* back when I was human, I have to do them at night."

"Isn't that going to make you sad?"

There was a silence.

Nick blinked as a lightbulb went off over his head.

Then some part of him relaxed.

Ah. That's what was bothering her.

He almost wondered if she'd picked up something from him.

Shoving that aside, Nick tried to really think about her question, to answer honestly.

"Maybe," he admitted. "It might make me sad."

"So why do it?"

He could hear the worry in her voice again.

Strangely, he felt himself relax even more. Maybe it was because he now knew what was bothering her, why she'd been reacting.

"I don't know." He remembered the vampire at the stadium, the one who was so damned sure he knew him, and frowned. "I feel like there's *something* here... something I want to understand better. Brick never sent me back here. Not once the whole time I was with the White Death. He never seemed to want me to come here at all. I know he hates nostalgia, so I thought maybe it was just that... but, you know... maybe it wasn't."

"What does that mean?" she asked.

He could hear her frowning, trying to read past his words.

Nick thought about that question, too.

He considered explaining his encounter earlier that night.

He considered just dumping all of that on her, right there and then. The weird vamp, how emotional he'd been. How he'd seemed genuinely sad to Nick as a vampire, even as he seemed delighted to see him again. He thought about telling her about the vampire's insistence around a wife and kids Nick had never had, a part of his human life he'd never gotten to lead, a dog he'd never owned... but he could really hear the fatigue on her now.

He didn't want to give her more reasons to worry and make up scenarios in her head.

He wanted her to turn off the virtual workspace and crawl into bed.

He wanted to talk to her... desperately... but not like this.

"I wish you were here," he said finally.

"I wish you were *here*," she countered.

"You're not ready to kick me out yet?"

He smiled as he said it.

Even so, the sharpness returned to her voice.

"No. Why? Are you changing your mind about moving in with me?"

Nick frowned. He fought not to react to her words, to her harder tone.

"Why on earth would I change my mind about moving in with you? It's been amazing, hasn't it? I thought we both agreed it was amazing?"

"It *is* amazing," she said, still sounding angry.

"Then why would you ask me that?"

She didn't answer.

Feeling her worry again, Nick clenched his jaw, then released it slowly.

"Wynter. Honey. What's going on? What's wrong? Are you really worried about me? You saw the fights... all three of them went fine. My back hurts a little, but honestly, it'll feel better if I walk it off a bit. I need to stay limber, since I've got two more fights tomorrow evening. And I really *will* look into getting a massage tomorrow."

"You should rest," she countered.

"Wynter."

He felt her about to say more.

He even heard her suck in a short breath.

Then, in that split second before she would have said whatever it was she'd wanted to say, he practically felt her change her mind.

He felt her pull back. He felt her fight to control herself, to control her heightened seer emotions, which were almost as crazy and volatile as vampire emotions.

He could almost see her expression as she held the inhaled breath, biting her lip.

She wanted to yell at him. Some part of her, at least, *really* wanted to yell at him.

She wanted to express *something* to him, anyway.

Maybe even she didn't know what it was.

Something about their interaction was giving him an odd *déjà vu* feeling though, like what he got when she said or did something that specifically reminded him of Dalejem.

It also brought up an affection he struggled to suppress.

"I love you," he said. "A ridiculous, embarrassing amount, Wynter."

Even he heard the love in his voice.

"And I'm bringing you here with me next time," he promised. "I'm still pissed that soulless psychopath wouldn't give you a few days off. I mean, I get the argument about the racial authority being different out here, but hell... why be obligated to a multi-national, uber-scary defense contracting conglomerate if they can't even arrange for an illegal fuck-weekend for me and my unregistered seer squeeze?"

Wynter didn't smile at that, either.

"It's not a good time, Nick."

"Why the hell not?" he growled.

He blurted it before he'd thought about how it sounded.

Now, when she didn't answer him, he felt his own nagging worry return.

"You're going to tell me what she has you working on one of these days," he said, his voice gruff. "Right?"

"I already told you what we're working on," she countered.

He blinked. "You did?"

Thinking about her words, hearing the truth behind them, he frowned.

"You're still hunting Yi's people?" he said.

"Of course." At his silence, she clicked at him with her tongue. "Nick, Yi had propaganda groups, political organizers, and terrorist cells seeded all over the world. It's not like Archangel has underground rooms crammed with trained seers to do this kind of tracking for them. Even with the amount of *regular* surveillance at our disposal, it's basically a full-time job for an entire infiltration team... meaning forty or fifty full-blooded and military-trained seers. Instead they've got me and Mal. We have maybe a dozen hybrids with varying degrees of *some* sight, but they desperately need training, and we don't have time for that, either—"

"Tai can't help you?"

"Tai's in school."

"You *work* at school," he growled. "For fuck's sake, Wynter... it's too much. You have to sleep. They can't work you twenty-four hours a day."

"I'll be all right, Nick."

"No, you won't—"

"Look, no one's *making* me do anything. I *asked* to do this. I *want* to do it, Nick."

His jaw clenched.

Like she had with him, only a few minutes earlier, he bit his tongue, forcing himself to remain silent.

He knew she was right.

This wasn't his call; it was hers.

He also knew Wynter might not tell him if she didn't have any choice.

"You and me," he began cautiously. "Lara hasn't mentioned—"

"No," she said, blunt. "She hasn't threatened me lately to have my boyfriend murdered if I don't do what she asks, Nick."

Nick's jaw tightened.

That was a little too on-the-nose with what he'd been thinking.

He believed her, though.

Mostly.

That didn't change the fact that Archangel had leverage over the two of them—leverage that Lara St. Maarten didn't particularly need to spell out at this stage of their relationship.

That leverage hadn't gone away, whether or not Lara chose to hold it over his wife's head in so many words.

Unfortunately, that leverage might *never* go away.

Unless the law changed, and the world changed, Nick and Wynter's relationship would remain illegal indefinitely. Wynter *herself* was likely illegal, just her very existence as a living being, since Nick deeply doubted she'd come up as "hybrid" in a detailed racial-cat examination by the Human Racial Authority, or H.R.A.

He didn't know for sure what they'd do to her, if they ever found out.

He knew *exactly* what they'd do to him.

Rogue vampires were not tolerated.

Nick would be tortured, questioned, and likely killed.

That, or they'd "reprogram" him until they no longer viewed him as a threat.

To avoid any of that, Nick would have to go underground with the White Death, and take his wife with him. That, or he'd end up in some underground black ops unit, working for Archangel.

Hell, he still might end up there.

He'd probably get assigned to one of their assassin teams, like Tai. Maybe he and Tai would even work together. He and the kid could trade "craziest hit" stories and teach each other more efficient kill techniques while he helped her with her math homework.

The thought made his teeth grind.

But there wasn't much he could do about Tai, either... or her brother, Mal, who also worked more or less at the whims of Lara St. Maarten and Archangel.

Mal, Tai, and now Wynter, were beholden to Archangel for their very existence, for even the semblance of a "normal" life.

It was something Nick had allowed himself to forget while they'd all been focused on stopping the telekinetic seer, Dimitry Yi.

Now that Yi was gone, Nick found himself thinking about it again.

He found himself thinking about it a lot.

He also wondered if maybe Lara might have a different plan for the two of them, now that Yi was out of the way and she no longer had to play nice. Or maybe, since Lara and Brick the vampire king seemed to be working together more closely these days, they'd worked out some kind of deal together, on what to do with the two of them.

Maybe they'd mapped out a detailed schedule on exactly how to share Nick and his highly valuable and technically extinct seer mate... and how to continue to blackmail them into cooperation without tipping Nick into murderous psychopathy.

He hadn't realized how quiet he'd gotten.

Not until Wynter spoke.

"We can't talk about this on here," she murmured. "Later. Okay?"

He nodded, as much to himself as her.

He knew the mechanism would pick up his nod and incorporate it into his avatar's mannerisms.

"Okay," he said.

"I love you."

He felt his fangs extend.

His chest clenched, overwhelmed briefly with that damned vampire emotionality.

"I love you too," he managed. "Go to bed, Wynter."

Without waiting, he hung up.

For another few seconds, he gazed out over the city of his birth, frowning.

CHAPTER 3

WANDER

Nick set out from his hotel, hands buried in the pockets of an expensive, designer, motorcycle jacket he'd bought for the promo-tour, his face covered with a black mask and a hoodie.

He managed to get out without attracting too much attention.

A few diehard fans noticed him in the lobby—fans who likely already knew he was staying at the hotel. Three other boxers were at the same hotel, but Nick was the big draw. He was the headliner, and the favorite for winning the entire two-day challenge match.

For the same reason, he had fans camped out in the lobby, at least when they weren't escorted out by security. They also had body scans of his body type, height, size, and even his gait programmed into their ident-finders on their headsets, so they were a lot more likely to notice him trying to sneak out, even with his face covered.

They weren't hard to get rid of, but he knew his brief interactions with a few of them would hit the fan sites and feeds. At least a handful of those hanging out in the lobby, hoping to catch a glimpse, snuck image captures and some video as Nick passed by.

Then two young fans approached him and he finally stopped.

He gave out a few autographs, let a few more take their photo with him, pulling down his mask so they could get one with his face.

Once he was out on the street, he pulled the mask up, slipped into vampire hunting mode, and did his best to make himself invisible. By the time he'd made it a few blocks up Market Street, he'd shaken the few humans who tried to follow him.

A few blocks more, and he was out of the main locus of the boxing tournament, in terms of bars, hotels, and the street brimming with fans and fighters.

A few blocks more, and he was in a different part of the city entirely.

After that, he didn't get a lot of second looks.

He tried to discourage that even more by pulling the hooded sweatshirt he wore under his designer clothes more tightly over his head. The insignia for Farlucci's boxing club lived on the back of that sweatshirt, but no one could see it as long as he left on his jacket. Between the motorcycle jacket, the hood, the mask, and his general vampire-ness, he was probably in more danger of being arrested for looking suspicious than he was of being recognized.

Well, unless he ran into more diehards out here, who had their headsets actively scanning for his exact weight, body proportions, gait, and so on.

He stayed on Market for the first dozen blocks, walking in the direction of Castro.

He told himself he didn't know where he was going.

He told himself he was just going to wander around, see how things had changed.

Maybe he'd meander his way down to the Castro, get a drink. See a few bands. See how much that part of the city had changed. He might even walk up to Golden Gate Park, then on to Ocean Beach, make his way up to the Presidio to check out the vampire enclave.

He could easily do a big loop around the top half of the city before morning.

But he didn't do that.

He didn't really wander at all.

He walked more or less in a straight line, until he reached Van Ness.

Then he hung a left.

He walked in a straight line again, now heading almost due south.

He told himself he'd check out the Mission first.

See how much it had changed.

But he barely looked at the Mission District as he passed through.

He made another left, this time onto 17th Street.

He walked through that corner of the Mission District as well, also without stopping, without really slowing down, or glancing around much at the buildings. He noted the old armory was still there. That was pretty much it, in terms of things he recognized. Most of the buildings looked completely foreign to him, and nothing like the Mission he remembered.

He walked out of the Mission District.

He walked a while longer.

He made at least one other turn.

Now he stood somewhere else.

Somehow, despite his walking there in a straight line, he still managed to be surprised when he found himself there.

He just stood there at first, staring at it.

He hadn't been here in so long, it felt like entering one of his dreams.

He wanted to tell himself he would be doing this anyway, that he would have come to see the old place anyway, regardless of whether he'd been accosted by a strange vampire or not. He would have come out of respect for his human parents. He would have come out of respect for his human sisters, and his human nieces and nephews… hell, his human life.

He would have come out of respect for Miri.

He even would have come out of respect for Black… and hell, Dalejem.

After all, all of them spent holidays with him and his parents here for years, even after he'd been turned.

It had nothing to do with what that vampire told him.

It had nothing to do with a strange vampire who claimed to know Nick as a human who raised human children here with a human wife.

It had nothing to do with any of that, Nick told himself.

That didn't really feel true, though.

Or maybe it only felt partly true.

It definitely felt like Nick was seeing the house in front of him with new eyes.

He stood outside the gate of a Victorian, two-story, three-bedroom house so achingly familiar, his chest hurt.

It might have been his heart that hurt… only Nick was a vampire, and his heart didn't work the way a human's did anymore. It didn't beat. It didn't circulate blood, at least not in the same way, and certainly not on its own.

It wasn't supposed to ache the way a human's heart ached.

It wasn't supposed to.

Glancing from the familiar gate up to the familiar, red-painted front door, he felt his grief so keenly, it honestly shocked him.

He'd thought he was past this… past losing his human family.

He'd been lying to himself.

He'd never be past it. Not really.

It would never go away.

He'd stayed away from San Francisco partly for that reason.

It had been pretty clear Brick didn't want him here, but he could have come in the years since. When he rejoined the force, his job never brought him here *specifically*, but hell, he'd lived and worked in L.A. for years, and he never came up to visit? Not even once?

Even while he was still with the White Death, Nick could have made it back here if he'd really tried.

He hadn't tried.

He'd stayed away entirely since the wars.

The few times he considered coming back, the thought brought up so much grief, he'd pushed it all away. After that nightmare of depression and suicidal thoughts after he lost Jem, he'd decided he needed to focus on the future, to not look back.

Looking back was death.

Looking back was how he'd end up in that black hole he'd barely crawled out of the first time… and then only by erasing part of his memory.

So when the war finished, when he left the White Death, Nick didn't come back to San Francisco. He didn't remember being here much during the wars, either… or really…

He paused, frowning.

Jesus. When *was* he last in San Francisco?

The question somehow snapped him out of his grief long enough to really look around at where he stood.

He'd wanted desperately to bring his girlfriend (*wife,* his mind murmured) back with him this time because it had struck him how little he'd traveled in the past few years, even outside of work. He'd hoped he and Wynter could make a vacation of it.

She could watch the fights from the hotel room if she didn't want to see that shit live. Then they could hang out downtown, go to clubs, eat ridiculously expensive food, shop for even more ridiculous souvenirs, fuck like rabbits in the fancy hotel bathroom.

Maybe Nick could even learn to like traveling again.

He wanted to make an effort to move past all his old hang-ups and bad memories, now that Wynter was back in his life.

Ever since they'd left London, he'd been conscious of how few places he'd gone since he left the White Death.

He'd been in Los Angeles.

Then he moved to New York.

Before that, before L.A…

Nick didn't remember a damned thing.

That must have been around where he erased things, because everything in Nick's mind just went dark. There were flashes, bits and pieces of the war, of the White Death…

He refocused on the house.

Hadn't his parents' house been destroyed? He had a memory of their house being flattened at one point. Everything being gone. He remembered crying with… someone. Had it been Dale-jem? Angel? Dex? Black?

Had it been Miriam?

Frowning, he pushed open the low, wooden gate.

It squeaked under his hands.

Even the squeak sounded familiar.

Nick made his way up the path to the base of the stairs. He climbed up the steep, creaky, still-wooden stairs, and walked onto a white-painted, antique, and obviously refurbished wooden porch. The red door stood in front of him now.

Succulent plants covered the porch in giant ceramic pots.

Those pots even looked Japanese.

He hesitated for a few seconds longer, just standing there.

Whoever lived inside the house would have him on surveillance by now.

This was an expensive neighborhood, even more than it had been then.

They'd know he was standing there, on their porch, like an asshole. They might even know he was a vampire, since he hadn't bothered to put in his contact lenses before he ventured out of his five-star hotel on Market, and he'd pulled down the face mask while he climbed up the wooden steps. He'd also pulled off his hood, figuring it would make him seem less like he was hiding his appearance from the cameras.

He'd been told San Francisco was a pretty vampire-friendly town these days, that no one would harass him, just for what he was.

Still, there was a good chance they'd call the cops.

He was a stranger.

He was a *big* stranger, even for a vampire.

He looked like a fighter, even without the hoodie.

But really, more to the point, he was a strange vampire in a human neighborhood.

At night.

Raising a hand, Nick hesitated just long enough to stand perfectly still.

Then he knocked sharply on the wood.

It didn't occur to him until later how odd that was.

No one knocked these days. It's what he would have done, showing up at his parents' front steps, back when he was human. But no one did that anymore.

No one.

Then again, few people had wooden doors anymore, either.

Most replaced them with organic metals fashioned to simulate real wood, even on old houses like these, houses that were officially declared historical monuments and more or less priceless now, especially if they survived the war looking like this.

How *did* the old house still look like this?

Why wasn't it gone?

Had someone really rebuilt it, from the ground up, exactly as it had been?

Who would have done that? Why?

Nick looked up and down the dark street.

Why wasn't *all* of this gone?

Before he could second-guess why he'd come, what he was doing there...

Behind him, the door abruptly opened.

CHAPTER 4

YOU CAN'T GO HOME AGAIN

Nick turned, blinking into artificial light.

Some part of him expected to see someone standing there with an old-school shotgun, maybe one loaded with vampire-killing bullets.

Instead, a young, friendly-looking human, backlit from a warmly lit house, blinked at him in surprise.

"Hey," he said. "You're a vampire."

Nick's vampire eyes adjusted to the sudden influx of bright light.

He hadn't fully realized how long he'd been walking in the dark.

"Yeah," Nick said. He adjusted his voice downward, and it turned gruff. "Yeah, kid. I'm a vampire."

He didn't mean the "kid" part in a condescending way.

It just sort of slipped out.

Anyway, any human who didn't have gray hair and a face full of wrinkles and age spots struck him as a "kid" these days.

Even a lot of the gray-hairs could make him feel old as fuck.

"Sorry to bother you," Nick added, when the kid just blinked at him. "I used to know someone who lived here. A long time ago.

I admit, I was pretty curious to see the old place back the way it was… it's a little surreal to see it looking like this again."

The twenty-something human blinked a third time.

He could have been one of Nick's young nephews or nieces back in the day. He even looked Japanese, with angular, high cheekbones, a full mouth, dark brows, evenly-toned skin. He had piercing hazel eyes, which used to be pretty rare among Japanese people from the old country, but did happen occasionally, even back before the old ethnicities from Nick's generation got even harder to pull apart.

Back then, Japanese people sometimes had hazel eyes, too.

Nick's mother had hazel eyes.

Eyes that looked a hell of a lot like—

"What's your last name?" he blurted, again without thinking.

"Tanaka."

Nick felt his whole body stop.

"What? What did you say your name was?"

"Tanaka." The young man put out his hand, tentative, but seemingly determined to not let Nick scare him. "I'm Derek Tanaka. I inherited the house pretty recently. From my aunt. But it's been in my family for ages."

Nick stared at him.

He found himself looking past the kid then, into the house.

"Can I look inside?" he asked.

He blurted that out without thinking, too.

Immediately, he heard the kid's heartrate speed up.

"Hey." Nick held up his hands in a peace gesture. "I swear. I mean you no harm. I'm sorry for being so forward. Maybe I could come back another time? I didn't mean to cold-call you like this. I'm just a little shocked to find all of this here. I'd heard this whole part of the city got wiped out in the wars."

The kid's face visibly relaxed.

It had never ceased to amaze Nick how the mere fact of being marginally polite could convince most people you wouldn't hurt them… even though the two things literally had zero connection to one another. It was one of those human quirks that vampires used to their advantage often back in the days of open hunting of humans.

Hell, who was he kidding?

Vampires *still* did it. A lot.

They'd probably been doing it for thousands of years.

Really, ever since there were vampires around and humans for them to hunt, they'd probably been using human psychology against them.

"No," the kid said now.

He stepped back, out of the doorway, swinging the wooden door inward.

"I don't mean no," he added quickly, a little flustered. "I mean *yes…* you can look. I meant *no,* you don't need to come back later. You're welcome to take a look now."

He gave Nick a short, polite bow of the head as he motioned him inside.

"My wife isn't here, so now's probably a good time, honestly. She gets a little nervous around vampires. She lost her great-grandparents in the war to vampires."

He said the last part apologetically.

It might have been darkly funny if Nick's brain had been remotely working.

As it was, Nick only stood there, hesitating for another half-second.

Really, it wasn't funny.

A hell of a lot of civilians died during the wars.

This kid's wife's ancestors could have been murdered in their own home, their children huddled in a panic room, or just lucky to be gone that day, sent to stay with other relatives.

Without letting himself think too clearly about why he'd asked, what he was looking for, or why he was doing any of this… Nick walked inside his childhood home.

He walked through an eerily familiar entryway.

His vampire eyes picked up and noted the various changes.

New, high-tech, semi-organic security system.

Virtual screen on part of the floor, reconfiguring into a field of waving sunflowers as he walked over the pressure tiles.

The gilded mirror had been replaced with another virtual painting, one that could no-doubt reconfigure into a mirror, or a news feed, or a view of whatever was going on outside the front door. A few antique pieces of furniture cluttered the hallway as well, but none from Nick's time period, and most of them post-war.

The closet was gone. Or at least, the door was no longer visible.

But the house's basic shape was the same.

The narrowness of the Victorian corridor was the same.

The high ceilings were the same.

When Nick walked into the living room, the main sitting area of the house, it was the same size and shape he remembered. It was decorated completely differently than the room his mother and father lived in, but he could see the bones of that room still.

He stared around at the modern, faux-fur couch that changed colors under a rotating overhead light. A glass entertainment center morphed colors in synchronicity with the couch. Above that, a wall monitor stretched from the sliding glass doors to the window near the corridor that used to lead to the three bedrooms.

The monitor currently displayed five different feeds.

Two of those were straight news.

The third looked like a gossip or arts show.

Another showed a talking head on one of the political channels.

The last appeared to be a replay of Nick's final fight of the night.

Even with all the differences, Nick could almost see his mother's flowered sofa and loveseat set, with the two matching chairs and the antique Japanese coffee table that stood between them. He remembered the traditional brush paintings over his mother's upright piano, and that modern art abstract thing they'd gotten from Miri and Black one year.

He glanced to his left.

The wall there, opposite the door to his mother's old kitchen, had also been modified into a virtual screen, but this one was covered with family photos. Nick stared, watching the faces of children, adults, older people shift by.

The sense of familiarity in some of those faces was cloying.

Not just cloying. Disturbing.

"You're Japanese, right?"

Nick jumped about a foot.

He tore his eyes off the image of a woman that could have been his mother's twin.

Or maybe his mother's daughter.

Or maybe his mother's great-great-great granddaughter.

He stared at the young man, conscious again that some part of him was having a near-panic reaction to everything he was seeing.

"Your name's Tanaka?" Nick blurted. *"Derek Tanaka?"*

The young man with the retro, now-trendy, orange-rimmed eyeglasses blinked.

"Yes," he said, sounding surprised. "You've asked me that. Twice. Now three times. Why?"

"How long have you had this house?" Nick asked. "Your family, I mean?"

The man blinked again.

Nick remembered what the young human said at the door.

"You said you inherited it, right?" Nick added. "Recently? From an aunt?"

The man's expression relaxed marginally.

His mouth firmed as he thought about Nick's question.

"Well." Derek Tanaka pushed the orange-rimmed glasses up his nose, resting his hands on a slim but athletic waist. "It's only been a few months since *I* officially owned it, like I said, but it's been in the family a long time. I honestly don't know how long. I got it from my Aunt Tania, who died recently."

Nick heard the sadness in the young man's voice.

Clearly, he'd been fond of his aunt.

"But she inherited it, too," he added, a bit more brightly. "I know she got it from her grandfather, Hiroto—"

"Hiroto," Nick muttered.

Nick's human father was named Hiroto.

Nick's own goddamned *middle name* was Derek.

But the young Tanaka was still talking.

He hadn't stopped talking, the whole time Nick's brain fuzzed into static.

"...then before that, I think *his* father had it," Derek was saying now. "The family's had it for ages, is my point. Well before the war. I'd have to go back and look at the papers—"

"Do you have them?" Again, Nick blurted the words, cutting the human off without thought. "The papers? The original ownership papers for the house? Is there a copy of the old deed somewhere?"

The man blinked.

Now he looked a little wary.

"Why would you want to see that?" he asked. "Are you some kind of vampire historian or something?" Then, seeming to realize again what Nick was, putting two and two together with the fact that vampires don't exactly look their ages, he frowned. "Wait. You said you knew someone who used to live here. What was their name? Was it Tanaka? Is that why you keep asking me about that?"

Nick looked back at the morphing wall.

He stared at the changing images there, images of his own family.

They had to be his family.

"Do you know their name?" he asked. "The first Tanakas who lived here?"

There was a silence.

Nick looked back at the young man, who blanched.

Then Derek Tanaka seemed to pull himself together again.

His hazel eyes slid out of focus.

He appeared to be looking at something in his headset. Nick realized he was probably looking for the old deed, and didn't speak.

Some number of seconds later, Derek Tanaka smiled.

"Found it," he said.

Using hand gestures, he moved the information to the same wall as the family photos.

"I was pretty sure my mom had all that info in a file for our family," he explained, as the document grew larger, crowding out all the images of family members. "She was into all that genealogy stuff. She wanted us to know where we came from. And this house was kind of a social point for years. It was the holiday gathering spot, you know? Birthdays, graduations, Thanksgiving, Christmas…"

Nick barely heard him.

He was staring at the deed on the wall, and the handful of images that went with it.

Several of those images were of people.

"Hey," Derek said. "That guy looks kind of like you!"

But it was impossible.

All of it was completely impossible.

His oldest sister, Numi, bought the house for their parents after she made it big in corporate law. Nick moved here while he was still in high school. If this really was his family, it should be his parents' name and faces connected to that deed: Yumi and Hiroto Tanaka.

But it wasn't.

The kid was right.

The images were of him.

Nick's name was there, spelled out in black and white.

Naoko Derek Tanaka.

His chicken-scratch of a signature even looked the same. He

should know; he'd been writing it for hours that night, for everyone who wanted him to sign his real name and not just his stage-fighting name, "The White Wolf."

The photos of Nick showed him as a human, and he looked older in them than he did now, but he couldn't have been much more than thirty-five.

But it was all wrong.

His parents had already lived in this house for years by then. Nick used to visit them here while he was on leave from the military. Then later, when he was a cop, and then a detective for the SFPD, he came by nearly every weekend.

But it wasn't even that. It wasn't any of those things.

This house was gone.

The connection to Nick's family should have been severed.

This house had been leveled.

Nick remembered a time when most of San Francisco had been taken out. The house was destroyed. There'd been a damned crater here. His family had been targeted specifically, *because* they were his family, and because Nick was classified as a traitor to the group that started the fighting out of San Francisco. Nick couldn't even remember which group that had been.

He never came back here and bought the house.

He never came back here again.

But thinking about those years didn't clarify anything.

All of that felt so confused now.

Who the enemies were. How he had memories of fighting with seers, and memories of fighting alongside vampires, and even with large groups of humans. He remembered fighting shoulder to shoulder with Brick and his people, and he remembered times where he infiltrated vampire groups, pretending to be one of them only to rip them to pieces.

But if he'd betrayed Brick, Brick would have killed him by now.

Brick had a long, long memory for betrayal.

Anyway, none of it was clear, even within the same snapshots of war. In some of those memories, the groups switched back and forth too quickly for Nick to follow, much less make sense of. He'd see himself fighting with vampires, and he'd see himself fighting next to seers, sometimes in the same battles.

None of it made sense.

But Nick remembered looking at a crater where this house had been.

He remembered standing in the middle of the wreckage, fangs extended, blood on his mind as he looked around at his parents' home.

That happened.

Nick was sure of it.

His parents, his sisters... Nick's memories told him they'd gotten out. They'd all moved to Europe. They'd stayed in Europe.

Nick wanted to believe that part was real.

He wanted to believe that part really happened, and wasn't just his mind rewriting reality into a history he could live with.

He wanted to be *positive* they'd all survived, but really, he couldn't be.

There was no way to be.

He did remember that whole mess was what convinced him to join the war.

That part, Nick believed.

Them targeting his human family was part of the reason he enlisted.

Hell, it *was* the reason he enlisted.

Nick just wasn't entirely sure who "they" were, or why he'd been targeted.

Could someone really have built a new version of his parents' old house?

Some distant nephew who looked like him? Who had the same name? Why?

Nick only had sisters. By the time Nick got turned, none of them had the last name of Tanaka. They'd all taken their husbands' names, as used to be the tradition. Nick's parents would have been long dead before the war ended. Who else could it be? Some grand kid who decided to take his grandmother's surname?

Had Nick done it himself, using a human alias of some kind to bypass the vampire codes? Was the photo faked? Was that why his name and face were on the deed?

Was all this part of his memory he'd erased?

But Nick was a vampire. He couldn't have kids.

He couldn't have grandkids.

Anyway, he could see the date on the deed.

It said November 11, 2008.

That was the old date system. That was the date system he'd grown up with.

Nick would have been thirty-four years old.

He would have just gotten his detective's badge.

None of this made sense.

Absolutely none of it made sense.

He was about to turn to the human again, to ask again about his family, ask him where the hell they came from, whether they'd ever lived in Europe, how they'd gotten the house, what he knew about his family history…

…when his headset pinged.

Emergency channel.

Gertrude, the NYPD's artificial intelligence avatar, grew visible in the top right of his screen.

"Detective Midnight?" Gertrude inquired politely. "You are being requested to call in. Security Access Code: 8819201C-12. Detective James Vincent Morley would like a call-back to Detective Damon Jordan at your earliest convenience."

Nick muted the A.I., turning to face the human.

He had more questions.

He had a hell of a lot more questions.

But it would have to wait.

Maybe Nick even needed it to wait.

Maybe his head would explode if he tried to ask them now.

"I'll be back," he muttered.

He was already heading for the front door.

The human, Derek Tanaka, didn't move from where he stood in the middle of his modern-styled, verging-on-trendy living room. He only turned his head to watch Nick leave out the front door, gaping a little.

From the look on his face, he wasn't quite sure what just happened.

CHAPTER 5

BRICK'S STORY

"WHAT DOES THAT MEAN?" NICK FROWNED, LOOKING UP AND down the street as he crossed Van Ness.

He was moving a lot faster than he needed to.

He could feel some part of himself trying to put distance between himself and the house on Potrero Hill.

His body still felt tense with shock. It didn't seem to be getting better, no matter how fast he walked, or how many steps he put between himself and the young man who could have been his nephew... or maybe his great-great-great-great grandson.

Nick shoved it out of his mind with an effort.

"Jordie?" he said, a little sharper. "What are we talking here? More illegal vampire tech? Fake venom? What?"

He'd walked at least eight or nine blocks before he called his partner back.

It took him that long to unscramble his brain enough to make the call.

It took him that long to sound reasonably normal to his partner and friend.

He still struggled to switch hats, to bring back his cop brain.

It was hard enough doing that these days, just switching from Nick Tanaka, increasingly famous underground fighter known as

"The White Wolf," to Nick Midnight, grunt vampire detective and decidedly *not*-famous blood-sniffer in the employ of the human NYPD.

Jordan was his partner.

Well, technically, Nick couldn't really *have* a human partner.

Any human on the force could give him orders, and tell him what to do, which more or less made the "partner" thing moot. Thanks to the inter-species laws of the Human Racial Authority, Nick was lower on the ladder than any human in the police hierarchy, including the guy in the mail room.

Really, technically-speaking, Nick had a lower legal status than any human who lived by human rules in the human world.

Since Jordan was cool, Jordan *felt* like a partner, though.

He hadn't in the beginning, but he sure as hell did now.

Damon Jordan, NYPD Homicide Detective II, was probably Nick's best human friend, despite some bumpy patches they'd had here and there, even recently, but especially when they first met. Jordan and Morley—Morley being the human who felt like Nick's *actual* boss—were definitely the two humans Nick trusted the most right now.

Well, them and his twenty-something tech-punk pal, Kit Fiorantino.

In his earpiece, Damon Jordan sighed.

"I just know the little bit they sent me," the human detective said. "Gertrude gave me a transcript of the summary recorded by the uniforms who got to the scene first—"

"And where was that?"

"Some ritzy apartment place along the park."

"Central Park?"

Nick practically heard Damon roll his eyes.

"Of *course* Central Park. If it was any other park, Tanaka, I would have said so."

"And they found... what, exactly?"

"Dead people. Apparently. Well, technically dead vampires."

"Vampires?" Nick frowned. "And the NYPD is prioritizing this?"

"Well, yeah, so here's the weird part. From what the summary said, they appear to have been turned recently. As in, really, *really* recently. They all came to New York as humans, something like three weeks ago."

"Oh." Nick's brow cleared. "So this is more about them being turned?"

"I think that's part of it, yeah. There's a few mucky-mucks in the bunch. Rich people, I guess. And maybe a few who worked for pretty big companies. Someone turned them into vampires, entirely without authorization, of course—"

"Unwillingly?"

"Well, yeah," Jordan said, like that was obvious. "From the lab reports, they'd only been vamps for maybe a week or two. But they think this group, whoever it is who turned them, has done it before. Something about the exact type of venom it was—"

"Wait. So someone's *making* vampires? On purpose? This wasn't some kind of venom overdose? Someone getting sloppy with their blood-type?"

"They don't think so, no." Jordan exhaled a longer sigh. "I wouldn't say that's conclusive yet, but the prevailing theory is that they were turned deliberately by someone… really some group… and that it was done on purpose."

"And you can't tell me why they think that?" Nick asked.

"Well, I mean, this isn't exactly my area of expertise, Tanaka," Jordan said dryly. "But to my human, non-science-guy, non-vampire ears, my understanding is that it's got something to do with the mixture of venom used to turn them."

"*Mixture* of venom?"

Jordan's avatar nodded. "Yeah. I guess it came from more than one vampire. Like it was something the attackers had in storage, versus a single vamp turning them… which is more likely to be the case when it's a sex thing gone wrong, or some kind of accident."

Nick frowned.

Vampire venom was tricky when it came to making new vampires.

Kind of like human blood types needing to be compatible for transfusions, human blood had to be the *right kind* for a vampire to turn a human into a baby vampire. Some people's genetic typing wasn't compatible with the process at all.

Some humans could be turned only by vamps who had a very particular type of blood… or possibly venom… or both, maybe.

A few lucky human genome-types could be transformed by pretty much any vampire.

Those were usually the ones vamps could sniff out and target.

They generally even tasted better than regular humans.

Seers didn't fare so well with vampire venom-based transformation. Seers generally died during attempts to turn them.

Some hybrids could turn.

Like Zoe, Miriam's sister… she started off as a hybrid.

Then again, Zoe might have been Brick's first fully-successful attempt to turn a seer-human hybrid into a vampire without killing them.

Or, well, driving them insane.

Nick himself had been a tricky turn.

Brick had been bound and determined to do it, so he'd more or less tied Nick to him, making their lives interdependent, but only for the first twenty or so years of Nick's vampire existence.

Of course, Brick… being Brick… lied to him about that.

He initially told Nick the blood-dependency between them was permanent. Presumably so Nick would do everything in his power to keep Brick alive, Brick told Nick that if he, Brick, died, then Nick would die too.

Brick then informed Nick that the reverse was also true.

In doing so, of course, Brick heavily implied that Nick should be forever grateful that Brick would risk such a thing, just to make Naoko the vampire into his personal pet.

Because Brick was just that kind of manipulative asshole.

In any event, Nick found out later it wasn't forever.

That dependency only lasted until Nick's body fully adjusted to the transformation, which took anywhere from fifteen to thirty years.

"So who's this group making vampires?" Nick asked. "Do we know?"

"We do not."

"How many?" Nick asked. "How many bodies are we talking?"

"Four. No, wait... five. Five humans changed. Five new, baby vampires now dead."

"And it says here in the report they were all here for some conference? Some annual tech symposium at the Met?"

"Yup. That's what they told us."

"So all of them were tech guys?"

"Well. All of them were here for the conference. I'd have to confirm their exact roles, but presumably they were at least tech-adjacent."

Thinking about this, Nick felt his stomach drop.

"It's not the White Death, is it? Building up their ranks after what Yi did? Is there any indication they're making that kind of move?"

There was a silence.

Then Jordan's avatar frowned.

The expression looked funny, almost cartoonishly exaggerated.

"Do they *do* that kind of thing?" Jordan asked, incredulous.

Nick winced.

Another part of him rolled its eyes.

Of course they did that kind of thing.

Like... *no shit* they did that kind of thing.

Nick wasn't sure it was wise to be that flippant with Jordan on this particular subject, though. Jordan might be cool with Nick after all this time, but he still got twitchy about vampires in general. He definitely got twitchy when it came to vampire mafias who operated totally outside the law and ran most of the organized crime rings in all of the human protected areas.

Especially since they often did so with full immunity from law enforcement, not to mention the Human Racial Authority along their local enforcement arm, the Inter-Species Friendship Council... or "I.S. Fucked," if you asked a lot of vampires.

Nick wasn't about to make Jordan's paranoia worse on any of that.

Not on purpose, at least.

For the same reason, Nick made his voice more of a shrug.

"Well, sure. Sometimes, sure," he said diplomatically. "They'll go recruiting. Brick would generally have his people start by looking for specific humans. Humans with skill sets he wanted. Humans he thought they might be able to turn willingly, maybe with a little nudge. Then he'd try to talk them into letting themselves be changed—"

"Willingly?" Jordan broke in. "One, who would do that willingly? And two, why on Earth would Brick care about that? Didn't you say he was a sadist?"

"He is," Nick affirmed. "He *is* a sadist. But he's also strategic. It always works better to turn people if you get their buy-in first. If you can make them actually *want* it, all the better. They're less likely to die... or turn suicidal once they've gone through the initial transformation. Hell, they might even be grateful. Brick loves grateful..."

"Grateful?" Jordan let out another disbelieving snort. "People can't really be that soft in the head. Can they? Why in God's name would anyone 'buy-off' on that?"

Nick thought about that a second.

Then he rolled his eyes.

He couldn't help it.

"You're kidding, right?" He smiled faintly at his human partner, quirking an eyebrow. "Let's see. Immortality, eternal youth, eternal good looks, strength, insane healing abilities, being healthy forever... money. Lots and lots of money. The ability to act with impunity. Never having to work a regular job again. Fuck whoever you want. Go wherever you want. Get back at people you hate. Steal from people you're jealous of. You can't imagine *anyone* who might find that sort of thing attractive, Damon?"

"Jesus."

"Yeah." Nick exhaled. "Humans suck."

Jordan snorted a disbelieving laugh.

Then he seemed to think about what Nick had actually said.

"I mean... yeah, okay. I guess you're right," Jordan conceded.

Still thinking, the human went on in a harder voice.

"I mean, I get it, when you put it like that. But that totally ignores the racial authority laws. Given all *that* shit... the registration, the behavior-control crap, the forced relocations, the name affiliations, the restrictions on movement and association... not to mention restrictions on feeding and who you can have a relationship with... I mean, who's going to choose to be a vampire willingly, given all that?"

He paused, then seemed to realize what he'd said.

"...No offense."

Nick only shrugged.

He ignored the "no offense" part.

"Those laws don't mean much to a lot of vamps," he admitted. "They sure as hell don't mean anything to vampires who live like Brick."

There was another silence.

Nick could practically see Jordan frowning, thinking about this.

Then his partner sighed.

"So you really think that's what's happening with this? You think the White Death is doing that now? *Recruiting* people?"

Jordan still sounded half in disbelief.

"I think it's definitely possible," Nick admitted. "Yi killed a lot of vamps. I don't know how many, but I'm sure *Brick* knows exactly how many of his people he lost. He might have sent some of his more charming vamps out, looking for new recruits. He'd want to turn people with skill sets he could use, like I said, so a big tech conference makes sense. He would seed his people in the crowd. Get some hot vampire babes to talk up the potential recruits... male or female, depending on the preferences of whoever they were targeting..."

"These were all men. The humans. Preferences were mixed, from what we know."

"Well." Nick shrugged with a hand, seer-fashion. "There you go. They probably sent out a mixed group. If this was a recruiting operation, they would have done that even if they didn't have specific targets in mind. They'd send specialists to hunt through the crowds, feeling people out on immortality until they found someone who'd bite."

Nick frowned.

"I've never heard of them using some concoction of mixed venom before... but it's possible they did that to hide their footsteps. If they didn't want it to be traced to a particular vampire, maybe? Kind of strange, given how many he's got on his payroll, but I suppose it's not inconceivable..."

Nick trailed, trying to decide why Brick might do this, why any vampire might.

There was a longer silence.

"Yeah, but why now?" Jordan asked. "Yi's gone. Why would Brick give a shit, given that? It's not like the human authorities bother the White Death any."

Nick shrugged again.

Again, he kept his voice careful, unemotional.

"Maybe it's insurance," he said.

"Insurance?"

"You've met Brick." Nick grunted wryly, thinking about his sire. "Does he strike you as particularly trusting? Does he seem like someone who believes humans and vamps might overcome their mutual problems with presents and lots of hugs?"

Nick paused for a beat, then went on sourly.

"...Or does he seem more like someone who'd always be counting the number of people he has? Worrying it might not be enough?"

There was another silence.

That one was shorter.

Jordan grunted his own cynical laugh.

"Okay, point taken," he conceded.

"The thing to know about Brick is, he's old-school," Nick added in a more explanatory voice. "He might seem crazy, but he's not. He just thinks in terms of old-world power. Numbers. Weapons. Resources. Land. Yi was probably a bit of a wake-up call for him."

"A shake-up from complacency," Jordan offered.

"Exactly. Or he'd rationalize it that way, at least."

Hearing Jordan start to accept the things he was telling him, Nick relaxed into more of his real voice. Once he sensed Jordan following along without overreacting, Nick stopped being quite so careful about his exact wording.

"I know you've only met Brick a few times, but he's actually got something of an old-school military background, too," Nick continued frankly.

"No shit?"

"It's not something he advertises, or even tells most of his children... but he even fought in World War II as a human. It was towards the end of that war that he got turned."

Jordan whistled.

Nick knew that to the human, that was beyond ancient history.

It was akin to one of his friends telling him, back when he was human, that their dad rode to the Holy Land in the Crusades.

Or maybe that they'd gone to war with Alexander the Great.

Thinking about that, Nick grimaced.

"Unfortunately, those early experiences pretty much formed Brick's mental framework for war. Also for human behavior, not to mention what human beings are capable of. His human family

61

were Roma, and he lost most of them in the death camps set up by the Germans during the war. When the Nazis discovered Brick's ethnic background, he was going to suffer the same fate, even though they initially housed him as a regular prisoner of war. Brick only escaped with his life because a vamp wandered by, looking to feed on camp prisoners. That vamp took a liking to Brick... and, well, the rest is history."

Pausing to let Jordan absorb that much, Nick combed a hand through his hair.

Noticing a group of teenage girls looking at him, he turned away.

Without giving them a backwards glance, Nick walked deeper into the shadows, lowering his head as he stayed out of the brighter glow of streetlights.

"Anyway," Nick went on. "I'm telling you all this because Brick never shook certain mental images from those years. Even now, he trusts no one. He thinks most humans are shit. He thinks most of *them* are depraved monsters, if you can believe that. He also thinks they would kill him as soon as look at him. Brick really doesn't trust anyone."

"He trusts you though, right?"

Nick let out an involuntary laugh. "Hell no."

Thinking about that, he laughed again.

"No. Absolutely not."

"But he has alliances, right? People he works with?"

Nick shook his head, then shrugged.

"I mean, yeah. Sure. But Brick really doesn't rely on *trust* for his alliances. Brick's about power. Self-interest. If he had any kind of philosophy, it would probably be something like: *trust through strength.* Or maybe, to put it in a slightly more sophisti-cated framing: *trust through deterrence.* I don't think he'll ever lose that mental framing. I also don't think he'll ever stop wanting to be the guy with a few more guns, a few more sets of fangs, a few more bombs and a lot more money than anyone he views as a potential threat."

Nick grunted a little.

"…Which is pretty much everyone."

Jordan snorted a faint laugh.

Nick heard the understanding in the laugh that time.

"He'll also probably always want to hide those things," Nick added, his voice a touch more cynical. "He'll want to have a few more resources than anyone knows about, a few more booby traps, a few more exit plans than anyone might think to look for. Brick is about making sure he always has a way to win... eventually. If he can't win today, if he can't win *right now,* he'll sure as hell make sure he has what he needs to survive, so he can regroup and win *later.* Brick will always have a Plan B. He'll always have a hole he can slither into if things go wrong. Brick doesn't leave *anything* to chance. Not if he can help it."

"Like what he did in London," Jordan acknowledged.

"Yeah." Nick grunted. *"Exactly* like what he did in London. London was pretty much classic Brick. All the way down to the smirk at the end... after letting the rest of us think we were about to be ripped apart by a psychopath with telekinetic powers."

Still thinking, Nick watched an old-fashioned trolley go by on Market Street.

"Honestly?" he admitted. "I get it more now. He nearly got exterminated for his race even back when he was a human. Since then, he doesn't like leaving things to the whims of history. I wouldn't doubt that's why he crowned himself King. Brick wouldn't trust someone *else* to lead him. He's too much of a damned control freak. Also, he's just very, very conscious that things can go really, *really* badly... sometimes really fast... and sometimes from totally unexpected quarters. Sometimes from people or groups you weren't really paying attention to, not until it was too late."

Nick took his eyes off the buildings he was looking at.

He didn't recognize any of them.

They certainly didn't look anything like the colorful, wooden

Victorians he remembered from the San Francisco where he grew up as a human.

Most were morphing, squatting monstrosities now.

Made of semi-organic cement and glass, they were featureless and industrial-looking, despite how expensive they likely were. Virtual paint covered every gray, bland surface—no doubt meant to do the work of dressing up an essentially boring and ugly design.

Those paint skins changed color now as Nick walked by, the instant the motion sensors picked up the back and forth glide of his legs and feet.

Nick focused back on Jordan's avatar through his headset.

It occurred to him to wonder why he was telling his partner all of this.

On the other hand, maybe this little "talk" about Brick was overdue.

"Brick's often told me our entire race could get wiped out," Nick said, shoving his hands deeper into his pockets. "He's said it to me in all seriousness, a few times at least... that our whole species could easily be exterminated, and more or less overnight."

Nick's voice grew a touch colder.

"I think he really believes this, Damon. I think Brick genuinely *believes* he's the only thing standing between vampires and total annihilation. In Brick's mind, no other vampire would be wily enough, or watchful enough, or paranoid enough, or vicious enough, to do what needed to be done. In Brick's mind... without him, vampires would simply cease to be."

There was a silence.

Then Jordan grunted.

"Great. He sounds like a mad king."

Nick thought about that.

"He *is* a mad king," he admitted. "An immortal, psychopathic, ruthless mad king, whose maybe one redeeming virtue is that he gives a damn about his people."

Hesitating the barest instant, Nick added,

"I don't know if you know this, but according to our kind, Brick is also relatively young still. Back when I was first turned, Brick was considered *obscenely* young to be a king over our people. Too young, to many vampire minds. There are rumors he wiped out every member of the previous ruling class, when he first overthrew the old king. I know he spent a few years consolidating power, because I was around back then. I was human, and a cop, but I knew about it because I was friends with people who were trying to control him, even then."

Jordan grunted.

Nick got the feeling the idea blew his mind a little, despite his feigned nonchalance.

Thinking about that, remembering those years, Nick grimaced.

"He's still not very old," he muttered. "Not for a vampire."

Jordan grunted a second time.

"Great," the human muttered under his breath. "And how's that working out for him? Being the mad, immortal, psychotic vampire king?"

Nick thought about that, too.

In the end, he could only shrug.

He knew Damon's question hadn't been real, but he gave him a real answer.

"I mean... not *that* badly," he admitted.

Jordan laughed.

There wasn't much humor in it.

But it was a real laugh somehow, in spite of that.

"Right," the human said.

"I mean it." Nick hesitated, then went on cautiously. "Look at it from his perspective, Damon. Brick's still around. He's alive. He's free. He's rich as fuck. Moreover, he's still king. Not many vampires could have accomplished all that, particularly given the historical period we've all being going through for the past two hundred or so years."

Still thinking, Nick added,

"Maybe more significantly, our *race* is still around. And in much bigger numbers than we probably have any right to be. We weren't wiped out in the wars. We weren't forced out like the seers. We weren't relocated to camps. We even managed to broker a peace deal with the humans to end the war... a peace deal of sorts, anyway... even if big parts of it rest on a lie."

There was another silence.

Then Jordan exhaled audibly.

Nick heard it through his headset, along with the human shaking his head, fighting with how to answer what Nick just said.

Or maybe just fighting with how to answer it politely.

Nick had noticed Jordan tried to tone down his anti-vampire rants around Nick, especially when it came to vampires Nick knew personally, even Brick.

Nick probably needed to have a chat with his friend about that. Personally, he didn't give two shits if Jordan wanted to go off about what a psychopath Nick's sire was.

Brick *was* a psychopath.

It's not like Nick disagreed.

Even for a vampire, Brick was deeply fucked up.

Yet, maybe because he *was* Nick's sire, Nick found he understood Brick, too.

Even when he didn't want to understand him.

CHAPTER 6

BE A DETECTIVE

"So you need me to come back?" Nick cleared his throat, pulling them back to what the call had originally been about. "Is that why Morley wanted me to call you? So you'd have to be the one to tell me to come back for this humans-being-turned-into-vamps thing?"

He waited for a beat, but not very long.

"...Because Farlucci won't like that," he added sourly.

Thinking about that, he let out a dark laugh.

"In fact, that's putting it so mildly as to be utterly laughable," Nick added. "Farlucci will throw an absolute, goddamned *shit*-fit if I go back to New York before the last two fights finish up, which won't be until late tomorrow night. I strongly suspect he'd sue the NYPD, if it came to that. He'd definitely be on the phone with Acharya," Nick added, referencing New York's police chief. "He'd call the Governor. Maybe even the H.R.A., since they brokered the contract between him and the NYPD. He'd be out millions of credits. Probably more, depending on what kind of personal bets he's got down on—"

"No."

Nick saw Jordan's simple, semi-cartoonish avatar hold up a hand.

It was always deeply strange to see an avatar imitate a friend's mannerisms through the virtual program. Especially when you knew that friend well in real life.

"No?" Nick's eyebrow rose. He was back to glancing around his physical surroundings, now that he'd reached the edge of the Castro. "No to which part, Damon?"

"I don't mean no on what you said about Farlucci... I mean no, that's not why Morley roped you into this, and had you call me. That's not what he wants."

Again, the avatar tilted its head in a way that Damon, the human man, did in real life. Again, it looked weird as hell to Nick. There was an uncanny valley aspect to the AI program that made the avatar look both too much like his friend, and not nearly enough.

Jordan's avatar lowered its fake hand.

"No, man," Damon repeated. "Stop looking at me like that. Morley isn't going to get you in trouble with Farlucci. He doesn't want you to come back to New York before the fight. Not at all."

Jordan sighed, and the A.I. cartoon put its hands on its hips.

"The opposite, actually," Damon admitted. "Morley wanted to know if you could extend your trip by a few days. Turns out two of the human victims are from there... San Francisco, I mean. When they were humans, before they got changed, they lived and worked where you are now. As far as we know, they were only in New York for the tech thing. It was just supposed to be a working vacation. A long weekend. Then they were going home."

Nick grimaced again.

That time, it was for a different reason.

Something else had just occurred to him. A few, small words finally sparked something in Nick's brain. A part of this hadn't fully stuck before.

It did now.

"The tech thing."

Well, wasn't that a coincidence.

Who else did Nick know who spent a lot of her time obsessing on "tech things"?

Who else did Nick know who was based out of New York?

Who else did he know who recently entered into a partnership with Brick? Who might have her own reasons for feeling paranoid and wanting more muscle around?

"Archangel a big part of that tech thing, by any chance?" Nick asked drily.

There was a silence.

At the end of it, Jordan exhaled. His voice grew reluctant.

"We're looking into that," he said.

"We?"

"Homicide. Me and Morley."

"What the fuck is that supposed to mean?"

"Exactly what it sounds like, Midnight," Jordan said, exasperated. "We don't need you on that side of things. You're with Farlucci right now. Remember?"

"You don't want me to ask her? Lara, I mean?"

"Morley says no."

"What about Kit? She'll be discreet."

"No. Morley was specific. He doesn't want you asking your wife, either."

Nick got honked at by a passing car, and stepped back onto the curb. "Why the hell not?"

"Where are you, anyway? Why is it so loud?"

"Walking around. I'm in the city. Nightclub district."

There was a silence on the line.

The light changed, and Nick began to walk. Looking around, he again noted the silence on his headset channel as he strode quickly across the street.

He tried not to be offended.

"Damon? You can't really be pissed I'm walking around? You know I used to live here, right? I told you I was planning to check out how the city's changed. That doesn't mean I'm going out partying until dawn... or doing anything *else* until dawn, either."

More silence.

Nick fielded a few stares and realized he'd forgotten to put his mask and sweatshirt hood back up after he left the house on Potrero Hill. A number of people clearly recognized him, including a few who immediately started filming him. Nick saw a few others pointing, talking excitedly to the people they were with.

Maybe coming down here was a mistake.

The Castro was clearly still a busy district.

It was also clearly a nightclub district, like he'd told Damon.

And a bar district.

And a pick-up district.

When Nick turned the corner onto what had been the main strip, he got hit by a wall of virtual lights and writhing advertisements.

Most displayed on the outsides of bars and clubs. Some provided actual descriptions of entertainment, and special offers outside the various bars.

Others were designed solely to draw the eye.

The last category soon had all of Nick's attention.

A twenty-foot-tall cobra hissed at him, swaying back and forth to the left of a VR-panel-covered door. On the next block, a virtual cowboy wearing chaps but no pants, easily forty feet tall, threw a lasso, trying to wrap it around the head and neck of the snake.

A vodka brand had a Viking in furs running across the night sky, leaving lit footprints as it chased a virtual polar bear belonging to some hamburger joint across the street.

A mermaid beckoned to Nick as he walked past, swishing her tail in a huff when he didn't react to her pouting lips and winks.

When he looked at her a second time, she massaged her naked breasts, winking at him again.

Everywhere he looked, it was like a sensory overload.

It was a little like being in a porno amusement park mixed with a zoo.

Even as he thought it, he glanced up, and saw the fiery-footed viking getting fucked in the ass by the polar bear. The detail of their expressions, not to mention their grunts, pants, and the size of the bear's cock made Nick stare, in spite of himself.

He remembered when the Castro had famously been the gay district.

He didn't really see a lot of specific signs of that now.

No rainbow flags. None of the old club names or historic markers from that time. No pink triangles or anything else to indicate the old identity markers or symbols of pride.

Then again, that wouldn't really be a "thing" anymore.

No one but vampires and maybe a few hybrids would remember what a rainbow flag even meant. Most of the people living here, especially those born after the wars, probably didn't even know that same-sex and multi-gender identities and partners had been a big deal at one point. Big enough that people passed laws against it, and created neighborhoods to avoid being harassed by stupid dickheads because of it.

When people learned about other races, meaning vampires and seers, that kind of wiped out a lot of other issues.

A few assholes still tried, of course.

Some argued that only reproductively compatible pairs should be allowed to marry legally, with some bullshit excuse of promoting human-on-human breeding or whatever.

That kind of stuff went on for a few years.

Maybe even a few decades.

But once the wars started, no one cared.

Nick just stood there for a few seconds, at the top of the hill, remembering. As he did, he tried to decide whether he should stay in this part of town, look around a little more, maybe get a drink somewhere. He was beginning to think it would be a bad idea. There were just too many young people here, too many who clearly knew who he was. Young humans between the ages of fifteen and thirty-five made up the largest proportion of his fan demographic.

He was just too visible here.

He should probably head back to the hotel.

Or maybe he could go to the beach, like he'd been thinking before.

He could walk up Castro to Divisadero and then Geary. From there, he could hang a left, and walk west through the Richmond and towards Ocean Beach and Land's End.

Hell, he could walk up most of the streets perpendicular to Divisadero, aim west and make his way to Golden Gate Park.

He was still thinking when a new voice rose in his headset.

He'd almost forgotten he still had an open line.

James Morley pointedly cleared his throat.

His older, deeper, more cultured voice rose in Nick's ear.

"Are you giving my detective a hard time, Midnight?" he asked.

Nick blinked. "Not that I'm aware of."

"Are you walking around the streets of San Francisco, discussing police business?"

Nick scowled, rolling his eyes before he could stop himself. "Depends on what you mean. I'm using sub-vocs, boss. But yes, I guess you could say I'm *technically* doing that."

"What's this about you wanting to go to Archangel?" Morley asked, blunt.

Nick blinked a second time.

Then he exhaled.

This was definitely feeling less like teasing and more like a dressing-down.

"I just wondered why I *wouldn't* go to her," he said. "Or Kit. Or Wynter, for that matter. It's not like St. Maarten won't know you're investigating her. Hell, we could frame it as needing their help to find possible vamps infiltrating the tech conference."

"No. We're not doing that."

"Why not?"

"Because I have absolutely no intention of asking them a direct question on the matter, Detective Tanaka. Not when I

72

know they will simply answer any question I ask with a lie." Morley spoke drily, a faint Southern accent twanging through his words, as it sometimes did. "We're making inquiries discreetly on this... at least for now."

Nick frowned.

He wasn't sure how to tell him.

Hell, he wasn't sure if he *should* tell him—

"That being said," Morley went on sourly, interrupting Nick's train of thought. "Since I imagine Archangel's got surveillance on all our hardware... and especially on yours... not to mention whatever surveillance the White Death's got you under, along with the NYPD more generally... I suppose you may as *well* ask her, Midnight. Since it's more or less one hundred percent probable she's listening to this as we speak. Or will be listening, soon enough."

Nick frowned. "Yeah. I was going to mention that."

"Sure you were."

"I *maybe* was," Nick admitted.

"Jordan wasn't really supposed to tell you about the Archangel thing."

"Well, in his defense, I asked."

"Figures."

There was another silence.

Then Nick rolled his eyes.

"So what am I doing again? Asking Lara? Or no?"

"No. I told you. We're making our own inquiries, via our own methods. And no, I'm not telling you what that means."

Nick glanced back and forth on the street.

He tried to decide again if he really wanted to deal with this many people.

He decided he didn't.

Shoving his hands in his pockets, partly to blend more with the humans around him, he began to make his way back to Market, turning his back on the flashing lights of the clubs and bars all up and down the lower part of Castro Street.

He saw a few more people point and stare as he turned, and crossed Market Street as well, heading for the part of Castro that went up the hill towards Divisadero.

Once again, he considered just hanging another right, heading back the way he'd come.

From there, he could make his way directly back to *The Hotel Vortex*, the five-star hotel where Nick was staying downtown, near the old cable car turnabout.

At least back at the hotel, he could relax.

Once he got past the lobby, he wouldn't have to deal with any more fight fans, or recording devices, or people gawking at him when they saw his face. He wouldn't have to deal with media drones, or Human Racial Authority drones, or I.S.F. drones, either—or hell, White Death or Archangel surveillance or spies—or anyone or anything else that might have reason to piss him off and track his every move.

He could maybe even do some research into this case.

He wasn't sure he was ready to go back to the hotel, though.

After the barest hesitation, he shifted direction a second time.

He started walking up the hill, aiming his feet towards the Western Addition.

Maybe he'd go by and see if Angel's place was still standing.

If he was going to do this torturous hike around memory lane, might as well go all-in, rip the Band-Aid off all at once. Heck, why not *really* make himself feel like shit? Why let himself miss anything that might slip that dagger deeper into his heart?

He wished Wynter was there, with him.

Not to torture her, but to change the way he saw it.

At least then, Nick could maybe justify his fucked-up, depressing tour of his own past. He could make it more about sharing himself with her, showing her more about him, about the people he'd loved, about his family.

He could even pretend he was using it to jog Wynter's own memory a bit.

Hell, maybe it *would* help her remember.

That old seer who showed up in London, Yi's father, definitely seemed to think Wynter would remember more about being Jem eventually.

Realizing Morley was still on the line, Nick sighed.

"So?" he said. "What *am* I doing here for you, James?"

"A bit of detecting. If you don't mind."

"You don't want to be more specific than that?" Nick glanced at a line of houses overlooking the street from up on the hill. He noted the line of trees, the zig-zagging roads up the side of the steep slope. "You want me to look into the guys who got turned? Or is there something else over here that interests you?"

He found himself scanning windows, looking for Angel's house.

Of course it wouldn't look the same as it had then.

Even if the lot and some of the original design elements of the house remained, it still wouldn't look the same.

The Potrero Hill house had been a fluke.

A freak fluke, one he would also investigate when he got back to the hotel.

"I want you to talk to the people who knew them, yeah," Morley said over the line. "There's a husband here I want you to interview. Work colleagues. Friends. It's all in the file, Midnight. We could do it over virtual, but I think you'd get a lot more if you showed up on their doorstep unannounced."

Nick nodded.

He knew that was probably true.

People were a lot different face to face than they were behind the relative safety and anonymity of a screen.

It was just the way human beings were wired.

"Am I looking for anything in particular?" Nick asked.

"You mean besides the usual detecting things?" Morley retorted.

Nick rolled his eyes.

He glanced at the houses on the other side of the road.

Some of those looked more familiar.

Nick remembered walking up this hill with Dalejem a few dozen, hundred times. Usually they'd been heading back to Angie's after going out for dinner, or coming back from a bar, or multiple clubs. He remembered walking this hill with Angel, with Miri, even with Miri and Black. He remembered walking Miri's dog along here, too, a giant Irish Wolfhound with the somewhat incongruous name of "Panther."

He remembered going to see *Vertigo,* the Hitchcock film, with Jem down at the old Castro movie theater.

He remembered seeing a few films with Jem down there.

"Hello?" Morley's voice sharpened. "You there, Midnight? Or am I interrupting your vacation by the bay?"

"A little of both," Nick muttered.

"Did you hear what I said?"

"No," Nick confessed, blunt. "Not a word."

"Look into the two guys who are from there," Morley said, sighing a little dramatically. "Do a deep-dive on their contacts, their families. Follow anything that seems off to you. See if you can figure out why they might have been targeted... either for murder or for being made into vamps. If you think their families are at risk, tell me, and we'll arrange for protection from the SFPD."

"You know this is all the stuff you usually pass off to uniforms," Nick grumbled. "Can't you get someone in SFPD to do it?"

"I don't *want* SFPD to do it. I want *you* to check them out. You're in town. Do some damned detective work while you're there. Keep your mind sharp, Midnight. Maybe you'll keep it from going too soft from all that fist-pummeling."

Nick grunted, mostly to himself.

"So?" he said. "I take it you don't want me to wander the streets, asking random strangers if they knew the guys. You got names? Addresses? Places of business?"

"Smart ass."

"You're not giving me much to work with here, boss."

"Sending it all your way now. Try not to share it with everyone you meet over there. Try to remember you're a damned *cop* still... not just some head-inflated, celebrity jackass."

Nick grunted a soft laugh.

He saw a pulsing light in the corner of his headset screen, letting him know he'd just received a data transfer to his confidential NYPD file. That file was supposedly coded specifically to him, and accessible to him only, via his DNA and his specific police ident number.

Given everything they'd just talked about, about Archangel and the White Death, the thought was laughable, of course.

Confidential his ass.

"So tell me more about these bodies," Nick said. "You said they were human when they arrived in New York. They got turned at some point while they were there... then, what? Someone just murdered them? With an alligator, or—"

"Alligator," Morley confirmed. "Right."

"So why turn them at all, if someone's just going to kill them?" Nick said.

"Well," Morley said drily. "We're thinking there's probably two sets of people there, Nick. That maybe the people who turned them into vamps *aren't* the same people who ripped their cold, vampire hearts out of their chests."

"Really? You don't say." Nick rolled his eyes. "You're saying the first group didn't know they were being followed by the second group? If it was the White Death who turned them, I find that highly unlikely."

"We don't know that yet."

"Anyone else go missing during this conference? Show up a different race than they were when they first got there?"

"We're looking into that."

Nick gritted his teeth. "So what *do* you know? Who are the players?"

"If I knew who did this, do you think I'd be spending my Friday night talking to your surly, old-man, vampire ass right now? Trying to get you to do actual police work?" Morley grumbled under his breath. "I may be old, but I'm not dead. I could at least be out getting a drink or something. Playing bingo at the local church."

Nick rolled his eyes in real annoyance that time.

He knew the A.I. avatar would pick it up.

He didn't care.

Morley's old man schtick was a load of crap, too.

"You know what I mean," Nick growled. "Vampire rivalry? Humans versus vamps? More of Yi's cultists? What?"

"Again… are you asking me if I've solved the case already, Midnight?" Morley queried. "Are you wondering if I'm just wasting your precious, boxing-celebrity, wander-down-memory-lane, me-time? Sending you on a wild goose chase for shits and giggles?"

"I'm asking what you *think*, James. Jesus H. What the fuck is wrong with you? What's the working theory? What does the evidence say?"

"It's… inconclusive."

Nick frowned. "Did you send me this inconclusive evidence?"

"I did."

"Am *I* going to find it 'inconclusive,' boss?" Nick retorted.

There was a silence.

Then Nick swore he heard Morley smile.

"I have a feeling you won't find it so, Detective Tanaka," he said emotionlessly. "In fact, I strongly suspect you'll have some real opinions about what you find in that mess."

Nick frowned.

Morley wasn't finished.

"…But then, you always seem to think you're smarter than the rest of us. Don't you, Midnight? Maybe you could prove it, for a change. For once, you being an arrogant, know-it-all, show-boating ass might actually be *useful* to the NYPD. Instead of just irritating. Although I'm sure it will still be irritating."

Nick frowned.

He could definitely hear it that time.

Morley had some opinions all right.

Opinions he didn't want to share over a line he knew was tapped.

Morley clearly didn't want Nick to share any more of his opinions, either.

He also didn't want to tell Nick much of anything overtly.

Nick wondered about Morley's tone in most of the conversation, too. It almost seemed like Morley wanted whoever was listening to think he, Morley, didn't entirely trust Nick, or that they had some kind of antagonistic, boss-and-underling relationship.

They really didn't.

Usually, Morley and Nick would be having those Friday night drinks together, and often at Morley's place, where they played chess or watched old movies together after Nick made tacos, or sometimes homemade pizza.

Wynter had mused a few times that Nick liked having Morley as a friend to be a regular "old man" with, and she wasn't entirely wrong.

But Morley clearly didn't want to telegraph the real nature of their relationship now.

Maybe he even wanted whoever was listening to think he didn't like Nick.

Or that he really thought Nick was an insubordinate, arrogant ass who cared more about his boxing fame than police work.

Related to that, Nick suspected Morley hadn't been entirely joking when he expressed annoyance over Jordan admitting they were looking into Archangel. Morley might have been even *more* annoyed that Jordan said he, Morley, didn't want Nick involved.

Which meant Morley probably *did* think Archangel was involved.

That, or Morley *knew* Archangel was involved.

Likely, if Archangel was involved, so was the White Death.

It might also mean Lara St. Maarten double-crossed Brick.

Or it could mean she accidentally interfered with one of Brick's recruitment operations, and killed a bunch of his baby vamps.

Or maybe Morley didn't think Archangel had anything to do with it at all.

Maybe he believed the White Death was behind all of it, and he didn't want to spell that out, either.

Either way, this could easily blow up in their faces.

Nick hesitated, trying to decide if there was anything he could ask without jeopardizing any of those things Morley was trying not to say. Nick opened his mouth, in the process of forming words, but his mind didn't work fast enough.

Before he could expel his held breath, Nick's headset beeped.

There was another, lower tone.

Then the line went dead.

James Vincent Morley, Homicide Detective IV for the NYPD…

…had hung up on him.

CHAPTER 7

NOT SEEING IT

Nick didn't wait until he got back to the hotel.

He opened the file at once.

As he scanned the summaries and the first few sets of interviews, Nick didn't slow his steps down what had now turned into Divisadero Street.

If anything, he walked faster as he began to organize everything Morley sent, pulling the file apart in chunks and expanding the various segments inside the virtual screens of his headset.

Once he had everything downloaded to the portable memory, he shut off the network connection, in the hopes he could scan through it all without some asshole back in Archangel analyzing his every move, and staring at all the same screens he stared at.

Once he was off the network, no one should be able to see it but him.

In theory.

Nick kept a small part of his vampire mind focused on where he was walking.

It didn't take much. He just had to make sure he didn't walk out into traffic… or into a tree. Luckily, being a vampire helped with both things.

He could smell trees.

He could hear and see cars faster than any human.

If worst came to worst, he also had the inhuman reflexes and healing abilities to make it easier to avoid dying, in the event he didn't manage to avoid danger altogether.

He walked and scanned text, flipping through images.

He started with the police reports.

Five bodies, just like Damon said.

He compared the reports to the photos, and he walked.

He continued to walk along his sketchily-planned route, but now he didn't pay much attention to exactly how he got there. He hung a left when he reached Haight, but more because his mind had already decided to do that before he hung up with Morley.

He continued to look at files as he hiked up the hill towards the previously famous neighborhood of Haight-Ashbury. Without thinking about it much, he decided to walk all the way through to Stanyon Street, and head into this side of Golden Gate Park.

Up here, everything looked different.

The lights from the city below were shockingly bright.

The few times Nick glanced around at the neighborhood itself, he saw nothing he recognized at all.

Only a handful of semi-Victorian buildings even remained in this part of town.

All of those Nick saw were covered in virtual panels that made them appear different colors under the glowing street-lamps, but those colors were obviously fake, and changed to accommodate the virtual advertisements running up and down the block. All of the crooked, multi-colored wooden houses Nick remembered from his childhood were gone.

There were no panhandling hippies.

He didn't see any street art or any of the ceramic wall art or mosaics he remembered, or any of the sculptures or rock posters or art galleries from the 1960s or 1970s, either. None of the used clothing stores or record stores or hookah places remained.

No graffiti decorated the walls.

Like on Market, he saw a lot of flat, metallic buildings covered in VR skins.

The streets were relatively quiet, especially compared to the strip on Castro.

Even so, a number of bars had virtual advertisements morphing and blinking outside. Most of those were more subtle than the ones he'd just seen down in the clubbing district, but a few were jarring enough that he stopped to stare up at them, maybe because it was weird to see it here, in a place he'd known so much better before the war.

One virtual display turned an entire building into a ship in a storm.

Nick watched the building appear to roll up and down in crashing, tsunami-like waves, so realistically, it might have made him seasick if he'd been human.

Another virtual illusion turned a building into a haunted mansion, complete with crooked gables, ghosts in the windows, a graveyard on the shake roof, and a confusing array of cast-iron balconies, candleholders sticking out of walls, paintings with moving eyes, and weathervanes. The virtual skins elongated the building's appearance and distorted it, so it looked like it leaned and loomed creepily over the street.

Virtual storm clouds gathered around the top of the highest tower, complete with thunder and lightning, not to mention fake rain that only fell around the doorway of the building.

The illusion of rain made patrons squeal and laugh as they got hit by the iridescent and instant-drying, not-water raindrops. Those raindrops somehow, miraculously, never damaged their clothes or mussed their make-up or hair.

Nick glanced at another building that had a virtual skin making it appear entirely underwater. Fish swam and floated by large windows. An enormous manta ray undulated over the patrons dining on the roof, which was covered with hanging string lights in gold and green.

A lot of it was beautiful.

Compared to the Castro, Nick guessed this was the high-end version of San Francisco nightlife... one version of high-end, at least.

None of it reminded him of the San Francisco of his youth.

None of it reminded him of Haight-Ashbury.

A some point since the last time Nick had been here, the Haight had become an expensive, exclusive-feeling neighborhood—filled with private clubs, boutique designer stores, waiting-list restaurants and bars, prohibitively expensive houses, and spotlessly-clean streets with no messy art or music to bother the rich people.

Nick saw one or two fetish shops closer to the park, but even those looked weirdly high-end, with tasteful posters done in retro styles and retro-looking ticket booths.

Posters advertised burlesque acts and unique dance shows, interspersed with celebrity humans doing comedy and magic, or sometimes singing or playing instruments.

Sex acts at those places featured exclusively seer-hybrids and vampires.

Which was all just polite-speak for hooking half-humans who fucked for pay in sweaty back rooms. The pole-dancing, burlesque, magic shows, and player pianos were all just a way to give the whole thing the appearance of highbrow legitimacy.

Nick suspected the cover charge for these places was significantly higher than for any of the clubs he'd glimpsed in the Castro, though.

He couldn't help thinking about how it all worked in New York.

Or in Los Angeles, for that matter.

He had to hope it was better here.

San Francisco was supposedly more friendly to the not-entirely human.

In New York, a lot of the hybrids who worked in those places only did so because they basically had no choice.

He thought about Wynter and what might have been for

either one of them, under different conditions, and felt himself starting to sour on this part of the city.

Maybe he should go back to the hotel after all.

Once he reached the end of Haight, he made up his mind.

He crossed over Stanyon, entered the park, and immediately hung a right.

He felt himself relax as the dark branches and trunks erased his silhouette from the street, even though he knew he couldn't stay there for long. Avoiding the road as long as he could, he walked over the grass and through the trees until he reached Fulton Street.

At that point, he crossed back over Stanyon.

Pulling up his mask and hood, Nick began making his way down Fulton and back towards the Western Addition.

He caught one of the old-school style trolleys when it slowed alongside him.

He was maybe halfway down the hill at that point.

Seeing it slow, realizing it had done so for him, he jogged a few steps and swung onto the back, remembering there was never any trolley here before, when he lived here as a human.

A mechanized voice inside Nick's headset asked where he was going.

Nick told it the name of his hotel.

When the A.I. prompted him, Nick flashed his barcode at the fare system.

It came up as taking zero credits off him, and he remembered that as a public employee, a Midnight, even in a different Protected Area, he rode for free.

He slumped onto a bench.

Gazing out the window, he tugged his hood a touch higher, covering more of his head.

He only looked over at the rest of the car once, to stare at the map.

Gaos. He was in luck.

The map showed a brightly lit line of its route. The damned

thing would take him all the way back to his hotel. It was basically dropping him off at the front door.

The line coursed down the map from Stanyon to Fulton to Van Ness, to Market.

He could jump off anywhere along that part of Market. Or, assuming the trolley continued on in a straight line, he could take it all the way to the old Ferry Building and walk along the bay for a few minutes before heading back to his room.

Nick decided he'd make up his mind when he got there.

Setting up a trigger in his headset to let him know when the trolley was about to reach that part of Market, he focused back on the files Morley sent him.

He went through the basic info on the two male humans from San Francisco.

Gordon Murami, forty-eight years old. Systems engineer.

Kelvin Johns, twenty-six years old. Consultant for artificial life.

Murami worked at Suntrode Virtual Systems. Johns at Norolog, which appeared to be some kind of weapons manufacturer, although Morley made a note they'd gotten famous from some new, semi-organic chip that had a few times the processing power of its predecessor.

They didn't have any obvious connection to one another.

Different companies.

They lived in different parts of the city.

They didn't share any obvious interests.

Johns was twenty years younger. He was single, ran marathons, and was pretty big into the club circuit and illegal inhalants. He was currently fucking a number of people, male and female. None of his sexual partners appeared to know about any of the others. Several, during initial interviews, indicated they'd believed he was dating them exclusively.

What a peach.

Murami, in contrast, appeared to be a genuine family man, living with his male, human partner out in the China Beach area.

He was seemingly faithful, in a relationship where they'd each taken monogamy vows. His husband, who he'd been with for several decades, was a public defense attorney and activist by the name of Alan Rickson.

Rickson had an equally squeaky-clean profile.

Fifty-two years old. Born in the Northeastern District. Went to Stanford for undergrad and for law school. Moved to San Francisco in his twenties.

The two of them met over drinks through mutual friends, when Rickson was twenty-nine, and Murami was twenty-five.

They now had three kids: one boy and two girls, ages twelve, ten, and seven.

Out of the five vics found in New York, none had shared family connections.

None appeared to be religious, or particularly political.

None appeared to be working on projects related to what the other was doing.

Two maintenance workers found all five of them, including Johns and Murami, dead in an exclusive apartment complex in New York City, after being turned into newborn vampires.

Along with the other three bodies found in the same location, Johns and Murami were found on an antique Persian carpet. That carpet lay on top of an original set of white and black, Italian stone tiles that had been installed on that floor over three hundred years earlier.

Chests gaping and bleeding, hearts missing, the five vics lay in no particular pattern Nick could see, sprawled in front of a real, working, wood fireplace.

The wood fireplace, Persian rug, and authentic Italian tile all made the whole thing seem unreal. Apparently, none of that was unusual for an apartment at The Dakota, however, an extremely high-end apartment building in the "River of Gold" section of Manhattan, on the lower west side of the park.

Even Nick had heard of The Dakota.

It constituted one of the few truly famous apartment buildings left around Central Park from the pre-war period.

Nick had no doubt The Dakota had been refurbished over the years, possibly numerous times, likely from the ground up. Even so, its longevity still made the building impressive. It also marked The Dakota as a deeply nostalgic and deeply iconic landmark in New York City.

Hell, at this point, it bordered on an ancient ruin. The original was built in the Gilded Age, sometime in the late 1800s, using the old, pre-war calendar system.

Funnily enough, Nick remembered it for a totally different reason.

The Dakota had once been a prime shooting location for a movie he'd liked as a kid. The director used the outside for his horror movie, *Rosemary's Baby*... a movie Nick suddenly remembered going to see with Dalejem, also at the Castro Theater.

It had been one of Nick's absolute favorites back in high school.

Maybe he would make Wynter watch it with him when he got back to New York.

Right now, however, Nick was getting frustrated.

So far, he wasn't seeing what Morley had seen.

He wasn't getting this "strong opinion" about who or what had killed these people that Morley seemed to think they would get when they spoke over the network.

All he felt was angry, especially about Murami.

Three kids. A husband.

Motherfucker.

Whoever did this, they destroyed a family.

Whoever killed him, Nick intended to find them and make them pay.

CHAPTER 8

QUIET AND SOUND

Nick was still immersed in the files when his headset let off a low tone.

Nick looked up.

Then he looked around at the segment of Market Street the trolley was passing by.

He could already see his hotel out the window.

It startled him, frankly, that he could be here so soon. But then, he'd probably been staring at the stats for Murami and Johns, the two now-dead newborns, for longer than he realized. Also, he was alone on the trolley, and no one else had climbed on board while he rode it down here, so there hadn't been any other stops.

The trolley more or less took him straight here.

Nick considered going the Ferry Building again, then decided against it.

Tomorrow maybe.

Right now, he wanted to spend more time on these files.

He sent an impulse to have the trolley stop.

The powder-blue car had already begun to slow down, so its A.I. likely had Nick's destination logged from when he boarded.

The trolley rolled to an idle in front of Nick's hotel. Once it came to a complete stop, the front lights blinked warmly to illuminate the doors closest to where Nick sat.

He slipped off the faux-wood bench, aiming his feet in that direction.

Seconds later, he found himself standing in the street.

As the trolley pulled away, Nick looked up and down the sidewalk.

He tugged his hood a little further down to hide more of his eyes and forehead. Once he got that arranged, he pulled the mask up to cover his mouth.

Then he hunched his body in the expensive jacket, shoved his hands in the pockets to cover more of his chalk-white skin, and headed for the hotel's giant, organic-glass doors.

He thought he might make it through without incident…

…when there was a sudden, sharp, half-hysterical scream.

Nick jumped, looking around.

That was a mistake.

As soon as he did it, Nick realized it was a mistake.

Sadly, it was one of the hazards of being back in cop brain; Nick's cop brain definitely reacted differently to screams.

But this person wasn't screaming because someone was trying to murder them, or because they were in danger, or even because they were afraid. The painfully young, maybe seventeen-year-old girl was staring straight at Nick… and screaming her fool head off in pure disbelief and excitement.

Wide-eyed, an enormous, face-splitting grin showing her dimples, she screamed again.

She pointed straight at Nick.

She screamed a third time.

Nick now felt like he was in *Invasion of the Body Snatchers*.

He also felt his age. Keenly.

And not only because of his mind's old-as-dirt movie references.

The teenaged girl's friend turned.

Another young person, this one male, with bright blue and

red hair, he followed her eyes and that piercing sound to Nick's face. The second teenager was followed by a third. Then a fourth. Then a fifth.

By the end, Nick saw eight young people's stares aimed in his direction.

They saw Nick, and their eyes collectively widened.

They widened so much, it looked disturbingly, freakishly cartoonish. In those few seconds, their faces looked more unreal to Nick than some of the virtual landscapes he'd just witnessed outside.

"OH MY GOD THAT'S HIM! HE'S THERE! RIGHT THERE!"

A young male's voice carried even further than the girl's had.

"OH MY GOD! OH MY GOD! THAT'S REALLY HIM!"

Nick hadn't fully realized how relatively quiet it had been in his head for the last however-many hours he'd been out walking. Since he left the hotel the first time, he'd barely had to deal with any strangers at all.

Really just one.

Just that kid in Potrero Hill.

Now, it all came rushing back.

The screaming crowds. The people jostling for his autograph. The young fans who stared at him like he was some kind of comic book superhero who could shoot laser beams out of his eyes. The people who wanted something from him. The people who wanted to fuck him. The people who wanted him to bite them.

The people who looked at him and saw *whatever* they projected onto his face and body, good or bad, and expected him to play the role they'd assigned him.

Vampire. Fighter. Celebrity.

Killer.

Seeing the group heading for him now, Nick knew what Farlucci would want him to do.

Farlucci would want him to play nice, sign teenaged breasts, show them some fang, let them take selfies and buy him a few drinks.

Farlucci would want him to put on a good show.

Nick knew that, but right then, in that moment, Nick didn't care.

He also felt no shame.

Truthfully, he really didn't think at all.

He ran.

He just ran.

HE RAN AWAY FROM THEM, STRAIGHT FOR THE ELEVATORS.

It wasn't like the old days, where you had to hit a button to summon an elevator—at least not in a building as new as this one. Which was a good thing, because his vampire ears pricked when he heard them coming after him.

For humans, they moved damned fast.

He was considering making a run for the stairs when the first set of elevator doors slid open in front of him.

Nick practically leapt inside.

He ended up feeling mildly ridiculous when he got curious looks from two couples leaving the elevator, both heading in the direction of the lobby. They were dressed up, possibly for the fancy bar on the lobby level, or possibly to attend a late-night show.

Nick didn't make eye-contact.

He stepped into the car and immediately out of the way of the open doors, into the hidden area near the elevator's control panel and its emergency alarm. He waved his ident tat in front of the sensor, then cursed in seer when it took two tries to take.

It did take, though.

The doors silently closed.

Only then did Nick exhale in relief.

He found himself glad as hell he hadn't taken the stairs.

Farlucci had him staying on the forty-fourth floor, the penthouse suite.

He was a vampire, so he *could* have done the stairs, and without stroking out, but it would have been hell, it would have taken forever, and further, he had his doubts he could even access the penthouse that way.

He likely would have been stuck calling the concierge to let him onto the elevator from a different floor. Or worse, he'd get locked in the stairwell. Then he'd either have to break himself out, probably triggering the security protocols in the process, or he'd (again) have to ask the front desk to send someone to come get him.

Either way, he would be avoiding the stairs.

Nick leaned his back into the mirrored wall that filled three sides of the elevator and tilted his head and jaw towards the car's ceiling. He watched the virtual numbers appear and disappear as they slowly counted upward through floors.

It seemed to take too long, even going this way.

He had time to think about how hungry he was.

He pinged the front desk, still watching the numbers continue to go up.

Those numbers had reached thirty-three now.

"Hey, yeah." He was in the elevator alone, and these weren't state secrets, so he didn't bother with sub-vocals. "I'm the guy in the penthouse. Penthouse 1A. I was wondering about room service. Specifically, food."

"Of course, Mr. Tanaka. You have the entire inventory of the hotel at your service, sir. There is a complete virtual menu you can access via your headset by imprinting on the green light showing at the bottom left of your screen..."

"Got it." Nick's eyes scanned through the list.

It never seemed to end.

After a few seconds, he exhaled, more to make the point.

"This is too much for me right now," he admitted. "Can you recommend something? For a vampire. I'm not picky."

"We have an extensive collection of fresh blood for all of our vampire guests, sir. We also have the best selection of live feeds of any establishment in San Francisco. They are all employees of the hotel, and have fully-vetted security vouchers and consent forms, which allows them to stay with our guests for as long as both parties desire—"

"No," Nick cut in hastily, a little shocked, in spite of himself. "No... thank you. Thank you. But no. That won't be necessary."

He didn't add: *my wife would remove my spleen with a spatula if I tried it, and then probably have sex with another vampire in front of me, just for good measure. She'd probably blow the guy while I bled out all over the fucking floor.*

"...Nothing with a person still attached," he added grimly. "If it's fresh, that's great. You can send up whatever you want, in terms of blood bags or containers. But I'd like a fair amount. I'm pretty hungry."

"Of course, sir. Do you have a preference on blood type?"

"No. Anything's good."

"Ages? We have a new category for 'barely legal,' as well as—"

"NOPE," Nick said, again a little shocked. "Nope. Legal-legal works for me. I'm really just trying to keep the machine running."

"Of course, sir." The person on the other end smiled, and Nick suddenly remembered they knew exactly who he was. Hell, they'd probably bring him a live baby if he asked, given that Farlucci would cover any legal issues. "We will bring that up for you the very moment we've finished with extraction..."

The elevator let out a soothing ping.

Nick exhaled when it did.

He exited out the retracting doors as soon as he could squeeze through the opening.

He'd never wanted to get back to a hotel room so badly in his life.

Well, not one that didn't have Wynter in it, anyway.

"I'm at my room now, so anytime is good," he told the room-service person.

"Of course, sir. On our way."

Nick disconnected the line.

He waved his arm in front of the panel over his door, and exhaled again when it popped open.

He walked inside, moving fast—

—and something hit him, *hard as fuck,* on the back of the head.

There was a sharper sting, somewhere in the vicinity of his vampire heart.

Nick went down hard.

Nick went down fast.

He went down so fast and hard, he didn't have time to think about how weird that was, that he was going down at all.

CHAPTER 9

ROBBED

"Oh my goodness! Sir! SIR! Are you all right? Oh my GOODNESS! Sir!"

Fingers gripped Nick's bicep.

They tugged on it, pulled on it, turning him over.

Nick fought to accommodate them.

It felt like trying to wade through a kiddie pool filled with Jello.

He fought to open his eyes.

He fought to look around, to look for danger, for threats.

He could barely see past the pain.

"Sir! Please, sir... don't try to stand up alone. Please, let me help you, sir. Please! You don't look well at all..."

Nick hadn't fully realized he'd been trying to climb to his feet.

Now those same hands he'd felt before were gripping his arm again. Before he knew it, they were helping him get up, pulling his body where he'd already been trying to go. He leaned heavily on a slight form, but it didn't crumple.

Warm. Small.

Smelled human.

Strangely, he didn't question whether he could trust the person he sensed there.

They didn't feel like danger.

He continued to look for danger, to try to sense it, but he felt nothing like that coming off the kid whose entire body now propped him up.

The kid.

Human.

He could definitely smell that they were human.

Young, maybe early-to-mid-twenties. Male.

Heart beating too fast.

Scared, but not of him.

Scared *for* him, maybe, but not of him.

Groggy, fangs extended, Nick used the kid as leverage and counter-balance to lurch his way to the wall. He squinted around, trying to get his bearings. Hotel room. He wasn't all the way inside yet. He was in the foyer.

He pulled himself along the wall, stopping when he reached the end of it, and the space opened up, showing the living room-type area of his suite, with the balcony in the background. He just stood there, looking around, fighting to see.

His vision still blurred in and out.

He couldn't see anyone.

Pain clouded his mind.

His eyes were flushed with scarlet. The added color didn't help; it only made it more difficult to see, more difficult to think. He didn't feel particularly aroused, in any sense of the word. He wasn't hungry anymore.

He was too nauseated to be hungry.

He wasn't feeling aggressive, or all that ready for a fight.

The fangs and the red eyes likely happened mostly because of the absolutely *insane* amount of pain he was in.

His jaws hurt.

His teeth hurt like hell.

He felt sick, weak.

He felt like he might throw up, but vampires didn't really do that, either.

"Sir… I'm calling a medical tech up here right now. Just hang tight, sir. They'll be here right away. We have vampire anatomy specialists on call, twenty-four hours a day, seven days a week." There was a short pause. "…There. The doc is already answering my summons."

Nick held up a hand, waving him off.

He felt some part of him struggling to protest, but he couldn't make himself talk, and the person with him didn't seem to be paying attention anyway.

Nick could see the guy now, squinting into the gold-tinted light.

Young, like he'd smelled. Twenty-something, like he'd smelled.

The human coded male, with white-blond hair and dark skin, shocking, blue-green enhanced irises and a tattoo covering most of one side of his face.

Nick couldn't make sense of the tattoo, but it made his eyes stand out, in part because it was the same color as the kid's enhanced irises.

He also had a number of piercings on his face.

His voice, his presence, everything about him was gentle.

Nick had an overwhelming desire to thank the kid, but he still couldn't speak.

He wondered if he should let himself be seen by the hotel's vampire tech, then wondered why he was even questioning it. He should absolutely let someone look at him. He had no idea what had happened to him, even now.

He had no idea what would make his face and jaw feel like they did.

More to the point, Wynter would fucking kill him if he didn't let a tech look at him.

He tried again to speak to the guy holding him up.

That time, his throat managed to make semi-coherent sounds.

"My face," he croaked.

He grimaced in pain, even just from voicing that much.

"…What does my face look like?" he managed.

The human blinked at him.

Briefly, his enhanced eyes glimmered in confusion.

The young man cleared his throat.

"Sir, you are absolutely beautiful," he said sincerely. "Absolutely stunning, even for one of your race. Everyone I know thinks you're the most handsome—"

"No." Nick shook his head, grimacing. "Fuck. No. Goddamn it…"

He gasped, but he didn't need air.

It was pure pain.

He shook his head, trying again.

"I mean right now," he said. "What does my face look like *right now?* What did they do to me? My whole fucking face hurts. I feel like every tooth in my mouth is broken or bent. I feel like my jaw is broken. Like my skull is smashed…"

He gasped, and realized some part of him was trying to breathe.

He was a vampire.

He didn't need to breathe.

"You could tell me my whole face was smashed in, and I'd believe you," Nick added in another gasp. "I want to know. What's wrong with me? It's not… normal. For a vampire to be in pain like this…"

Understanding flickered in those blue-green irises.

Nick saw that understanding coupled with a more confused mixture of disappointment and relief. Then a warmer sympathy grew there, as the young human seemed to understand what he was seeing on Nick's face, and maybe hear in his voice.

It was pain.

It was deep, unescapable, horrible pain.

Once the kid got that much, he clutched Nick tighter.

"Sir, I'm so sorry. Come just these few feet. There's a bench here. I really think you should sit. I'll look, okay? But you should sit down, first."

He tugged carefully on Nick's arm, pulling him to his right.

Nick followed his guiding fingers without protest.

After a few steps, the kid came to a stop.

He pressed on the top of Nick's shoulder.

"Sir," he told him gently. "Please sit now, sir. If you bend your knees, there's a bench right behind you. I won't let you fall."

Nick did as he was told.

His knees bent obediently.

His legs and ass landed on something firm but soft.

Immediately, he felt a pale kind of relief.

He just sat there, unmoving, as the young human walked around him where he sat. The hotel employee examined Nick's face, looking at him from only a few inches away. He straightened to look down at the top of his head. He reached out cautiously, then, when Nick didn't move, he felt over part of Nick's skull.

He touched a few fingers to Nick's neck, as if looking for blood, then looked at his shoulders, his chest, his body more generally.

"I really can't see anything at all, sir," the human said seriously. "There's no blood. I don't see any bruises or burns. No lumps indicating you were hit."

He paused, giving Nick another once-over.

He made his voice even more cautious before adding, "I really think you should let the technician do a thorough examination of you. I'm going to call Mr. Farlucci, as well. He'll likely want to bring one of his own people over here to check you out."

Nick grimaced, but didn't argue with that either.

That time, Nick didn't have any desire to argue, not even in knee-jerk instinct.

Everything the kid said made sense.

Of course Farlucci would want that.

Farlucci would be screaming to high heaven if no one called him.

For the same reason, Nick only nodded, closing his eyes.

"Would you like the blood you ordered, sir?" the human asked politely.

Nick winced. "No. Not yet. I'm pretty sure I'd puke it up."

Of course, saying it out loud only made him feel more nauseated.

"Your wife?" the kid ventured. "Would you like someone to call—"

"No," Nick cut in.

Even as he said it, he frowned.

Maybe he should the kid call Wynter. If the doc knocked him out, at least he could explain to his wife what happened first.

The thought horrified him, though.

He pushed it from his mind a few seconds later.

He knew he'd need food, probably soon, but he'd give himself a few minutes for that, too.

He just wanted to sit.

Sitting, he could manage.

There was a knock at the door.

The human jumped to his feet.

Nick hadn't even noticed that the young man had dragged over a second chair to keep an eye on him, not until he leapt up to answer the door.

Now he walked promptly to the suite's entrance, unlocking and opening the panel without asking who was there. Nick didn't move, didn't open his eyes, but listened as the young human with the curly white hair spoke to whoever stood there.

After listening long enough to determine that the new person was, one, someone the young human obviously knew personally, and two, obviously had to be the technician, based on the questions they asked... Nick tuned them both out.

He didn't try to listen.

He felt like his head was being cracked open slowly with a vise.

He hadn't been in this much pain in a long time.

Maybe not since the last time someone tried to kill him. Or

maybe not since the last time someone had nearly *succeeded* in trying to kill him, anyway.

He wanted to scream, but he was afraid to move, to make a sound. It felt like even the slightest movement or change in his position would only make everything hurt more.

No, it felt worse than that.

It felt like it might actually kill him.

Maybe he really was dying. How the hell would he explain that?

How would he explain it to Morley? To Farlucci or Jordan?

How *the fuck* would he explain it to Wynter?

He remembered a few other times he'd almost died.

Just thinking about that made the pain worse.

It made him more nauseated, trying to remember.

Grimacing, he shoved the images from his mind.

Someone was feeling over his body now. Skilled, precise hands, checking him for broken bones, feeling over his veins, feeling under his jaw and over his throat. They felt his wrists, his fingers, the back of his neck.

They kept going back to his jaw.

Something about the probing fingers there, pressing at spots under the bone, made him shudder, even though nothing those fingers did actually hurt him.

He could feel something else, too.

Electronic feelers of some kind.

Whatever it was, it felt both mechanical and animal.

The tech must be using some kind of organic machine to scan his body. Whatever it was, the pulses it sent out touched his skin, from head to foot.

It vibrated his flesh, his bones, looking for damage.

Again, nothing the machine did hurt him.

It was all psychological, all fear of something going wrong. It was an instinctive terror of something happening, accidentally or on purpose, that would make the pain worse.

Even the slightest touch made him recoil.

It also made his fangs extend painfully in his mouth.

After a long-feeling silence, the person standing over him spoke.

"Huh," a female voice said.

Nick scowled. He clenched his jaw, squinting as he stared up at the tall female in front of him. Even the dim lights of the hotel suite hurt his eyes.

They made his teeth grind, which made the pain in his head sharper.

"Huh?" he growled. "That's the best you can do?"

She didn't smirk at him, or even smile.

She looked disturbed as she stared down at him.

For the first time, it hit him that she was a vampire.

Her cracked-crystal irises glowed faintly in the ambient lights.

"Come on, doc," he grumbled. "What is it?" He scowled again. "If I'm dying you better call my wife. Then you'll need to pass me the phone so I can tell her it's not your fault… and not the hotel's fault. So she doesn't murder all of you."

For the first time, the vampire doc looked at him directly.

Her narrow lips curved in a faint smile.

"I don't think we're quite *there* yet, brother," she said. "But I suppose it's good to know you can joke about it."

"Who says I'm joking?" he muttered.

But the doc wasn't really listening to that.

The frown tightened on her lips as flipped back into clinical mode. She glanced at the human room service attendant, who still stood in the room, Nick realized, looking worried.

"Is he going to be all right, Cherry?" the young human asked.

"He will be," she affirmed. She looked back at Nick sourly. "… But you'll definitely have to cancel your fight tomorrow night," the tech added. "You won't be fighting at all, White Wolf, not for the next month."

"What?" Nick stared up at her. "Why?"

The technician blinked.

Then, for the first time, she gave him a real smile. "Well.

104

Doesn't that just figure. Zero problem making jokes about your homicidal girlfriend when you think you might be dying... but tell a guy they can't fight, and it's all shock and disbelief."

"I just meant..." Nick scowled, shielding his eyes as the pain worsened from his agitation. His head pounded so hard, it deafened him. "Fuck. What's wrong with me?"

The tech sighed.

She sank gracefully into the chair in front of him, the same one where the young human had been sitting. The retro, round-backed thing with gold upholstery looked like something Nick's parents might have owned back in the seventies.

The female vampire bent towards him, perched on the edge of the cushion.

"Someone's taken all of your venom, brother," she said seriously. "They knocked you out and drained you dry. I have no idea *how* they did it, but they were damned thorough, and from the cracks in the base of your teeth under the gums, I'm guessing they used some kind of illegal extraction device. Your teeth are badly damaged, but they will repair themselves sooner than your venom will replenish."

She gazed at him sympathetically.

He could feel her watching him though, gauging his reaction to the news.

"You're going to be weak as a kitten for a while," she added when he didn't speak. "And I'm not at all surprised your teeth, face, and head hurt. I can give you something for the pain, but, well... you know our constitutions, brother. You'll burn off the painkiller before the pain stops. You'll need regular doses to even make a dent."

"How long?"

She paused.

Nick saw her glance at the young human, then back at him.

"It varies somewhat, from vamp to vamp... but my guess would be a few weeks, at least. More likely, more than a month, as I said. I'll need to bring you in and do a more thorough scan to see what the actual venom sacs look like. The hand-held gives me a rough idea, but it's more like an ultrasound. I'd need to use a nanotech camera to get a real look."

Nick grimaced. "That sounds… lovely."

"It's really not," she smiled. "But we can keep you unconscious for it, if we use an IV. We promise not to pluck your hairs or toenails out to sell to your rabid fans. If that's at all reassuring."

Nick knew she was teasing, trying to make him smile, but he couldn't answer.

Truthfully, he was still lost in disbelief.

He was about to speak, to ask something more—

—when the door to the suite burst inward.

Before he could blink, people poured into the room.

A familiar voice boomed over all the rest.

"WHAT THE FUCK HAPPENED? WHAT HAPPENED TO HIM?"

Nick winced, clenching his jaw.

The cavalry had arrived.

CHAPTER 10

THE WORST OF IT

"ANSWER ME! WHAT HAPPENED? WHAT *THE FUCK* HAPPENED TO MY FIGHTER?"

Nick clenched his jaw, closing his eyes.

Farlucci's voice was like a drill-bit, grinding its way into the bones of his skull.

At that point, he just wanted to crawl into the bedroom, and disappear into the dark.

Maybe for the same reason, he just sat there, unmoving, while they talked over him. He heard the female vampire tech explaining everything she'd told him, only in more detail, getting into things like gland location and showing him the images she'd gotten from scanning him.

Nick had a second person feel over his jaw and neck, then take more scans of his teeth and face.

Farlucci tried to talk to him.

Thank the gods, both techs—the one employed by the hotel, and the one Farlucci brought to the room—more or less dragged the fight promoter away.

Nick still heard Farlucci in another part of the suite, yelling at various people.

He yelled at the hotel for their "shitty security."

He yelled at someone in the phone, saying "what do you expect me to do about it?"

He yelled at someone who might have been Morley, or someone else at the NYPD.

He yelled at more people... police... press... the handlers for the other fighters...

Nick really didn't know.

Whether Farlucci was the one to call them or not, the police showed up.

One Midnight, four humans.

Nick was getting the celebrity treatment, even as a vampire.

If he'd felt even a little bit better, he might have bared his fangs at everyone in the suite, police included, and threatened them all until they went away.

As it was, there was nothing he could do but sit on the padded bench, staring at the floor while the argued and accused one another and asked the hotel employees questions. Nick had a vague idea that they were watching surveillance footage at one point.

Then the other Midnight knelt down next to him, the one sent by the SFPD.

She asked Nick what he remembered.

Nick told her, in stilted words, the basically nothing he could tell her.

She nodded, telling him that everything he said reflected what they'd seen in the surveillance footage.

Nick would have liked to say a few things to that.

Like, why the fuck did you ask me, if you have it all on the live surveillance footage?

Oh, and why the fuck do you have live surveillance footage in here?

But he knew why.

Farlucci would have requested it, to keep an eye on his expensive toy.

David Farlucci had way too much money invested in Nick to

grant him something as provincial as personal privacy, not while they were in town for a big fight.

Farlucci was convinced the whole thing was about him, of course.

Sabotage. A way of throwing the fight.

They were jealous. Farlucci was being plotted against. By his enemies. Other fight promoters. Rival fighters on the circuit.

It was all a way to make it look like Farlucci and his "over-hyped" fighter were weaseling out of the challenge match, and maybe the North American championships next month.

Nick didn't give a shit.

The only people he didn't mind being in the room right then were the kid with the blue hair, who picked him up off the floor, and the vampire doc who worked for the hotel. Nick had no idea if they were still in there or not, but he wouldn't have minded if they were.

The rest of them could fuck all the way off.

At some point, someone must have remembered Nick was there.

Nick had a memory of a needle.

He saw someone hold an amber liquid up to the light.

They jabbed it into his leg.

Then nothing.

Oblivion.

Sweet oblivion.

HE WOKE UP LYING IN THE HOTEL BED.

He woke up, and pain ripped through his skull.

It wasn't light out yet.

Too many fucking people were still in his room.

He heard voices.

None of them noticed him at first.

They milled around, talking to one another.

Nick heard Farlucci, other voices he knew, but names he couldn't put a face or name to. He heard a woman on the phone nearby. Was it the Midnight, from before? The vampire doc who worked in the hotel? Someone else?

Someone noticed he was awake.

Maybe he had his eyes open.

Maybe he made a sound.

Maybe he even told them to fuck off that time, instead of just thinking it.

Someone jabbed him with another needle.

They jabbed him in the ass that time.

He didn't mind.

Nick disappeared again.

He jerked in bed, and let out a shocked gasp.

His fucking teeth.

Goddamn it, they hurt.

"Here." A soft voice murmured in his ear, surrounding him, cocooning him in warmth. "Drink. You need to drink, baby."

He obeyed.

He sank his fangs into the offered arm.

He drank. Goddamn, it tasted good.

It got him so hard, he whimpered.

"Okay," the voice said. "Okay. That's enough."

He stopped.

He slumped back on the bed.

Gaos, his mouth hurt. His teeth hurt. His head hurt.

His fucking skull hurt.

He was so tired of this. He wanted to go outside.

He wanted to lie on the grass. Look up at the moon.

He must have voiced at least some of this out loud. He still couldn't hear her. He couldn't hear a damned thing through the blood.

"I know, baby," she murmured. "I know. The venom's gone. Remember? So we can't hear each other."

"It hurts," he growled. "It hurts… and I want to fuck…"

"I know it hurts," the familiar voice said. "And no fucking yet, Nick. You need to get better first, or you're going to bite me and break off your teeth."

He frowned, eyes closed.

Was that true?

It might be true.

He wanted to believe it wasn't true, but it probably was.

"Here," she said. "They gave me more. I just wanted you to eat first."

A sharp prick jabbed into his skin.

The needle entered his neck that time, making him wince.

"Take it easy," she murmured. Her breath kissed his ear. "Sorry about the throat. It seems to work better there. It's closer to your teeth maybe. Closer to where everything hurts…"

He let out a groan.

Her voice was maddening. It made him want to bite her.

It made him want to fuck.

It was also growing softer, harder to hear.

Her voice grew quieter and quieter as she spoke.

And for the first time, he fought against falling asleep.

He fought…

He really tried to stay awake…

It didn't make any difference.

CHAPTER 11

NO LONGER ALONE

"Have *you* eaten?" he grumbled, when she offered him her throat. "What are you even doing here, Wynter?"

She gave him a look.

That look said she wasn't sure if she should dignify either of his questions with an answer.

Then, seeming to change her mind, she sighed.

She rolled to her back on the king-sized bed. She arranged her body on top of the covers, and exhaled again, turning her head to look at him.

"Farlucci called me," she said.

He blinked at her in open surprise.

She shifted her head sideways, so she once more faced the ceiling. She folded her hands and fingers over her sternum, and exhaled.

"Then St. Maarten called me," she added. "Then Kit called me. Then Morley called me. Then *Jordan* called me—"

"Jesus fucking Christ," he muttered. "I'm going to kill all of them."

She turned her head, looking at him, her mouth pursed.

"You don't want me here? Because Farlucci said you more or less *demanded* he call me. He said you *demanded* that he buy me a ticket out here, or you'd never fight for him again. He said you were threatening everyone. That you wouldn't take blood from anyone. They could barely get you to drink from a blood bag..."

Nick stared at her.

Then, thinking about her words, he winced.

That sounded like him.

Something else occurred to him.

She couldn't have just skipped down the street to get here. It took Nick a full two days to get from the East Coast to the Bay Area Protected Zone.

He doubted she would have flown. There weren't a lot of coast-to-coast flights, and even Farlucci likely wouldn't have sprung for that.

Brick maybe could have done it, but his was about the only name Wynter hadn't mentioned.

Anyway, if Wynter flew across the country with Brick and a plane full of his gangster vampires, Nick was going to freak the fuck out.

The more likely scenario was that she got here by ground.

She would have taken an underground train.

Those trains were damned fast, but that still would have taken her ten hours, minimum, to get from one coast to the other.

Nick's took longer because they made a few stops to do brief press tours, but all trains stopped at several major hubs across the country. She was also starting from the furthest point north on that side of the continent, in what used to be Maine or Vermont.

"How long have I been out of it?" he asked, blunt.

"It's been six days," she said.

"Six... days?"

"Since you were attacked."

Nick stared at her.

His mind wouldn't compute that number at first.

"Wait. Seriously? I've been unconscious for nearly a week?"

She looked at him, shaking her head a little incredulously.

"You really *have* been out of it, haven't you? I honestly

114

couldn't tell sometimes. You'd act so reasonable, like you are now... then you'd want to do something crazy."

"Something crazy?" He lifted one eyebrow. "Like what?"

Staring up at the ceiling again, she grunted.

"Well. Let's see. I've practically had to wrestle you to the bed at least once, every single one of these past five days since I got here. You tried to walk to the elevators... stark naked, I might add... twice. You wanted to go *swimming,* you told me. My best guess is that you were trying to cool off your face and head when they started to swell."

Grunting in irritation as she seemed to be remembering, she turned her head, meeting his gaze across the few inches between them.

"Let's see. You wanted to go to the park. And you asked to go to the aquarium to watch the fish. You asked me to take you surfing a few times. You wanted me to drive you to Santa Cruz. When I said no, you wanted me to go with you to Ocean Beach."

Thinking about that, she grunted a half-laugh.

"You probably would have made it, too," she added, once more meeting his gaze. "But Brick sent some of his people here, as well... ostensibly to guard you, in case whoever it was came back. The big guy who's out front right now more or less tackled you to the carpet. Twice. Then he helped bring you back here so I could jab another needle in your ass..."

Nick grunted, half in disbelief.

"Jesus."

"Yeah," she said, smiling faintly now. "I'm not sure you can blame the gods for this one. But someone sure has a lot to answer for."

"You're not blaming this on me?" he asked incredulously. "Are you?"

Her smile faded.

"No. Of course not."

He felt the tension rising in him abruptly relax.

"Do they have any idea who did it?" Nick touched his own jaw gingerly, wincing a little, then relaxing when it didn't hurt as bad as he'd expected. He felt over his face, which still seemed to be a least mildly swollen.

"Or *why?*" he grumbled.

When he glanced at her that time, she looked murderously angry.

Not at him.

He found it strangely fascinating, maybe partly *because* it wasn't aimed at him.

If she'd been a vampire, her eyes would have been a dark, shining, bloody red. Her fangs would have been fully extended, her skin flushed crimson with heat and bloodlust.

"The second part, I can answer," she said coldly. "Brick informs me that—"

"Stay away from Brick," Nick growled. "And stay away from vampire bodyguards who can tackle me to the ground—"

She barely missed a beat.

"Don't be ridiculous," she said, dismissive. "And that vampire never would have been able to do what he did if you weren't such a mess right now. Heck, *I* probably could have tackled you to the ground, those first few days, at least."

"Then *you* do it next time," he retorted.

She ignored that, too.

She seemed to know his weird vampire emotions were coming back on line.

"*Anyway...*" Wynter rolled her eyes.

Nick wanted to bite her for that.

Partly because it was damned adorable.

"...Brick informs me there's a booming sellers market in illegal vampire venom right now," she went on, giving him a flat look. "Particularly *celebrity* vampire venom. Yours goes for a disturbingly high price, Nick. The thinking is now, that someone saw their chance, with you being a visitor in town, and staying in this room alone. They somehow got through security and broke into your room. Then they waited for you to come back here, then speed-harvested you with some kind of brand-new, state of the art, venom-extracting machine, after using some kind of industrial-strength vampire tranquilizer to knock you to the ground."

"Someone hit me," Nick said. "I remember that much."

"Yes." She nodded, once, seer-fashion. "They got that on surveillance, too. Two fully masked intruders wearing scramblers and anti-DNA suits were waiting just past the first wall of your suite. A third intruder hit you over the head, but that was mostly distraction... the guy in front shot you in the chest with the tranq-gun when you raised your head. They found a puncture wound from what they think was a *really* big dart."

She cleared her throat, shrugging.

"...They took the dart with them," she added.

"Fuck."

"Yeah." Wynter sighed. "Indeed."

"What the hell do they want my venom for?" Nick said. "Those three asshole brothers, the ones working out of the underground rings in New York... they were after vampire *blood,* not just venom. You know the ones. They nearly killed me, after dumping my body in a freezer unit?"

"I remember, Nick."

"Is this like that?" he growled. "Are they getting humans and hybrids high off vampire venom alone, now? Using celebrity names to jack up the price?"

Wynter frowned.

She opened her mouth, then closed it, as if thinking better of speaking.

"What?" Nick growled. "What, Wynter?"

"Well, Brick seems to think that isn't the *primary* reason they would want it, no."

"What's the 'primary' fucking reason, then?"

"Calm down, okay?"

"No." He forced his voice lower. "Just tell me the reason, Wynter."

She studied his eyes for a few seconds, then nodded.

"Okay," she said. "Brick tells me there's a recent trend of using celebrity vampire venom to turn rich people into vampires." She paused, throwing up her hands. "And yes, I know how frickin' ridiculous that sounds. But it appears to be a real thing. Morley confirmed it. So did St. Maarten when I asked her about it."

She turned her head.

Again, she studied Nick's face, her blue-green eyes worried.

After a pause where she seemed to be watching him react to her words, Wynter went on, her voice still carefully matter-of-fact.

"You might be underestimating just how much this venom is going for, Nick. Particularly for someone like you. We're talking a black market luxury only the *truly* wealthy can afford. I don't mean the ordinary rich douchebags, like Lara St. Maarten's ex-husband, or most of the parents of the kids who go to Kellerman."

She gave him a grim look, her peacock blue eyes flashing.

"I'm talking the *really deeply grossly* decadently wealthy people, Nick. The ones who own their own Protected Areas, and maybe have their own extra island somewhere, like villains from an old spy movie. These are the rich people that rich people whisper about. Apparently some of them cottoned onto the brilliant idea of paying top dollar to live forever."

She shrugged again, still studying his eyes.

"To these people, paying a significant chunk of their estate for a brag-worthy sire name to go with their immortality… it's worth the cost."

Nick frowned.

He didn't doubt her words.

Everything she said made sense.

It struck him as a hell of a coincidence, given the case in New York, but it all made sense.

There must have been rich assholes who'd done this before.

Whatever Brick told Wynter, this couldn't possibly be a new thing.

But maybe the celebrity venom part was relatively new. Maybe one of them got the bright idea of paying for bragging rights to a "cool" sire, and now all of their rich friends wanted their own cool sire, too.

And maybe this kind of thing was becoming more common.

The thought was almost darkly humorous, when Nick coupled it with his knowledge of vampire-world, as well as its erratic and extremely deep-pocketed king.

Nick wondered just how many of those rich idiots had gotten a visit paid to them by Brick not long after turning, where Brick explained the facts of life to them in vampire-land, along with who was *really* in charge, and just how much tribute that person felt he was owed by anyone stupid enough to volunteer their way into his domain.

But celebrity venom?

Venom was venom, right?

"I talked to Morley yesterday," Wynter added. "He sent you more files. He still wants you to pursue a few things while you're here, if you feel up to it."

She gave Nick a dark look.

"I told James to get bent, of course. But he assures me this is purely research, maybe with a few light interviews of the victims' family and friends. He says you'll be, and I quote… 'safe as houses.' I am quoting because I have absolutely no idea what that expression is supposed to mean."

Nick grunted half-humorously.

His words came out serious, though.

"Does Morley think what happened to me is connected to the guys being turned in New York?"

Wynter frowned, looking at him. "Is that the case he has you working on? The tech conference guys who got illegally turned?"

Nick frowned back at her.

He'd forgotten he wasn't supposed to tell anyone that.

Well, he wasn't supposed to tell anyone working for Archangel about that, which unfortunately included his wife.

Then again, fuck the NYPD.

Morley had to know he told Wynter everything.

Well. Mostly everything.

He told her everything eventually.

"Yeah," Nick admitted, briefly closing his eyes. "Morley wanted me to chase down more info on the two guys who were from here. He specifically asked me to do in-person interviews. He didn't want the SFPD to do it for some reason."

Nick opened his eyes again, looking at her. "Did he ever figure out if they were turned willingly?"

"I don't know." Wynter sounded wary now, though.

When he opened his eyes a second time, she'd gone back to staring at him.

"You think maybe these assholes jumped you because of this case?" she asked, pointed. "I admit, I just assumed it was because of who you are... because you're a celebrity. It never occurred to me that it might be because of whatever Morley had you looking into."

Nick shook his head.

Unfortunately, that made it throb a bit, so he stopped.

He started to sit up, and was shocked at how weak he felt.

He stopped a second time, rested for a few beats, then heaved himself up the rest of the way. Once he got his upper body more or less vertical, sitting on the mattress, he looked around. He blinked into the sunlight streaming through the vampire-safe glass.

"Weak as a kitten," he muttered, remembering what that female vampire medic said. "Hey. Where's the kid who found me? The one with the white-blond hair? Face tattoo?"

Wynter blinked. "Simon?"

"I never got his name."

"It has to be Simon." She sighed, fingering her dark hair with the colored streaks out of her eyes. "He's been up here every day, asking about you, bringing special blood bags just for you. It's positively adorable... even if I'm pretty sure he's got a full-blown mad crush on you." Glancing over at him, she added, "I can't complain. He brings me the most amazing cappuccinos and cupcakes whenever I call down there."

"He's a sweet kid," Nick said. "Call him up. I want to order breakfast for you."

"Oh?" She clicked at him bemusedly. "Do you, now?"

"Yes," he said. "Then I'm going to look at all the crap Morley sent me while you eat it, and probably listen to about three hundred of my messages before I get pissed off and delete the rest of them." Grunting at the thought, he added, "You said Brick's got a guy outside?"

Wynter nodded, quirking an eyebrow at him.

"I guess I'd better go talk to him first." He swung his legs over the side of the bed as he said it, wincing as his feet rested on the floor. *"Gaos.* I feel like I aged about two hundred years overnight. You might have to bathe me, Wynter."

She snorted. "You wish."

He shrugged. "It was worth a go."

Her voice turned more serious. "They said it could take a few weeks to be back up to your full strength—" she warned.

"I know. I remember that much from that night."

Seeing her questioning look, he explained, "There were a few minutes of actual lucidity there, with the hotel vampire tech and the kid, Simon. Before Farlucci and the rest of the media circus showed up and made me want to blow my brains out."

Wynter chuckled, but her eyes remained shrewd.

"You still want to do this?" she asked. "Look into these guys for Morley?"

"Have they really not advanced the case at all? In six days?"

"I assume they *must* have, at least a little," she said. "Especially since Morley called me this morning and told me to have you check your messages and the secure server coded to you by the

NYPD. But I have no idea where they are with it, Nick. It's not like they would tell me the status of an open case."

Nick nodded, but even so, something felt off.

He'd wait to react until he saw the actual files.

"What about you?" Nick asked then, turning to look at her. "Have you made any progress on it? Obviously you know what happened with these bozos being turned during the big tech conference. Has St. Maarten been looking into the case, too? Did she put you on it?"

"Bozos?" Wynter asked.

"Yeah. Bozos. If they got turned on purpose, they're bozos."

Wynter sighed, acknowledging his words with a seer's finger-gesture.

"To answer your question," she said next. "St. Maarten does have some of her people on it. Not me… not technically, anyway. Not Mal, either. She wants all of the available seers looking for Yi's people still. But I've heard some of the chatter. I got the impression she's mostly been working that end of things with Brick."

"Chatter, eh?" Nick raised an eyebrow. "You mean you've been reading her. And her people, presumably?"

"No, I mean actual chatter. Mostly from her employees."

Seeing Nick's skeptical look, she threw up her hands.

"Jesus, Nick. She wears electronic shields most of the time," Wynter said, unapologetic. "I *can't* read her, Nick. Believe me, I've tried. I suspect she now has vamps protecting her mind a lot of the time, too. But sure. I mean… I know who I work for, Nick. I do what I can to figure out what I'm not being told, and how much of what I *am* being told is a lie."

"Good," he muttered.

"There's a lot more security around her building now. With Brick and her working on a lot of things together, it's like a fortress."

Nick snorted cynically. "Of course it is."

Wynter shrugged.

"I've seen vampires around the offices more, too," she added, pursing her lips. "Even in virtual. So I'm reasonably sure she and Brick are working on more than just the conference thing together. That said, I *do* suspect she's using vamps for that. She's definitely not using seers. Mal told me she instructed him specifically that both of us should stay out of it."

Nick frowned.

He was about to ask...

...when something else occurred to him.

Something that should have occurred to him a hell of a lot sooner.

He motioned around the room, frowning, and Wynter rolled her eyes.

"Kit," she explained. "We're okay to talk right now."

"Oh."

"Yeah... oh." She smiled. "Are you going to take that shower? You stink."

"Vampires don't stink," he informed her loftily. "We emanate."

"I'm going to dump you in the hot tub," she told him. "And dump a bunch of flowery shampoo and aftershave on your head. Then you can 'emanate' all you want."

He grunted.

He tried to gauge his equilibrium while sitting down.

Then, mostly confident, he lurched to his feet.

For a few seconds, he just stood there, carefully testing his balance.

He looked out the long, sliding glass doors to the balcony, and the hot tub, and the view over the bay. The blue sky of the dome reflected on the bay's water, along with patches of sun and curls of white foam. Nick gazed over the expanse of what he still thought of as the "new" Bay Bridge, which had probably stood there over a hundred years by now.

San Francisco may have changed entirely, the uneven skyline most of all, but it was still a beautiful city.

It was still gorgeous here.

More so, when the sun came out.

For those few seconds, he let himself just soak up the view.

He let himself appreciate the fact that his head no longer hurt. His skull no longer felt like someone had taken a chisel and a hammer to the back of it.

His teeth ached a little, but nothing like before.

He also let himself soak up something else.

Wynter was here.

She was really here, not just a voice in his headset.

Smiling faintly, he stretched out his arms, then each of his legs and feet. Once he felt reasonably steady, he walked around the bottom edge of the bed in the direction of the enormous bathroom.

He'd just remembered it contained two showers and a deep jacuzzi tub.

He felt Wynter's eyes on him the whole way.

He knew if he'd been feeling better, he would have tackled her.

As it was, he only smiled.

CHAPTER 12

CHOSEN

N<small>ICK THREW ON A JACKET, ARRANGING IT OVER HIS SHOULDERS.</small>

He'd spent most of the day re-orienting himself around everything that had happened while he'd been out of it.

He glanced out the long window at the light of the setting sun.

That yellow and orange tint slanted through the vampire-safe windows; it illuminated and colored the main living area of the room, washing it a burnt gold.

Nick knew the sky and sun came from an artificial dome, that the sun was no more real here than it was back in New York, but somehow, he had to remind himself of that a hell of a lot more often here. Despite decades of living under domes, of not having a real sun overhead, or a real sky, his mind wanted to *make* it real here.

It didn't seem to matter how much that skyline had changed.

It didn't seem to matter that he hadn't been to San Francisco since the war.

This was no longer the city he remembered from when he was a kid, or even when he'd last been here as a vampire. But his mind didn't seem to care. His mind wanted it to be that old city, so it just skimmed past all the evidence to the contrary.

Gaos. Was he really homesick?

How delusional was that?

Which brought him around to something else.

"There's something we need to talk about," he told Wynter.

He finished with his jacket, and turned to face her.

She focused more on his clothes than his words, noting the boots on his feet and the jacket he'd just thrown over a dark blue T-shirt.

"You're going out? Now?" she asked, frowning.

"Not without you."

"Nick—"

"I really need to talk to you Wynter. Before we go anywhere. It's important. After that, we can talk about where we're going tonight."

He saw her eyes relax marginally at his liberal use of the word "we."

He took her hand, and led her over to one of the suite's long, velvet-upholstered couches.

He sat down, and tugged her fingers.

She sat down beside him.

"Is Kit still watching our surveillance?" he asked.

She glanced up from where his fingers held hers, startled.

Then her eyes slid out of focus.

They clicked back a second later.

"Yes. It's okay to talk, Nick." She sounded faintly worried. "What is it? What's wrong?"

"Nothing's wrong," he said, seriously. "But I need to tell you something. I probably should have told you as soon as it happened, but I wanted to look into it more first. Then the venom thing happened, and now here we are."

Still frowning faintly, she nodded slowly.

"I'm listening," she said.

Without waiting, Nick began to speak.

He told her all about the vampire who'd come looking for him after the fights.

He told her everything the strange vampire said.

He told her about going to his parents' old house in Potrero Hill, and what he'd seen, how chillingly *the same* the house looked, despite what Nick remembered happening to it at the start of the wars. He recounted every single word he remembered exchanging with either of the two males, the vampire at the arena, and the young human now living in his parents' house.

He told her about the deed with his name and face on it.

He told her about the names of the kid and his family members.

He told her how all of the dates matched up.

He told her how everything was completely wrong inside those dates.

He told about Victor the dog, Victor his friend in Afghanistan, his mysterious "wife" and four kids, the trips to Hawaii, the cruises, the *Bay-to-Breakers* runs, the weekly surfing trips with a guy he'd never seen before in his life.

He told her how that guy claimed to have met Nick as a human in his fifties, even though Nick had never seen fifty as a human being.

He told her how odd it was, that this guy knew so much about a version of Nick Tanaka that Nick had never been, but that echoed his life anyway.

He told her how goddamned *sure* the vampire had been.

He told her how genuinely sad Corey Scotsman seemed when Nick didn't remember him, and how sad Nick himself was when the security team came to take him away. He told her how damned *guilty* he'd felt, like he *should* know him.

When Nick finished talking, Wynter's eyes were wide.

She stared at him, her expression openly stunned.

"You really have no idea who he was?" she asked. "That vampire who claimed to know you, back when you were human?"

Nick shook his head. "No idea whatsoever."

"You couldn't have forgotten him?"

"With everything he said?" Nick shook his head. "No. Hell, no."

"Even if you'd erased that part of your memories?"

Nick thought about that, frowning.

But it still didn't make sense.

None of it made sense.

"I was turned almost a decade earlier than he claimed to know me as a *human,*" Nick reminded her. "He said I had a *wife,* Wynter. And four kids. Four. Kids. I mean... *gaos.*"

Combing a hand through his hair, he shook his head.

"None of what he said makes any sense. Everything was well thought-out, I'll give him that... but none of it made sense."

"So you think he was a crackpot?" she asked.

"I don't know." Thinking about that, he shook his head, sighing. "No."

"So how do you explain it?"

"I can't, Wynter. I literally *can't* explain it."

"You think Brick could have sent him?"

Nick frowned. "What? Why?"

Thinking about that, Wynter exhaled.

"I have no idea," she admitted.

When he looked at her, she returned his worried look, watching his face.

"You believe him," she said. "Why?"

Nick's mouth pursed in thought.

He remembered the guy's eyes.

He remembered how hurt Scotsman looked, how genuinely sad he was when Nick said he didn't know him.

He remembered thinking he *didn't* know him, but that Corey Scotsman was someone Nick *would* have been friends with, in a different life. He was someone he would have surfed with. Someone he would have run in San Francisco's goofiest not-marathon with, *Bay-to-Breakers.* Someone he would have gone to Hawaii with and gone on cruises with.

Someone he would have had over for barbeques with his family.

But that was insane, right?

Thinking that way was totally nuts.

"Nick?"

"I honestly don't know."

He shook his head. Resting his hands on either side of him on the purple velvet couch, he looked at her, wishing he had a logical explanation. "I really don't know how to answer that, Wynter. I just know he didn't seem crazy, and something about his story was weirdly... believable. Even though it was all wrong."

She nodded, not speaking.

He couldn't help noticing how pale she looked.

Resting a hand on her thigh, he shook her gently.

"Hey," he said. "I didn't tell you to upset you."

"I know."

"I guess I'm just thinking we have to make a decision," he added.

She looked up, frowning.

Then her brow slowly cleared.

"Whether to look into it, you mean," she said. "You want to know whether we should go find this Corey Scotsman and talk to him again. You want to know if you should investigate yourself, your own past, while you're here in San Francisco."

She paused, studying his face. "Is that right?"

"Well." Nick felt a flicker of embarrassment. "Actually, I was more thinking which thread we should pursue *first*. Morley's case, or—"

"Or your own. Got it."

For a moment they just sat there, both of them thinking.

Then she looked up.

She smiled at him, a little bemusedly.

"Let's do Morley's first," she said.

He glanced up from his clasped hands, a little surprised. "Okay. Why?"

Wynter shrugged, glancing out the hotel's curved windows. Nick followed her gaze, looking out over the tops of the nearby buildings. The sun had finally gone down for real. The last of it turned the bay's waters purple and dark red, but even that light was dwindling now.

Lights were coming on inside all the nearby buildings.

More lights flickered on in the streets, including virtual projections.

The new Bay Bridge shone with iridescent virtual glows, all along its curved suspension cables. They flickered and morphed, twisting and writhing in a way that made it seem like the whole thing was held up by two giant snakes.

Wynter spoke, pulling his eyes back to her.

"We can do it however you want, Nick. It's your life. And it's your job. You choose." She tore her gaze off the window, turning to look at him. "Anyway, you've got at least two weeks before you're ready to fight. So we have time. We can stay as long as we want."

"Why'd you say Morley first?" he asked, curious.

Smiling wryly, she shrugged. "I don't know. Somehow, I suspect the actual *murder* case is less likely to end with you getting killed. Maybe that's why."

Nick nodded slowly.

He didn't disagree… exactly.

He just wasn't sure if he wanted her to be right.

In any case, the decision was made.

Whether she knew it or not, she'd already chosen for both of them.

CHAPTER 13

FIRST INTERVIEW

REACHING UP, HE HAMMERED HIS FIST ON THE DOOR, GLANCING AT Wynter as he did.

"No one knocks anymore, Nick," she murmured. "He's going to think you're here to beat him to a pulp... especially if he's a fight fan."

Nick realized she was right.

Again, he felt disoriented, like some part of him was lost in a time warp here.

Some part of him really seemed to believe the clock had swung wildly backwards, depositing him in the middle of his human life, something like two hundred years ago.

Some part of him wanted to blame the vampire, Corey Scotsman for that.

Or maybe San Francisco itself.

A larger, more sane part of Nick didn't believe it was quite that simple.

Or maybe that part of Nick thought it was a lot *more* simple.

Like all of this was just some weird coincidence, something he'd made into more in his head. Like he'd let two unconnected, bizarre occurrences get twisted into a single, elaborate fantasy... out of exhaustion, out of missing his mate... and later, out of getting conked on the head and having all of his venom extracted by psychopaths.

But that less logical and less rational part of Nick wondered.

To that part of him, it really felt like he was in some kind of bizarre energy vortex here, where time and race and history didn't matter... or maybe all converged to a single point.

Maybe Nick *was* that point.

Then again, maybe not having his venom was making him punch-drunk.

He had to admit, not having his venom probably made everything a lot weirder right now.

He kept wanting to bite Wynter, so he could feel her mind...

...then he would remember how that wouldn't even help.

He couldn't hear her at all right now, even while he fed on her.

The venom was what established the blood connection.

The venom was gone.

Nick had *known* that he needed his venom for that, intellectually at least, but he'd never actually had to deal with the *reality* of it before.

Certainly not like this.

He clicked on his headset, looking for a number for the occupant so he could buzz the guy through his regular security system, explain who he was, what he was doing there. He was still going through the contact info Morley put in the files he'd sent, when the door abruptly opened in front of them.

For an instant, all three of them just looked at one another.

Nick watched the man's expression grow startled.

"Hi." Warm brown eyes looked from Nick to Wynter, then back again. "Can I help you?"

"You're Alan Rickson?"

"I am."

Nick flashed a virtual badge, displaying his ident number and designation as a Midnight.

"I apologize for coming to your residence without contacting you ahead of time," Nick said, before Alan Rickson could react. "We wondered if we could speak to you. It's about your recently-deceased husband, Gordon Murami."

Alan was staring at Nick now, though.

He pointed at his face.

"Aren't you—"

"Designation Midnight," Nick said, cutting him off. "Tonight, at least. I'm here on business, sir. Could we come inside? Or would you rather speak out here?"

There was a silence.

Then Alan Rickson looked behind him, into the warmly lit house.

Hesitating, he turned back to look at Nick and Wynter.

"Outside would be better," he said.

He slid his long, narrow form through the opening between the door and the jamb. He motioned them to his left and their right, pointing towards a cluster of tables and sofas around an antique wood table in an enclosed porch.

"Is that okay?" Rickson asked. "The kids are here."

Hesitating before he stepped all the way outside, he looked at Wynter.

"You're human."

Wynter didn't correct him.

"Do you want anything to drink?" Rickson asked. "I've got coffee. And some fruit juice. Cran-blueberry, I think. I might also have some apple juice somewhere. Synth, of course." He smiled apologetically. "Sorry, kids in the house. My drink choices pretty much revolve around juices, milk, and keeping myself awake."

Nick winced a little, internally at least.

This guy had just become a single dad.

The thought hardened his resolve.

"I'll take a coffee," Nick said. "Milk and honey, if you have it."

"Me too," Wynter chimed in.

Both of them ignored the surprised look Rickson gave Nick.

Then the tall human nodded. Without waiting, he receded backwards into the strangely adobe-styled house.

Nick walked across the porch after the human disappeared, sitting on one of the outdoor cushioned seats. Wynter sat in the chair next to his, leaving the love seat for their host.

Rickson returned a few seconds later.

He had a tray with him, which might have made Nick feel guilty in other circumstances. Right now, however, he strongly got the sense that the human found it a relief to be distracted by mundane things. Like making coffee for visiting vampires and their hybrid mates, and serving it to them on his enclosed porch with the floral cushions.

Rickson voiced a command as he set down the tray, and golden fairy lights rose around the railings, winking in and out gently in the dark.

Rickson plopped down on the love seat.

Without waiting, he leaned over the tray.

He set coffee cups with saucers in front of both Nick and Wynter, then indicated towards a beehive-shaped container of honey, and a cow-shaped container of milk.

Jesus. No wonder Nick felt like he'd fallen into some kind of space-time vortex.

He couldn't remember the last time someone served him coffee with real ceramic cups and saucers, with a ceramic creamer and honey jar.

He couldn't put a date to that last occurrence at all.

But it had been a long, damned time.

"Thank you," Wynter murmured.

Leaning over, she grabbed the ceramic cow, and poured a thick dollop of milk into her cup. Before she took a drink, she held up the black and white, hand-glazed mug to the blinking fairy lights. She turned it from side to side, admiring the shape.

"This is lovely. Is it an antique? It almost looks handmade."

Sadness rose to the warm brown eyes.

"Gordon made it," Alan replied. He clasped his own cup in

both hands, holding it between his narrow knees. "Ceramics were a hobby of his. Especially the antique style. He was a member of a local kiln society... he was really a big geek about it."

Wynter smiled politely, nodding. "Well, he did fantastic work."

"He really did," Alan agreed.

There was another awkward silence.

Alan looked at Nick expectantly, watching him put the finishing touches of honey and cream in his own coffee cup.

Nick took a sip, then looked Alan in the eye.

"I'm really sorry for your loss," he said, holding the human's gaze.

When Alan's eyes turned abruptly bright, Nick fell silent.

After a beat where he let the human emote, and then compose himself, Nick went on talking in that gentle, soothing voice.

"...And I'm really sorry to bother you, Mr. Rickson, truly."

"Alan," the human said. "Call me Alan. Only my clients call me Mr. Rickson." He gave Nick a pale smile, lifting the mug to his lips. "Most of them are criminals, so I figure it's good practice in that case. But you don't have to apologize, Detective Tanaka."

Nick smiled in return.

He admitted, he appreciated the guy using his real name.

"Okay, Alan," he said agreeably, nodding. "And you're welcome to call me Nick. I really appreciate you being willing to speak with us. We want to catch whoever did this... which means following any lead we have, no matter how unlikely. We'll try to be as unobtrusive with you and your family as we possibly can."

Alan was already nodding.

"No," he said, shaking his head. "It's fine."

Alan Rickson took one hand off the coffee cup, wiping his eyes.

"I understand," he said next, clearing his throat. "I work as a prosecutor, so I know how this works." He met Nick's gaze, his brown eyes a touch harder. "I want to help. I'll do anything I possibly can to help. Ask me anything you want, Detective Midnight."

Nick nodded slowly.

"Okay. Well, let me get this out of the way first." Nick paused, still watching the human's eyes. "Were you aware of any reason why Gordon might want to become a vampire, Alan?"

Rickson flinched.

Then, abruptly, his eyes widened.

He looked from Nick to Wynter and back again.

Clearly, he hadn't expected that particular question.

"No," he said, adamant. "Why? Why would you ask me that?"

"You're aware of the condition he was in, when he was found deceased?"

Rickson's lips pinched.

He looked between them a second time.

Nick thought he saw a glimmer of understanding there.

"I know he was found at The Dakota," Alan said. "Where those movie stars used to live, back in the pre-war period. They told me the eighth floor. They said the apartment was currently vacant, and was listed as being for sale, after the previous tenant died." He paused. "Why would you ask me if Gordon wanted to become a vampire?"

"Because he'd been turned," Nick said carefully. "He was a newborn."

"A... what?"

"A newborn vampire." Nick's mouth hardened. "When he was killed, he'd only been a vampire for a short period of time. A week. Two weeks, at most."

"He was there for a work convention—"

"Yes, we're aware. Did he tell you anything about that?" Nick said. "About the convention itself? Maybe after he arrived?"

"What do you mean?"

"I mean, did he meet anyone?"

"No."

Nick glanced at Wynter.

He looked back at Rickson, lifting an eyebrow.

"At a convention?" Nick asked. "He didn't meet anyone at all?"

"No. Not that he said to me."

Nick kept his voice and face expressionless.

"Did he tell you about any speakers?" he asked. "Any events he attended? Any people he met for drinks? Any meetings or business he conducted?"

"Who is she?" Alan pointed at Wynter, his mouth curled in a faint frown. "You showed me your credentials, but not hers. Why is she here?"

Nick hesitated.

Alan Rickson was either a lot more observant than Nick had banked on, or a lot more wary of the nature of his partner's death, or both.

Clearly, he wasn't an idiot.

Nick should have remembered the guy worked in the system. As a public defender, he was used to looking for breaches in protocol. They were often his best means of winning his cases, particularly when his client was guilty.

"She's my wife," Nick said after that pause.

"Lovely. Why is she *here?*"

Nick opened his mouth, about to answer, but Wynter got there first.

"I'm technically employed by the defense conglomerate Archangel Industries, Mr. Rickson," she said politely. "Due to the nature of the relationship between my employer and the government of the New York Protected Area, I'm authorized to work with my husband on some of his cases… with the approval of my bosses at Archangel, of course, and his bosses with the NYPD."

"Work together in what way?" Rickson asked warily.

"We share intel. Observations. Sometimes interviews… like this one."

"May I see the contractual status?" the human asked.

Nick's eyebrow rose.

Wynter didn't miss a beat.

"There's not a formal relationship in place at the moment, Alan."

"Security clearance?" he queried.

"I'm afraid that's classified, Alan," she replied diplomatically. "My employers consider the official security status of certain subsets of their employees to be proprietary information. Therefore, I'm not authorized to disclose anything about that status with anyone who hasn't received explicit rights and signed the appropriate NDAs with my employer, Archangel Industries. I apologize."

Pausing, she added,

"That said, you are welcome to ask me to leave, Mr. Rickson. Since I'm not officially authorized to be here, and cannot present you with a warrant or other order that would require you to tolerate my presence, you may revoke permission for me to be on your property at any time. You are under no obligation to give me permission to listen in on this interview, either. If you would like me to leave, I'll simply wait for my husband back at our hotel."

The silence that time felt a lot more loaded.

Rickson leaned back in the loveseat, still clutching his coffee cup.

"Archangel Industries." The man gazed only at Wynter.

"Yes," she said. "That's correct."

Wynter crossed her tanned legs in the white summer dress she wore, pulling Nick's eyes. He didn't get the impression she did it as a means of distracting either of them, but he couldn't help watching his wife's mouth and legs as she lifted her coffee cup to her lips to take a sip. Her sandals showed off pale blue toenail polish on each of her toes.

Nick found all of it distracting as hell.

Alan Rickson barely seemed to notice.

"They do a lot of genetics work," he said. "Archangel, I mean. Including with vampires?"

"I'm afraid I'm not at liberty to discuss that either, Alan."

He nodded, his eyes faintly bemused.

He stared at her face, studying her, mouth pursed, like he was trying to read behind her expression to whatever she wasn't saying.

Then he glanced between her and Nick.

"Is this to do with Gordon's work? The stuff he was doing with vampire venom?"

Nick felt his whole body tense.

For the first time in several minutes, he looked away from his wife.

"What?" he said.

CHAPTER 14

PROSECUTOR

"W ELL." A LAN R ICKSON ADJUSTED HIS HEADSET, HITTING A pressure trigger on the side. "I'm probably not *really* supposed to talk about this, but no one's specifically told me *not* to talk about it, and really, no one's asked me much of anything since telling me Gordon was found dead…"

He sounded distinctly bitter at the end.

Then, as if to brush it off, Alan Rickson made a noncommittal gesture with his hands.

Somehow, that vague flutter made one thing crystal-clear.

Alan Rickson wasn't feeling all that obligated to whatever or whoever might not want him to say anything about Gordon's work.

"Anyway, no one even bothered to tell me they'd turned Gordon into a *vampire.*" Rickson said the last words angrily, then winced, as if the reality of them was still hitting him in stages. "I can't help but wonder if *that* could really be a coincidence."

"It seems unlikely," Nick agreed, giving Wynter a dark look.

She never took her eyes off Alan.

Nick strongly suspected she was reading the human.

For the same reason, he didn't look at her for very long.

He focused back on Rickson.

"Gordon talked to you about his work?"

"Well. Sure." Alan looked at Wynter, then back at Nick. "Clearly you two have that kind of marriage, as well. Gordon and I shared everything. No exceptions."

That time, it was Nick's turn to wince.

He bit his tongue, mostly to keep from telling the human again how sorry he was.

He *was* sorry though.

He was also angry.

"But you're a lawyer, right?" Nick pressed. "You can't tell him everything."

"Everything I could tell him, I did," Alan said, his voice a little harder.

"Of course." Nick cleared his throat, his own voice gruff. "So what was this project? The one involving vampire venom?"

"I'm getting to that," Alan said.

A light erupted from one side of his headset.

The light sent a projection out from the camera by his ear.

Rickson leaned back, and a three-dimensional image unfolded over the coffee table that stood between the loveseat and the two chairs where Nick and Wynter sat. Nick looked up, adjusting his spine in the patterned cushion, squinting up at what looked like a warehouse by a large lake. He didn't recognize the building, or the lake, or the surrounding land.

"Where is that?" he asked.

"Seoul," Rickson answered promptly. "It's where they first discovered it. Or designed it, I suppose. It took them a bit longer to realize what it could do."

Nick opened his mouth to ask, then shut it again.

Clearly Rickson intended to tell him.

Nick strongly got the impression he'd learn more if he kept his mouth shut.

"I confess," Rickson said, glancing again at Nick, then at Wynter, then back at Nick. "I *had* wondered if there was some connection with Gordon's death. Even before you told me what they'd done to him. Once I saw the names of the people in the room with him when he'd been found... I suspected this *had* to be about that. It was simply too much of a coincidence. It *had* to be about the project Gordon was working on at the end."

Nick sat up straighter. "You recognized them? The other victims?"

"Yes."

"All of them?"

Rickson nodded again. "Yes. All of them. Several have been to this house, but I know all of them from different industry events and so forth."

Five detailed insignias rose into the visuals over the table.

They looked like company logos.

Nick squinted up at them.

He recognized only two.

Alan went on in the same calm, explanatory voice.

"Gordon told me the whole project was super-crazy hush-hush. They were working with a few other groups besides this core group of five, but none of it was logged officially on the books for the first year... not even internally, within each company. As far as I know, at the time of their deaths, they *still* had absolutely no explicit agreements in place."

"Why?" Nick asked, blunt.

Rickson sighed.

Then he held up his hands.

"I can only speculate," he offered. "I'm guessing it allowed them to experiment before the discovery might have impacted the markets. I also would assume it's more dangerous to them, in terms of risk, if things were to go wrong. So they preferred to do their work quietly at first. No electronic trail."

He gave Wynter a wry smile, quirking an eyebrow.

"...sort of like you, Mrs. Tanaka."

Wynter grunted a bit, smiling politely.

Otherwise, she didn't answer.

Leaning back in her chair, she took a sip of her coffee, one elbow balanced on her crossed arm. Alan smiled back at her.

He looked more seriously at Nick.

"Gordon was the top systems development engineer at Suntrode," he said. "His boss pulled him into the project personally. Viraj Das laid the whole thing out… what it was, what was at stake, what they were risking, the potential payoff. I admit, Gordon was pretty excited about that last part. He really wanted to buy a house…"

Nick glanced at the house behind where the human sat.

Alan waved him off.

"We're renting this place. I make an okay salary, and Gordon made a great one, but this project would have let us buy this place outright… in cash… or something comparable. Without touching what we have saved for the kids."

Nick nodded, noncommittal.

"What was the project, Alan?" he asked.

Alan sighed, picking up his own coffee.

"Gordon's old boss is well-connected. Super rich." Alan waved a hand, pursing his lips. "He had university connections with this huge lab in what used to be South Korea… in the protected area of Seoul. That's what I just showed you… the main labs of ColdArt Creation, the biotech firm. They had a bio-engineer there, Laks Boorman, who claimed to have developed a form of synthetic vampire venom."

"Laks Boorman." Nick flipped through his own files. He remembered the name. "That was one of them, wasn't it? One of the victims in New York?"

"Yes."

"And could I get the boss's name again? The one who connected Gordon with ColdArt?"

"Viraj Das. He's Senior VP of New Product Development at Suntrode."

"Got it. And what was Gordon supposed to be doing on this project? What was his understanding of his role?"

Rickson shrugged, gripping the coffee cup more tightly.

"I think Das mostly wanted him to check it out, at least initially," the human said. "See if the project had wings. If it did, then Gordon was supposed to assess whether he could get Suntrode in on the ground floor. If everything looked good, the company would invest at a higher amount... and work out a deal for production and distribution."

"And this was for synthetic venom?" Nick frowned. "What kind of market were they looking for? Synthetic venom is illegal."

Alan Rickson nodded, clearly not surprised by that.

"I know. But they thought they'd found a commercial application. Something they might be able to petition for use with a carve-out license of some kind." Exhaling, Alan took another sip of coffee, then shrugged. "Initially, I really didn't understand all the secrecy... or the novelty, frankly. It just seemed paranoid and weird. I told Gordon not to get his hopes up."

Nick was frowning, though.

"I still don't get it," he said, blunt. "Did Boorman come up with some new way of synthesizing the previous versions of synthetics? Of mass-producing a new kind? Because the black market has several high-quality versions already. At least one has been available for purchase in large quantities for a few years now. The original came out of a Russian lab, but the formula got out, and now everyone has it."

Alan Rickson was shaking his head.

"No," he said. "That's what I thought, too. But it's not the same."

"Meaning what?"

"It's not the same tech, Detective."

Nick frowned.

He considered asking it again, then decided to change tacks.

"You said it's a form of synthetic vampire venom though, right? With the same functionality as the kind available on the black market now?"

"I didn't say that, no," Rickson said. "And no. It's not."

Nick stared at him. "So what is it?"

When Alan didn't answer right away, Nick paused, studying the human's face.

For a human, Rickson was surprisingly difficult to read.

"Either way, it's insanely illegal," Nick said, his voice faintly warning. "I have no idea why a company as big as Suntrode would risk something like that, much less any of these others..."

He motioned towards the company logos still rotating overhead.

"Synthetic vampire venom is classified as a bioweapon, Alan," Nick added. "Specifically as a *terrorist* bioweapon under the Human Racial Authority code. That doesn't even get into Protectorate laws or the laws of specific territories. Just being found with a small amount on your person is a minimum ten-year sentence. Since it's also considered a racial hate crime to possess the stuff, you could conceivably get as much as thirty years, depending on the judge."

"They weren't interested in any of that," Rickson said dismissively.

"Which part aren't they interested in?" Nick asked drily. "You know what it's used for, right? It's primarily utilized as a means of controlling large groups of people. Human people. In ways that completely strip them of their free will."

"Yes. I'm aware of its current uses, Detective Tanaka."

When Rickson didn't go on, Nick's frown deepened.

Was this guy fucking with him?

Why wouldn't he answer the question?

"My point is, why in the gods would they risk that?" Nick asked flatly. "Are they really so desperate for novelty defense contracts that they'd risk probing for a commercial use for something like that? For a bioweapon that could mean the end of human civilization?"

Alan Rickson was already shaking his head.

"No, that's really not what this is about, Nick," he said, his voice still dismissive.

146

"Then what is it about?" Nick frowned. "Are you going to tell us?"

"This isn't that," Alan said, his voice a touch warning. "I mean, you're right about the vampire venom currently on the market... and the legal issues they were risking, while they put the new tech into the testing phase. But they had no interest in crowd control, Detective, or in anything that could be used as a weapon... against either race."

Exhaling, Rickson combed a hand through his thinning hair.

"In the beginning," he added. "Gordon was working with their top genetic designer on the machine side, trying to remake Boorman's formula in a way that would enable mass-production. But that was only one tiny piece of what was going on. They had other people working on other components. Testing, mostly, to make sure the substance could do as Boorman promised. A few people from Norolog worked on that side, refining the organics, and working on designing it with the artificial life components needed to make it viable—"

"Johns," Nick cut in. "Kelvin Johns."

"That was one of them, yes. I believe he was leading their artificial life team."

"Norolog is also based out of San Francisco?"

"Yes. They have offices in the SOMA area. I believe they have another campus in South San Francisco... and one in Chicago."

Wynter spoke up, causing both men to turn.

From Rickson's face, he'd practically forgotten she was there.

Nick suspected Wynter *wanted* him to forget.

Which made it all the stranger when she spoke.

"You need to explain it to him." She stared at Rickson alone. Her voice was blunt, her eyes uncompromising. "You need to explain what it does, Alan. You need to explain what it is that Boorman is claiming to have made... and why."

"It's venom, right?" Nick stared at her, then swiveled his gaze back to Rickson. "What is she talking about, Alan? What did they make?"

Alan Rickson sighed.

Leaning back on the loveseat, he brought his cup of coffee to his lips, slurping a thick swallow of the dark liquid.

It occurred to Nick for the first time that they were drinking real coffee.

Real. Fucking. Coffee.

He honestly couldn't remember the last time he'd had it, or even smelled it.

The fact that he hadn't even noticed until now only proved again what a weird time-warp his mind had been in, ever since he arrived in San Francisco.

"Alan?" Nick prodded.

"Look, they weren't interested in the military applications for this type of venom," Alan said, exhaling. "Boorman more or less bred those out of this strain entirely. This was strictly meant to be a *commercial* product. It wasn't for getting other people to do what you wanted. It wasn't meant to be administered to anyone but the client themselves."

Nick frowned. "It's not to turn people, is it?"

Alan held up a hand.

"No. Definitely not." He set his cup and saucer back down on the coffee table, still holding up his other hand. "No, this was meant to *avoid* that possibility, actually. It was meant to do the *opposite* of turning people. Once administered, it should have protected them from being unwillingly turned. While still conveying to the affected customer most... if not all... of the, well, *benefits*... of that altered state."

"The benefits," Nick repeated.

"Yes. You know. All of the *good* parts of becoming one of your kind. From a human perspective," the man added.

"Are you talking about a youth serum of some kind?"

Alan's expression relaxed.

"In a manner of speaking, yes. It's more than that, but yes."

"So a kind of hyper-vitality youth serum? Youth serum with a lot of added kick?"

"Yes." Alan nodded vigorously. "That's exactly what I'm talking about."

Nick looked at Wynter, who raised an eyebrow.

Nick looked back at Alan Rickson.

"So, let me make sure I'm understanding you correctly." Nick leaned over to rest his arms on his thighs, clasping his ghost-white hands. "You're talking about *all* of the physical benefits of being a vampire... presumably through this specific, special type of modified, boutique-designed venom Boorman invented... but without the blood dependency, without the death, without actually *becoming* a vampire. Is that correct?"

"Yes." Alan Rickson nodded, even more emphatically. "Yes. That's it. That's exactly what Gordon was told."

"So immortality, but still eating and tasting human food, able to walk around in broad daylight on a sunny day—"

"That's right. All of that. That's *exactly* correct," Alan said. "All of the benefits. None of the downsides. That's what Gordon was going to help them mass-produce."

Nick's mouth twitched.

He couldn't help it.

He managed to keep the rest of his facial expression neutral.

"What about the heightened senses and reflexes?" he inquired lightly. "Hearing? Smell?"

"Yes." Alan nodded. "Those, too."

"Physical speed? Healing abilities? Would those be affected at all?"

"It's my understanding that anyone who fulfilled a course of the venom treatment, which could take anywhere from two to four months, would acquire all of those things by the end, yes. More or less at the same rate and ability of a real vampire."

"While remaining human?"

"Yes."

"Without a blood dependency?" Nick repeated.

He looked at Wynter. She held a poker face even better than he did.

His eyes returned to Alan Rickson.

"…Just so we're clear."

"Absolutely. Without a blood dependency. Without *any* of the negative aspects of your…" Rickson paused. He seemed to rethink his wording. He gestured towards Nick, and Nick felt the warmth from the human's skin as he flushed. "…you know. Your state. Your exact form of existence."

Nick looked at Wynter.

Again, she didn't so much as blink.

Her eyes remained on Alan Rickson, her lips pinched, but Nick couldn't tell if she was reading him anymore. She might have been thinking about something else entirely. No one could hold a blank, inscrutable face like Wynter could.

Looking back at Rickson himself, Nick took a sip of his coffee.

He felt a brief glimmer of regret that he couldn't fully appreciate what was on his tongue, or even absorb the full taste of the very *real* coffee their host had given them.

He couldn't even fully smell it.

Not accurately.

But that couldn't be helped, either. Nick had a vampire's palate now.

He'd had it for over two hundred years.

He could distinguish between thousands, tens of thousands, hundreds of thousands of variations in blood taste, skin, and other animal scents. He could pick out detailed information from those smells, pulling out possibly millions of data points over the course of his very long life.

But Nick couldn't fully taste a cup of finely-ground and roasted coffee.

Not even real coffee.

Not even a cup like this, which would probably go for over a hundred dollars if he'd ordered it in a restaurant.

Carefully, so as not to spill a single drop, Nick set the saucer and cup on the antique coffee table. He leaned back in his chair, making the real-wood frame squeak under his vampire weight, which was probably two or three times what a human his size would weigh.

He looked Alan Rickson directly in the eye.

"Bullshit," he said simply.

He wasn't expressing amazement.

He wasn't being argumentative.

He wasn't feeling the slightest bit defensive.

He was simply expressing the God's-honest truth.

CHAPTER 15

MAGIC BEANS

"Look," Nick said. "I'm not trying to be a dick…"

He made an effort to shift his voice lower.

He also fought to make it less harsh.

"…but I *am* telling you that what you're saying they invented isn't a thing," Nick added. "It's just not. For the simple reason that it's absolutely not possible."

At the human's continued silence, Nick cleared his throat.

He gestured politely towards Rickson's still form.

"Look, there's no shame in being taken in," Nick said. "I mean, shit. How could you have known? How could Gordon? He's a systems engineer, right? Not a geneticist. He'd have no idea how vampire physiological functions operate."

Grimacing at his own words, Nick added,

"Believe me, I get it. The concept sounds amazing. The commercial possibilities, if such a thing were feasible, would be positively through the roof. The problem is, it's really *not* feasible. There's really no good way to say it, other than to tell you that anyone who knows the first thing about vampire physiology would know that Boorman's claim is nonsense. It really *is* impossible. He's a fake. He may not even be a geneticist—"

"No." Alan shook his head. "You're wrong."

153

"I'm really not."

"You are." Alan turned on him, his eyes cold. "You didn't see what I saw. There's proof. Gordon showed me *proof* that it worked. They had recordings. Blood samples. They had hours and hours of scientific tests they conducted—"

Nick interrupted him, as gently as he could.

"Look. I don't want to argue with you," he said. "But it's honestly not up for debate. I'm trying to explain to you that this *had* to have been a hoax of some kind. What Boorman claims to have invented is impossible. There's no conceivable way it can be done. Trust me."

"Just because a thing *hasn't* been done before…" Alan's voice shifted a touch higher and more imperious. "…doesn't mean it cannot *ever* be done."

Nick chuckled.

"Except when it's bullshit," Nick said pleasantly. *"Gaos.* I'm sorry to be the one to tell you this, friend… I really am. But someone sold your husband a great big bag of shit. The vampire-blood-to-immortality scam is one of the oldest in the book. It's the equivalent of a bag of magic beans. Or being sold your own, personal deed to the Brooklyn Bridge. There's no possible way they designed some kind of 'modified venom' that does what you say it does."

"Why the hell not? Why *can't* it be true?"

Alan looked flustered now.

At the same time, clearly he was listening.

Because of that, Nick took the time to explain.

"To have any of these things you listed out—immortality, eternal youth, healing powers, enhanced sensory perception, enhanced strength and reflexes—to have *any one* of them, your human body has to die," Nick said flatly.

Wynter flinched.

Nick glanced at her, then looked back at Rickson.

He held up one of his chalk-white hands, displaying his fingers.

"This flesh, these bones…" Nick rotated his hand in front of the human's face. "…technically, they aren't human at all anymore. Technically, they aren't flesh. Technically, they aren't bones. They aren't even made up of the same material as a human body."

Seeing the angry frown coming to the human's face, Nick sighed.

Lowering his hand down to his lap, he explained in a patient voice.

"Look. Vampire genetics are still a fuzzy area. They're still a pretty big damned mystery, truth be told, even to vampire scientists. But we do know a *few* things. For one, we know vampires don't have genes or DNA or blood or cells or flesh at all."

His voice turned even more matter-of-fact.

"We also know that the building blocks that make up a vampire body are *entirely incompatible* with the oxygen-rich cells needed by humans to live. We don't generate blood. Technically, we aren't even male or female, despite our superficial sex organs. We don't sweat. We don't shed our skin or hair. Famously, we don't breathe or have a heartbeat, but those two things are symptoms of much more fundamental differences. Differences in the very nature of the kind of sentient consciousness we represent."

Nick could feel Wynter listening to him intently now, too.

He stared into Rickson's eyes, his voice blunt.

"No amount of 'designer venom' is going to keep a human being alive once a bunch of vampire cells start proliferating in the host body, Alan. Vampires, as a lifeform, are essentially parasitic. Their organic matter is deadly as hell to human beings, at the *molecular* level."

Leaning back in his chair, he held out his hands.

"There are really only two options for a human host after the point of infection," Nick went on seriously. "Either the human dies and never wakes up again, or the human dies and wakes up a vampire. When the second one happens, every single human cell in their body has been replaced by a vampire 'cell'… which isn't really a cell at all, but something else. Something we don't even have a good fucking name for yet, Alan... although there are a few floating out there, attached to this hypothesis or that one. In any case, we haven't mapped the vampire building blocks anywhere *near* enough to be able to manipulate their form, like we have with the human genome."

Still studying Rickson's face, Nick went on in the same blunt tone.

"*If* a vampire-infected human wakes up after death, they wake up in a completely different body. One that's only *loosely based* on the original, human body. One that has no measurable portion of the original organic material that *made up* that human body. That's not to say nothing carries over. There are a few notable, very important exceptions. There are some real mysteries about that part of the process still, like I said... the largest one being how the host body retains the memories and personality of the human it colonizes."

When Nick glanced at Wynter that time, he caught her looking at him.

The heat in her eyes made him smile faintly, even if he didn't fully understand it.

He looked back at Rickson.

Throwing up his hands, Nick went on in that same quasi-academic voice.

"There are a number of competing theories around that, Alan," he said calmly. "But the predominant one, the theory most vampire scientists subscribe to *right now,* is that the parasitic vampire lifeform, *sapien vampiricus,* doesn't have any interest in the higher functions of mind, so it leaves that part of a human being alone."

Nick shrugged again, leaning back in the garden chair.

"At base, a vampire is an animal that doesn't need to fuck to reproduce... so it's all about food, Alan. It's all about eating. You can think whatever thoughts, and feel whatever feelings your little heart desires, and the vampire organism couldn't care less.

You try and stop feeding the animal what it needs to survive, and it *will find a way* to get fed. Believe me."

When Nick focused on Alan Rickson that time, the human had paled.

"So you're saying—"

"I'm saying it's impossible, Alan. Someone sold Gordon a river of pure, unadulterated bullshit. It sounds like pretty elaborate bullshit, with a lot of extra bells and whistles, but it is what it is. Whatever Boorman and the others were up to, at base, it was a scam. A deeply stupid and dangerous scam, considering the playground they chose to grift in… but a scam nonetheless. A scam of epic proportions, really."

Alan continued to frown.

Nick could see him turning over everything Nick had just said.

He could also see Alan Rickson wasn't fully convinced.

That, or he didn't *want* to be convinced.

"They did tests," Alan muttered. "I saw the results."

Nick shrugged.

"If you still have them, I'd be interested in taking a look… but I can guarantee they aren't real."

"How *else* could they have done that?" Alan looked up. "Those things I saw? How could they *fake* something like that?"

The growing anger in his eyes told Nick the human was probably starting to believe him.

Nick's words had sunk in, or were starting to, anyway.

Looking at the human now, though, Nick almost wondered if Alan *had* known.

Suspected, anyway.

He didn't really seem all that surprised.

Pissed off, maybe… but not fully surprised.

Maybe he'd known and hadn't wanted to admit it to himself.

"How?" Alan demanded. "How did they fake all those tests? I saw some of them in person. Are you saying that was all some virtual field? An elaborate lightshow?"

"Maybe," Nick said, shrugging. "But you might be over-thinking it, Alan. There's a far easier, much more obvious way they could fake something like that. A way that would be a hell of a lot more convincing... especially in a live demonstration."

"Which is what?"

Wynter answered the question before Nick could.

"They could turn the test subjects into *actual* vampires, Alan."

Rickson turned, staring at her, his jaw hard.

That time, it was Wynter's turn to shrug.

"They could use make up to alter their complexions," she continued mildly. "Or possibly virtual filters for that part, since those are more subtle and harder to spot. Contact lenses for their eyes. Fake chest patches to produce a convincing heartbeat. Virtual skins to raise body temperature. There are a lot of small, relatively inexpensive things that can be done to make a vampire appear to be human. Vampires do it all the time... to travel freely, to gain access to human-only places, or just generally to pass in our world."

"You're saying the people I saw..." Alan's jaw hardened as he turned over her words. "Those people, they were really, truly turned into *vampires?* As in, they turned them for real? Made them into regular, blood-drinking—"

"Yes," she said. When Rickson looked over, Wynter shrugged again. "Why not?"

There was a silence.

In it, Nick watched Alan chew through everything they'd told him.

He saw him wince the hardest at what Wynter had just said.

Nick also remembered the man had just lost his husband a few days ago.

Thinking about that, in the context of all this, Nick grimaced.

It was hard enough knowing your partner died working on a revolutionary new cure for the worst parts of being both a human and a vampire. It was bad enough believing your loved one lost their life in pursuit of a noble (if profitable) cause, like extending the lives of human beings all over the world, and potentially ending the suffering of vampires themselves.

Maybe they even told themselves this could bring the two species closer together.

World peace. The end of racial wars.

Kumbaya.

The tech world had always loved to sing that song.

But just like all those other times, that's not what this was.

And really, it was a whole other thing to realize your beloved partner might have been taken in a centuries-old scam. To have to face *that,* that your whole family had been stolen from you by a bunch of greedy grifters, all because your husband bought into a story of a miracle cure that didn't exist...

Well. Most people wouldn't want that on their epitaph.

Killed by virtue of excessive gullibility. But he meant well.

That had to sting, even for Rickson.

After all, he'd loved Gordon Murami.

Given all that, Alan took the news pretty well.

"You're really sure about all of this?" the human said, wary. "The scientific side? You're absolutely certain?"

Nick exhaled.

"Yeah," he said, blunt. "Sorry, buddy. I'm definitely sure."

He paused, then made his voice more careful.

"Look. This might not be great to hear, but you've given us some really important information, sharing all this. We have a motive now. That narrows down the list of suspects considerably. It also might help us to answer some of the questions that were really baffling the NYPD about this case... like how these five victims were connected to one another... and why they got turned into vampires before they were killed..."

Nick activated his headset.

Using a mental impulse, he brought up headshots of all five of the victims.

All five of them were found in the living room of the same,

dark red, art-filled, multi-million dollar apartment at The Dakota on Central Park.

"So, can you identify all of these people?" Nick asked. "As well as their role in this 'designer venom' project Gordon was working on?"

Alan frowned.

Staring up at the images, he exhaled.

Then, without answering directly, he pointed at the first image, of a middle-aged, Eurasian man with a wide smile, brown hair, and dark hazel eyes.

"Well, that's Gordon, obviously."

He paused, biting his lip.

His finger moved on to the second image.

That one depicted a twenty or thirty-something blond male with brown eyes, dimples, shaved eyebrows, and tanned skin. His arms and shoulders looked athletic, but his expression was relaxed in a way that came across to Nick as more of an affectation.

Like he wanted people to *think* he was laid back, but he really wasn't.

His eyes were sharp, bordering on predatory-looking.

"That's Kelvin Johns, the artificial life specialist from Norolog." Rickson frowned. "A little prick, if you want the truth. He could have been in on it. I'm pretty sure he'd sell his firstborn if you offered him enough money."

Nick grunted.

He'd gotten the same impression about Johns.

Rickson's finger moved again, sliding further to his own right.

It stopped on a bald man in a dark suit, with a muscular neck, large shoulders, and thick, dark eyebrows. That person didn't smile, and his mouth appeared strangely small, almost disappearing in a soft-featured face.

He looked like he might have been late-forties, early fifties.

"That one is Lars Boorman. He's the genetic designer I told you about, working out of the ColdArt plant in Seoul... the so-called inventor. They called him 'Einstein.' I only met him a few times. Mostly at industry events. Once at a birthday party for Johann Nichols, the CEO of Suntrode."

Exhaling, a faint anger touching his words, Rickson pointed at the next face.

"That's Henrika Bleekman."

A pretty blond woman, maybe in her early thirties, smiled into the image capture.

"Gordon and I met her for drinks once, here in the city. I liked her. She was a corporate lawyer for Ubelis Bank, out of the Swiss Protected Area. Ubelis was supposed to be footing some of the start-up capital for the new product, as well as helping to set up distribution and production. Ubelis is who *technically* hired Gordon, on Viraj's recommendation. So Suntrode arranged for him to be contracted out. Presumably to put some distance there."

Nick nodded grimly. "Figures. Could Viraj have been in on it?"

"I honestly don't know. I always liked him, too."

Nick nodded. "Anything else you can remember?"

"Gordon worked with a small team. Ubelis set it up, hiring people from a number of different companies. Most of them were hand-picked from companies that were part of the Ubelis orbit, mostly in industrial real estate. They had Gordon working with building materials suppliers, construction PMs, architects. Ostensibly it was all to build that first plant… assuming the tests and legal paperwork all went through."

Nick grimaced.

Gaos. It was elaborate.

No wonder Gordon believed it.

Nick recorded all of that, nodding. "And where is she from? Bleekman?"

"Miami. She told us she lives in a suburb just outside of New Miami, Florida. Ubelis has branches all over. She came out here maybe five, six times a year."

Nick recorded all of that, too.

He pointed up at the fifth photo.

That one depicted the swarthy face of a heavy-set, Mediterranean-looking man, early fifties, with thick cheeks, large, hound-dog eyes, a genial smile, and thinning brown hair.

"And the last one?" Nick said. "Who's this guy, Alan?"

"Antonio Formi," Alan said.

His voice sounded a little reluctant that time.

"He's an investment banker from Rome. He's kind of known, at least in tech circles, as one of those big-deal angel investors. Some considered him a genius. He had a solid track record, backing various projects. He was the other big source of funding. I think he put down even more than the bank."

"Did you meet him, too?" Nick asked. "Did he come to San Francisco maybe?"

Alan gave Nick a slightly harder look.

"What are you implying, Detective Midnight?"

"I'm asking if you've ever met Antonio Formi in person." Nick pursed his lips. "It wasn't a trick question, Alan. There's no hidden message there."

"But what is the purpose of the question?"

Nick's eyebrow rose, that time without him willing it.

He shrugged, suppressing the impulse to look at Wynter.

"I'm trying to get a sense of how well the core team knew one another," he said.

Alan still looked suspicious.

After another few seconds ticked by, he seemed to force himself to relax.

"Them knowing one another wouldn't mean anything, you know," Rickson said next, subduing his voice. "The tech world is small, Detective Midnight. People within that sphere all more or less know one another, at least above a certain level. They meet all the time. For all kinds of reasons."

"Like what?" Wynter queried. "What kinds of reasons would those be?"

162

Rickson looked at her, scowling faintly.

"All kinds," he repeated coldly. "Engineers and inventors are always scrambling for funding for new ideas. Entrepreneurs are always looking for new projects, new break-through tech, new opportunities to form companies, or ways to get in on the ground floor of something that might take off. No one would think anything of it if they saw Gordon eating dinner with Antonio. Or Antonio having drinks with Ms. Bleekman. Or Johns playing golf with Lars Boorman. Those type of meetings go on every day in San Francisco. All over the world, really. No one would even notice... or care."

"They might care if they knew what they were working on," Nick remarked drily.

"But no one *did* know what they were working on," Alan said, his voice a touch harder. "Secrecy was paramount. They were insanely careful. All of them."

"Well, obviously *someone* knew," Nick said.

Alan opened his mouth, sucking in a breath.

Then he closed it, saying nothing.

He didn't seem to know what to say that time.

CHAPTER 16

GUTS AND GUESSES

NICK WAS ABOUT TO REDIRECT, TO ASK THE PROSECUTOR something else…

When a car pulled into the driveway below, blaring music.

They all turned their heads.

Nick stared down from the cave-like porch as three twenty-something, college-student-looking types tumbled out of different doors of the vehicle.

The music abruptly shut off.

Nick watched the three of them gather up crates in their arms, still talking and laughing to one another, clearly not yet seeing the three older adults sitting in the flickering fairy lights of the porch.

Nick opened his mouth, about to ask Rickson who they were, if Rickson was expecting someone, when the first of the three young humans turned abruptly from the driveway and traipsed up the stairs to the house. She reached the front door, and plopped the crate she'd been carrying unceremoniously down at her feet.

She waved her ident-barcode in front of the door's panel, and the doorbell inside the house went off, echoing through the house.

Alan was already climbing to his feet.

"Tricia," he said, raising his voice. "I'm in a meeting right now. You and the others can just leave everything there..."

The girl jumped.

She turned, eyes wide.

Seeing Alan standing there, she burst out in a grin.

She spoke a touch too loudly, like she was a little bit deaf.

More likely, Nick thought, she was listening to something in her headset.

"OH! Hey, Alan! I didn't see you. I'll tell the others." She pointed at the crate at her feet, still grinning. "We got the new signs! They are mondo-crispy-cool! You'll *love* them, Al-man! Definitely we need to figure out how best to use these babies!"

Alan Rickson smiled at her, pointing at his own ear.

"You're shouting, Tricia."

"OH! Sorry!" She must have done something to lower the sound in her headset. Her voice sounded normal when she glanced back at the rest of the recessed porch. "Oh! You have people here! Sorry!"

"You can leave it all here on the steps. Tell Brad and Marco to do the same."

She gave him a mock salute. "Will do."

Nick was staring down at the signs, though.

He didn't know if Wynter could read them, given the heavier shadows by the door and the distance from where she sat, but Nick's vampire eyes picked them up just fine.

"You're running for District Attorney?" he said.

Alan turned sharply, looking at him.

"Yes." Seeming to see something on Nick's face, he added, "It was planned before all this, of course."

Nick nodded, noncommittal. "That's a big job."

Alan's voice and eyes remained wary.

"That's why I wanted to do it," he said. "Gordon was fully supportive. So are the kids. We've been talking about it for years."

His eyes brightened, right before he shook his head, seemingly to shake away whatever wanted to overwhelm him.

"Anyway, I considered dropping out," he said, in a lower voice. "I still think about it. I think about it every day. But somehow, I keep going anyway."

Nick nodded. "I get that," he said.

He realized this interview was over.

He held out a hand, subduing his voice.

"Well, good luck," he said. "May the best man win."

Alan Rickson stared down at Nick's chalk-white hand.

Then he seemed to relax, from his shoulders down to his legs.

He took Nick's hand and shook it, smiling faintly.

"One always hopes," he said.

NICK WALKED DOWN EL CAMINO DEL MAR, LOOKING BOTH WAYS before he crossed over to 30th Street, heading in the direction of California.

"Well, that got... interesting," Wynter remarked, as she walked after him. "Especially towards the end."

Nick grunted, reaching for her hand as she began to walk down 30th alongside him.

"Indeed it did."

"You passing all of that on to Morley?"

"Most of it, yeah. I think I'll hammer out a bit more of a summary later tonight, but I sent him the raw interview file."

His voice lowered to a mutter.

"I think there's another one of those trolley stops up here."

His eyes clicked back into focus as he pulled his attention off the visuals inside his headset, mainly the map of San Francisco he'd been staring at.

He glanced at Wynter, gripping her hand tighter.

"So what do you think?" he said, frowning. "Not just on how weird he was being, but about the whole thing?"

Wynter exhaled.

She released his arm and hand long enough to finger her hair out of her eyes, stretching out the muscles in her arms.

"He's hiding something," she remarked.

"Yeah." Nick exhaled. "I noticed that. You get any of it off him?"

"Not really, no. I got a little bit around the artificial venom when he was hemming and hawing around what it was purported to do. Enough to nudge you to ask him about it, but he was difficult to read."

Nick frowned. "Shielded?"

"Possibly. Or possibly he's just on some kind of medication. Something I was struggling to get through. A lot of antidepressants and anti-anxiety meds make it really tough to read someone, and this felt a little like that. Like someone on a lot of meds."

Thinking, she shrugged, still swinging her arms a bit.

"He did just lose his husband. There's a good chance he's on something like that right now. Also, it could explain his defensiveness. He acted like someone who blamed himself. Like he felt he should have realized what was going on."

Nick nodded, thinking about that.

As he did, he winced.

"I probably hammered him too hard on the venom thing being fake."

"No," she said seriously. "It's good. I think he was pretty far gone in denial. It's probably better for him to see this for what it was. If nothing else, it will help him make sense of it later. It's almost always better to know the truth."

Nick nodded.

Something was still nagging at him.

He couldn't quite put his finger on what it was.

"So you believe him?" Nick said. "That Gordon Murami was totally clueless on the scam? That he was just an innocent engineer, in the wrong place at the wrong time?"

She shrugged. "Do *you* believe him? About Gordon, at least?"

Nick thought about that.

He tried to answer honestly.

"I kind of do," Nick admitted. "I have no basis for that whatsoever, of course—"

"No, I do, too. I just didn't want to say so, because I've got no basis for it, either." She paused, watching his face. "So we think Gordon is probably clean?"

Nick exhaled nodding.

It wasn't exactly a yes, but it may have been a conditional yes.

"Let's just say, I think there are other leads we could pursue first," he said. "I can think of a few, just from that conversation alone."

"His boss?" Wynter asked. "That Das guy?"

"And Formi."

"Formi?" She blinked. "Why him? Wasn't he from Rome?"

Nick gave her a grim look. "When Rickson talked about three of the vics in New York, he used only their last names. Once, he used a first *and* last name: Lars Boorman. There were only two victims he talked about where he didn't do that. Two where he used their first name alone. His husband, Gordon Murami..."

"...and Antonio Formi."

Nick nodded grimly. "Bingo."

"He called him Antonio?"

"He did. More than once. When he talked about hypothetical meetings between the various players, he said 'no one would think twice if they saw Gordon and Antonio having lunch together.' He listed a few more hypotheticals after that, but that was the first thing that popped into his head. Something about that struck me as kind of a tell."

Wynter nodded.

Glancing up and down the street, Nick looked for cars before crossing with her over to the other side of 30th, aiming for the trolley stop he could now see on California.

"I'm going to jump your vampire bones tonight," she told him calmly.

Nick came to a stop in the street.

He turned, looking at her. "Excuse me?"

"You were sexy as fuck tonight. I just thought I'd give you a little warning beforehand." Squeezing his hand as she slid her fingers back into his, she added, "I forgot how hot it is, watching you do your detective thing. I'd jump you right now, but it's been so long, we'd probably get arrested. Then there'd be the blood tests, and the being arrested—"

Nick's smile faded. "Don't joke about that."

"Not even a little? I thought cops were known for their gallows humor."

"We are. But don't joke about that anyway."

He glanced around in rote, looking for drones in spite of himself.

Gripping her hand more tightly, he aimed his feet in the direction of the trolley stand. He found himself listening to her heartbeat now, to her breath.

"How are you feeling?" she asked, her voice more subdued.

"Not great, to be honest."

"Still weak?"

He nodded, scanning the street with his vampire eyes.

"Definitely good enough to have my bones jumped. All of them."

"Even if they aren't really bones?" she teased.

"Still highly motivated to be jumped," he informed her.

After he'd looked up and down the length of the street, he ignited his headset's security protocol, switching on the scripts Kit wrote for him to specifically look for media and other drones, including Archangel's.

Including the kind Brick used for the White Death.

"Damn it. I've ignited your paranoid vampire thing. I can see it in your face."

Nick turned, looking at her.

He tried to relax. "Maybe a little," he conceded.

"Sorry."

He squeezed her hand tighter, not answering.

"Who do you think killed them?" Wynter asked, abrupt. "In New York, I mean. Those five bodies at The Dakota. Do you think Brick did that? The White Death?"

Nick sighed.

He wished they could just talk about sex.

Hell, he wished they could just go fuck.

Now that he'd passed all of that crap on to Morley, he felt obligated to find out a few things about the damned case, first.

He should have waited and sent the transcripts in the morning.

Thinking about her question then, he shrugged.

"I mean, it's not inconceivable," he admitted. "If Brick found out what they were up to, he might have done it. To send a message, if nothing else."

"A message to who?" Wynter asked. "The other people involved?"

"Conceivably." Nick shrugged a second time. "This was a pretty big group, from what Rickson said tonight. There's Das, Gordon's boss at Suntrode. There's the other people at Suntrode who signed off on sending Gordon to work under Ubelis. There's Formi's banks, who presumably helped him finance the whole thing. There's Norolog, whatever the hell their role was in this whole thing. Then there's whoever Boorman was working with to set this up, in terms of the fake lab, the fake tests, the test subjects, and so on."

Still thinking, Nick stopped at the trolley station, running his bar code over the scanning plate and glancing at the map on the wall.

He saw a trolley turn a few blocks up.

It began gliding their way.

"In terms of Brick's motives, there's also just the general warning others off from trying this kind of thing," Nick said, glancing away from the map to look at Wynter. "He might have meant it as a message to any other genetic scientists or human

171

con artists out there. Anyone who might be tempted to get involved in similar types of scams. Any tech companies who might be tempted to sell immortality to people with more money than brains."

Nick grunted, still thinking.

"Not to mention any vampire factions who might try to pull something like this without his authorization."

"Why would he care?" Wynter asked next. "Brick?"

Nick thought about that, too.

"Honestly," he said. "I can think of a few reasons. One, he sells a shit-ton of *real* vampire venom to rich assholes on the black market... not to mention real vampire blood to junkies, thrill-seekers, sex-fetishists, and vampire clubs. He might not want the competition, frankly. Also, Brick would feel it was humans impinging on vampire territory... if that makes sense. Like, go sell your own people's body parts. That kind of thing."

Wynter grunted. "Right."

She looked over at him then, her blue-green, jewel-like eyes serious.

"Do you *think* it's him, though?" She studied his eyes. "You, I mean. Nick Tanaka. What does your gut say on Brick being involved? Do *you* think he is?"

Nick had been asking himself that same damned question most of the night.

He'd asked himself the other night, too.

Before he got knocked out.

The answer had come up the same, every time.

That answer still surprised him.

"No," he said, his voice reflecting that surprise. "No, I don't really think it's Brick who's behind this. Or the White Death."

Wynter nodded slowly, absorbing his words.

"Okay. Who then?" she asked.

He frowned.

"I honestly don't know," he said, blunt. "Not yet. But I want to look up Antonio Formi. I want to know where he was in the weeks before he died. I also want to talk to that other guy at Suntrode… Viraj Das. The Senior VP of New Product Development. The 'well-connected' boss who supposedly hooked Gordon up with these guys."

Wynter frowned, nodding thoughtfully.

"Okay," she said. "Which one do you want to do first?"

CHAPTER 17

PACIFIC HEIGHTS

THEY SETTLED ON DAS. IT MADE SENSE TO GO SEE DAS FIRST.

If nothing else, they could use Das to corroborate parts of Alan Rickson's story.

They could at least see how Das reacted when they asked him about Gordon.

As for Antonio Formi and his potential connection to Alan, Nick sent a ping to Jordan and Morley, asking them if they could check it out.

In the same note, Nick described what he'd noticed in the Rickson interview.

He told them how and why he wanted them to take a second look, and admitted he and Wynter both wondered if Rickson might know Antonio Formi, angel investor, a little better than he let on.

Nick also asked the two detectives if it would be all right if he asked Kit to do it, if neither of them had time. He reminded them that network research was pretty much Kit's "thing," and that she'd probably be more than happy to do some sleuthing for them around who Formi was, and how he might be connected to Alan Rickson.

That seemed to wake Morley up.

Nick got a message back right away.

Morley didn't identify himself in the message, and the name was blacked out, but it definitely came from Nick's boss. It also said more or less exactly what Nick would have expected, given him and Morley's last conversation on the subject.

DO. NOT. INVOLVE. KATARINA.

YOU CALL THAT KID AND I WILL HIT YOU ON THE HEAD MYSELF.

DO NOT USE ANYONE AT ARCHANGEL.

There was a shortish pause.

Then Morley seemed to think better of that last message.

ONLY WYNTER. AND ONLY WHILE SHE IS OUT THERE WITH YOU.

A few seconds after that, another message came through.

Nick had to assume Jordan was with him, and they talked over the Formi thing.

JORDAN AND I WILL HANDLE FORMI. GO DO SOMETHING USEFUL. AND TRY NOT TO DIE THIS TIME. OR GET HIT OVER THE HEAD. AND USE THE DAMNED A.I. I DIDN'T GIVE YOU ACCESS TO THAT SHIT FOR MY HEALTH.

Nick snorted.

Still smiling a little, he rolled his eyes.

He had forgotten about the A.I., though.

He considered sending something snarky back, telling Morley exactly where he could shove his old-school caps-lock and his grouchy, old-man attitude problems. In the end, he thought better of it. He knew Morley well enough to know they were probably already looking up Formi and working on getting more information about who he was.

Nick didn't want to distract them from that.

Instead, he sent a second, more perfunctory message telling the old man that he and Wynter were right then going to talk to an executive at Suntrode Virtual Systems named Viraj Das, and that he'd update them after.

He also sent Morley the address in Pacific Heights.

Morley wrote back quickly that time, too.

Record it, he sent. *All of it, this time, Midnight. Don't think I didn't notice how you just sort of skipped recording the first half of that shit with Rickson.*

Nick snorted again.

Shaking his head, he clicked off the text function.

When he glanced over at Wynter, she was smiling at him.

"What?" he said.

"I can always tell when you're talking to one of your friends. You get this big smile on your face and start laughing to yourself."

"Not true," Nick proclaimed. "And those weren't friends. They were colleagues. Asshole colleagues," he added, glancing around for police drones.

Wynter rolled her eyes.

"Whatever. I can see your face. I know when you're horsing around with your buddies."

"Horsing around." Nick muttered the words, tugging on her hand before he squeezed it. "You sound older than me."

"So you've said."

They'd just climbed off the back of the lime-green trolley that picked them up on California Street.

Now Nick and Wynter were walking down Pacific Avenue, less than a block from where Viraj Das' documented residence should be located, according to the less-official version of the city map. Officially, Das had his residence completely shielded from all public directories and mapping programs.

Nick managed to get past that shielding by using the national police database and the SFPD A.I. to override it.

Morley granted him access to both things, just that morning.

Nick finally figured out how to use the trolley system here in the city, too.

It turned out, it wasn't like the old days, when he used to have to figure out the public transportation routes and schedules, and make sure he hopped on the right one, got off at the right time, and/or had to switch trains or buses to reach the destination he wanted… etc.

These days, trolleys and other forms of city transport went more or less wherever you told them to go.

Which explained how he'd gotten the door-to-door treatment the other night with his hotel, and why the tracks seemed to run over every street in the entire city.

They still had official trolley stops, of course.

If there were a lot of people on a particular trolley, the trolley car would use those designated stops instead, dropping groups of people off in pre-defined areas as close to the addresses they'd requested as the trolley car could possibly get them.

This particular trolley dropped them off only two blocks from where they needed to go.

Nick considered phoning ahead to Das' residence, since he got the phone number and the network address from the city's A.I. at the same time he got the man's physical address.

In the end, he decided against it.

He decided to surprise him, instead.

Somehow, he suspected Viraj Das would want to talk to him even less than Alan Rickson had wanted to talk to him. Anyway, Nick had long noticed that people tended to be less guarded if they hadn't mentally prepared themselves for your visit beforehand.

Now that they'd arrived, it was already looking like Nick was right.

Das certainly didn't seem all that enthused to talk to them.

When Nick swiped the ident barcode on his arm over the sensor panel beside Das' lower gate, he got nothing but silence. The tall, metal gate, which remained closed and locked, barred access to the stairs leading up to the front door altogether.

The house was completely lit up, but no one came to the door.

No one even spoke to them through the intercom system.

The security panel remained utterly dark.

Nick looked at Wynter, frowning.

Wynter looked at Nick.

Then he motioned up at the tall fence, which was curved outward at the top, towards the street. That would only discourage a human, though.

"Would you mind terribly?" he asked her.

She looked up at the thirty-foot iron bars.

She looked back at him.

"You're kidding, right?"

Nick shrugged. "I don't really want to come back tomorrow, do you?"

After a pause, Wynter sighed.

"No," she said, annoyed.

Nick nodded.

He leapt up for the curved bars.

Despite how crappy he felt, he'd managed to forget about having had all his venom drained. Or at least he managed to forget what that truly meant. He made it less than half the distance he normally would have, and immediately, his muscles screamed at him, tensing way beyond what they would have normally.

His hands struggled to grip tightly enough to hold on.

He also felt a sharp pain in his chest.

Nick gasped, renewing his grip, swinging a little on the curved bars.

When he glanced down, Wynter was shielding her eyes against the orange and gold streetlights, squinting up at him.

"You okay?" she asked.

"Not great," he admitted.

"You forgot about the venom thing. Didn't you?"

"Pretty much," he grumbled.

He was climbing now, working his way up the metal bars, hand over hand. He couldn't really get much purchase with his boots on the slick metal, so it was all pretty much his arms, abs, chest, and back. Despite how weak he felt, and how damned slow he was moving compared to normal, he managed to make his way all the way up to the top.

Once there, to get past the curve, he had to hoist up his upper body up, and climb the bars up and then down on the other side of the metal.

"Fuck," he muttered.

"That looks harder than usual," Wynter observed.

"Not helpful, wife."

Gasping, even though he didn't need air, he threw his body upward.

It took three tries to get enough of himself all the way up and over the looping metal.

Once he had his balance, he began easing his belly over the top of the highest curve in the fence. He spent a few seconds renewing his grip again.

Then he slowly began sliding down the metal poles, now going head-first.

"That seems like a bad idea," Wynter observed, folding her arms.

"I've got it all under control," he said.

"Sure you do, baby."

He fought not to laugh.

He made it down another eight or nine feet, to where the fence gradually straightened.

Then he stopped long enough to bring his lower body slowly and carefully down to one side, controlling it as best he could with his hands and arms. His shoulders strained, his neck muscles strained, his arms strained, his hands strained.

It hurt like hell.

Even so, he slowly turned himself around so that his legs and feet were below him, aiming down. He slipped down a few feet on the slick metal at one point, but by then he had most of his body where he needed it.

Catching himself, he aligned his body.

He looked down at the ground below, and rested for a second.

"That was... hard to watch," Wynter said.

She was back to squinting at him, one hand shielding her eyes.

He didn't answer.

He climbed down a few more feet, hand over hand.

Then he let himself drop.

He landed easily on his booted heels.

He resisted the urge to do a superhero landing, just to tease Wynter.

"I can see your face, you know," Wynter retorted, refolding her arms. "You should have just done the superhero thing. Now you're going to spend the night wondering if that was a missed opportunity."

Nick laughed quietly. He couldn't help it.

Then he held a finger to his lips.

"Hush," he told her. "You're going to get us both arrested."

"You know you must have tripped his security system already," she said, stepping closer to the fence, her arms still folded. "Honestly, I thought that was a lot of the reason you did it."

"It was," he admitted. "I thought he would have come out by now. So I could badge him and get all blustery and mean-cop-like."

She exhaled, looking up at the sky. "They've probably got police drones filming you, even now. Maybe putting crosshairs on your forehead."

"That's fine. They'll scan my ident chip, too. They'll contact me before they start trying to blow me away or anything... and Das is officially a person of interest at this point."

Even so, Nick thought about what Wynter had said, frowning.

He looked up at the sky, and imagined he saw fleeting glints of metal, gliding silently through the sky, here and there.

Realizing Wynter was right, that he was too exposed here, he scowled more.

"You're right," he said, blunt. "But we may have a bigger problem. Those might be police drones, but no cars are here. If he was home, Viraj should have called it in. Even if he *wasn't* at home, he would have gotten an alert from the system... and he *definitely* would have called the cops when he saw a strange vampire climbing his fence."

Impulsively, Nick activated his link to the San Francisco A.I.

Theirs was a male voice, unlike the NYPD version, Gertrude.

It was also weird as fuck.

Morley told him they called it "Butch."

"Hey," Nick said. "You there, Butch? This is Detective Naoko Tanaka Midnight. NYPD jurisdiction. Granted provisional jurisdiction in San Francisco City proper. Homicide Division. Ident tag: 9381T-112. Requesting authorization for investigation of a private dwelling under special circumstances."

"Hi there, Nick!" the A.I. said cheerfully. "How are you, buddy?"

"Err... hi."

"It is *Nick...* isn't it? My database tells me that you prefer to be called by this human nickname. All of your friends call you this, too. I am sorry I did not know this when we spoke before, Nick!"

"Yep, yep. That's great, Butch. Call me Nick. But right now, I really need your help with this. With my *murder* investigation, I mean. I have a potential situation here at the residence where my location tracker should have me. I need permission to investigate a private dwelling without the stated consent of the owner."

"OF COURSE, Nick!" The machine beamed in his ear cheerfully. "But before I help you with this, I need to ask you a few questions first! Okay? You ready?"

"I'm ready, Butch."

"Great! So tell me... what are these special circumstances you mentioned, Nick? The ones that require you to violate the sanctity of the legally-protected property and privacy codes for one of our beautiful city's private citizens?"

Briefly, Nick was stumped.

Then he shrugged.

"We came here, me and my associate, for a routine interrogation in connection to case Alpha-Alpha-Six-Nine-Two-Two-Alpha-Ten, out of New York Protected Area. Five bodies. Four male, one female. Definite, documented evidence of foul play. Two of our victims are full-time residents of San Francisco City proper. Viraj Das knows at least one of our vics personally, possibly more than one. There is suspicion he was involved in their deaths. There is additional suspicion of conspiracy charges in connection with a related crime."

"Understood. What are the special circumstances, Nick?"

"Subject was not answering door upon a regular summons, so I deliberately triggered the alarm system, in part to ensure that everyone living in the house is all right, due to the nature of the case..."

"Of course, Nick," the A.I. soothed. "Of *course*. We understand. After all, the work you do is important. You work in *homicide*, Nick. Heck, that's the most important job of all! OF COURSE you will worry if your interrogation suspects might be in danger!"

"That's exactly right, Butch. Exactly right. But I need that authorization now, buddy. No one has come to the door, despite my breaching the house's security fence. There have been no calls in to the SFPD. I wondered if I could get authorization to enter the dwelling forcibly... so I can make sure Viraj Das and his family are all right."

"Did you hear gunshots inside the house, Nick?"

"No."

"Any weapon discharges of any kind at all?"

"No."

"Did anyone call or scream for help, Nick?"

"No." Nick exhaled, resting his hands on his hips. "Requesting permission to go inside anyway."

"Denied, Nick," the A.I. said cheerfully. "But gosh darn it, thanks so much for asking! You'd be amazed at how many officers forget to do that!"

Nick gritted his teeth.

He was sure as hell wishing he "forgot," too.

He bet a lot of the officers around here had advanced cases of amnesia.

"Oh!" Nick said. "Oh! I just heard someone inside, Butch! They were yelling for help!"

"Are you lying to me, Nick?" the A.I. asked coyly.

"No. Of course not. Why would I do that?"

"Well," the machine said, wagging a finger at him in the virtual space behind his eyes. "*I* certainly didn't hear anything. And you've made it clear you want to go inside that house. Even though it doesn't fit protocol specs for you to do so."

"I'm a vampire, Butch. You're just going to have to trust me. I *definitely* hear someone in there. Calling for help. They could be dying, Butch... right now."

"All right, Nick," the machine said cheerfully. "Opening the door for you now."

Nick jumped, startled in spite of himself.

He heard a click, and the front door popped open about a quarter-inch.

That was a hell of a lot easier than he'd thought.

"Open the security gate, too," Nick instructed the A.I. "My partner's still out there. I need you to let her in."

"Authorization code?" the machine asked sweetly.

Nick growled under his breath.

"She's a consultant," he said. "She doesn't have one."

"Then I'm afraid I can't let her inside, Nick. *You* understand. If a violent incident occurred there, and your consultant was hurt or hurt someone else, this could put the SFPD in legal jeopardy. I'm awfully sorry about that, though, Nick—"

"Forget it. Whatever."

Giving Wynter a last glance, Nick decided he didn't have time to argue with this thing anymore. Truthfully, he was starting to really wonder why no one who lived in the house hadn't tried to speak to him or Wynter yet.

At the very least, he would have expected threats by now.

A strange voice ordering him off the property, and/or threatening to call the cops.

Turning back to the house, he began bounding up the stairs.

"Are you *kidding* me!" Wynter yelled, glaring up at him through the bars. "Motherfucker!"

"Don't say bad things about my mom!"

"Come back here!" she demanded, shaking the security bars. "Right now!"

"I'll be right back, sweetie!" he called out cheerfully, imitating the clinically-insane Artificial lifeform. "Just a quick pop inside, and I'll be right back out! I swear!"

"Nick, I'm not screwing around!" she snapped. "You're too weak right now. You're not even at half-strength... you're probably not even at *quarter*-strength. You shouldn't go in there alone! Not when you're still sick."

"Well, thanks so much for announcing that, honey! I'm sure any bad guys inside will definitely appreciate that information!"

"Nick! Goddamn it! I mean it! Wait for backup!"

He heard her. He listened.

He even felt a little bad.

But he didn't slow down.

He might be at quarter strength, but he was still a vampire.

He finished bounding up the stairs, and grabbed hold of the edge of the metal door.

Pulling it open, he walked into Das' house.

CHAPTER 18

THE OPEN DOOR

Nick stood inside an art-filled house with white, waterfall staircases. A house like this, in this part of town, probably would have cost a cool fifteen million, even back when Nick had been human.

He didn't even want to guess what it would cost now.

He walked across a pressure panel floor, and several of the wall installations flickered to life, possibly since they were sensing his barcode for the first time, and were set to trigger for people who had never seen them before.

Nick waved them off.

He stopped at the base of the stairs, glancing to either side to peer into the high-ceilinged rooms, both as tall as the room he was in, which had to be twenty feet, at least. A floating chandelier slowly expanded and retracted in the space between the staircase and the wide entryway into a larger room beyond, where Nick could hear water flowing, some kind of fountain.

He considered calling out.

Instead, he lifted his head, smelling the air.

Shit.

Blood.

A hell of a lot of human blood.

Maybe Das hadn't been blowing him off, after all.

Nick fought to hone in on where the smell originated exactly, inside the house.

Even that took him longer than usual, but he eventually got it.

Straight ahead.

Nick moved fast, walked silently through the wood and tile hallway. He slid into hunting mode without noticing he'd done it, following the increasingly pungent smell of blood, then the significantly less-pungent smell of just human, as in human skin, human bodies, human hair.

At least two.

No... three, probably more.

It was frustrating to realize even his damned nose was out of whack from the lack of venom. Fighting not to react to how blind he felt, he clenched his jaw. Maybe Wynter was right. Maybe he should have waited, called for backup.

The problem was, until this very instant, he really hadn't had any kind of probable cause.

Now, he definitely did.

He ignited the sub-vocals, pinging the A.I.

"Send at least one back-up unit to the Das house, Bruce," he told the thing silently. "Send an ambulance, too. I've got a strong smell of blood. At least one badly-injured human. No sounds that I can hear. The electricity and lights are all on. I can smell at least three humans in the house. Other possible races are unknown. I'm looking for the source now..."

"Unknown, Nick?" Bruce queried. "You cannot ID the race of the attackers?"

"Yes," Nick said, still silent. "Looking for the source now."

It occurred to him why the machine was confused.

The A.I. knew he was a Midnight.

Nick added shortly, "Be informed that my sensory abilities, including my sense of smell and possibly my hearing, are damaged from a recent injury. The same is true of my strength, reflexes, and stamina. All physical abilities in responding Detective Midnight should be assumed to be greatly diminished."

"Oh no!" Bruce cried in dismay. "That sounds DANGEROUS, Nick! I'm sending someone to help you…. right away! I'll make sure they bring a *fully-functioning* Midnight with them. That just sounds so unwise, you being in there alone! So very, very unwise!"

Nick rolled his eyes, internally at least.

"Yeah, my wife would agree with you," he told the machine silently.

He never took his attention off the brightly-lit room ahead.

He could just hear it now.

Panting.

Light, confused breaths, an even softer whimpering.

He darted forward, throwing caution to the wind.

He recognized those sounds.

He'd fed on enough humans to be intimately familiar with them.

Coming into the lit space at the back of the house, he was startled when the ceilings stretched even higher, most of them made of glass. The room was long and rectangular-shaped, running all along the back of the house. Nick's eyes found the fountain on one end, bubbling in front of a long, white-stone, lit fireplace. A blindingly huge wall-mounted screen covered most of the wall next to it, and a half-moon-shaped, cinnamon-colored sofa filled most of the sunken part of the living room, broken into segments with round glass tables between them.

Each of the glass tables were designed with glass shelves filled with individual headsets, small refrigerators, game boards, and an elaborate array of buttons, in addition to full-blown privacy shields to allow for individual play.

It was a geeky, tech-type family's wet dream.

Nick looked the other way, and saw that the rectangular room stretched just as far in the other direction. A long table and chairs stood at the far end, and he guessed the kitchen lived on the other side of that partition, connected through another of those tall, open corridors.

He couldn't remember the last time he'd seen so much glass.

More floating light fixtures morphed and slid through the space.

Still, Nick saw no one.

Then he felt a breeze.

He followed it, and realized the smell was coming from there.

A door was open.

Nick walked cautiously in the direction of the kitchen.

He walked around free-standing installations covered with jungle-like plants, a ten-foot fish tank built into the wall and filled with tropical fish. Another tank, even longer, held a shark, and a third, square tank held a giant, purple and gray octopus.

A fourth tank Nick saw in a recessed nook held a collection of bright pink jellyfish, which undulated in the five-foot cylinder, backlit in the dark space so that they looked like ghosts floating against a dark, empty sky.

Nick could smell the blood really strongly now.

He was beginning to understand part of why his nose was struggling, though.

The fish tanks were pungent, the jungle-like mountains of plants. More plants hanging from the rafters, some of them night-blooming purple and white flowers.

He had nearly reached the kitchen when another breeze wafted through the open sliding door. The smell of blood was cloying that time, overpowering.

It definitely came from more than one person.

A light blinked on the wall, likely attached to someone's head-set, telling the people who lived here that the door was open.

No one had turned it off.

Nick felt faintly sick now.

He could smell the blood a lot more strongly.

It was obvious a family lived here.

Not just adults. Kids.

He walked cautiously up to the door.

His vampire eyes picked out enormous trees in the distance, what looked like redwoods.

The center of the space was filled with a meandering, lagoon-style pool. An island in the center displayed several gentle water-falls, all of them illuminated with colored lights. The sound of the waterfalls wasn't the sighing sound he'd heard earlier, but it was distracting now that he had the door all the way open.

The shielding of the thick windows, and probably the acoustics from shape of the house itself made it difficult to hear the waterfalls in the pool until he got closer to the door.

Now that he stood on the deck, it all struck him as unnaturally loud.

Then there was a gasp.

It was a hell of a lot closer to Nick than he expected.

It shocked the hell out of him, how close it was.

Nick turned his head sharply to the left.

On a dark patch of grass, at the bottom of a series of stone and tile steps, Nick saw three bodies lying. A fourth body hung from the fangs of a male vampire.

The male was drinking hard, his eyes half-closed in ecstasy, his long, white fingers caressing his prey. From his expression, he was in absolute heaven, pulling the blood from the shoulder of what looked like a sixteen or seventeen-year-old girl.

The vampire had his hand down the front of her shirt, holding her to his chest and the front of his body like a lover.

She was the one who had gasped.

She stared at him now, eyes wide, pleading at Nick.

He snarled.

Nick didn't do it quietly.

For the first time, the vampire seemed to realize he was there.

He snapped out of his trance, long enough to stop drinking, and lift his head.

He blinked at Nick, completely doped on blood.

"Drop her!" Nick warned.

He reached for his hip in rote... then remembered he wasn't armed. He hadn't been cleared to carry a weapon here, since it wasn't his jurisdiction.

Great. Another thing he'd forgotten that might get him killed.

And from the frenetic, semi-psychotic look in his eyes, this asshole might be a newborn. At the very least, he appeared to be extremely young.

That meant he'd have an edge of strength over Nick already, even on a good day. Not to mention excessive amounts of sheer, psychotic *don't-give-a-fuck* force, which came with being a new vampire, and could be better or worse depending on the personality of the original human.

Newborns generally had a bit of an edge over most *normally*-powered vampires, especially in the first few months.

Nick wouldn't have worried about it excessively before.

He worried about it now.

This shithead was probably totally psycho right now.

He could also probably rip Nick apart.

"Put her down," Nick growled.

He felt his fangs growing in his mouth.

He kept his hand up, holding eye-contact with the strange vamp.

Bravado was about all he had.

"Put her the fuck down," Nick growled. "I'm a Midnight, asshole. More cops are already on their way. You face is all over their surveillance system... there's a fucking camera aimed at you right now. You're looking at reprogramming as it is... don't make me execute you right here."

That last was total bullshit of course.

He had to hope the newborn didn't know that.

Or at least that he didn't figure it out before Nick's backup arrived.

The vamp blinked at him, that cold, predatory stare unaffected.

He didn't look like much of a brain trust, this one, but Nick knew looks could be deceiving on that front, too.

The newborn's crystal-like eyes shone blood red in the backyard lights. His light-blue shirt was covered in blood, and it struck Nick that it was some kind of dorky polo-type shirt, like something that would have been hip back in the eighties, back when Nick was in high school.

"Put her down, asshole!" Nick growled. "Last warning!"

Movement pulled Nick's eyes to the dark stretch of lawn behind where the vamp stood.

Two more vampires emerged from a small grove of trees on the other side of the lawn, both female.

A fourth came out after them, another male.

That asshole was fucking huge.

They all stared at Nick along with the first vamp, the one he'd interrupted, mid-feed.

Their irises were all flushed red. Their fangs were all extended to razor-sharp points. The three newcomers looked just as psychotic and blood-frenzied as the newborn in front of him. They stalked forward slowly, watching Nick like lions circling a wounded gazelle.

Nick watched them position themselves to surround him, moving deceptively slowly as they joined their brother on the grass.

Shit.

He remembered Wynter stood at the front of the house, and his whole body tensed.

Goddamn it.

He wondered if she'd clear out if he asked her to.

If these damned newborns caught a whiff of seer blood, they'd lose their damned minds. They were still in the phase of early addiction to the high of drinking human blood. If they tried seer, it would probably turn them completely rabid.

They'd kill her.

Nick had absolutely no doubt of it.

They'd drink off her until they'd extracted every drop of blood from her body.

Then they'd probably rip out her bones to suck on the marrow.

Nick felt a sick panic growing in his body as he tried to decide what to do.

Then he noticed something else.

One of the females held a human child in her hands.

The newborn vampire gripped the long brown hair of a maybe seven-year-old girl in her clenched white fingers, forcing her head back. The kid's exposed neck displayed a torn bite mark on her throat.

The girl looked dazed, like she had no idea where she was.

The female vamp petted the girl's long hair while Nick watched, and something about the cooing sensuality of the gesture made him feel sick all over again.

Nick stared around at the four of them, and knew he was in trouble.

At the same time, the cop in him didn't switch off entirely.

He found himself noticing their clothes.

The two women wore business suits, both of them dark colors. One was a dark brown, with a cream-colored shirt and brown high-heels. The other was black, with a turquoise top. They looked vaguely ludicrous with the polo-shirt guy, but there was a consistency there, too.

They all looked like they belonged to the country-club set.

They at least looked like they *thought* they belonged to the country-club set.

Or like maybe like they *had* belonged to it recently, and hadn't quite figured out that they didn't anymore.

Their new vampire status made it difficult to pinpoint ages or how they might have looked prior to the change. The women, especially, wore clothes that now hung on them, showing they'd changed weights, possibly heights, and probably apparent ages in the process of transforming. The guy in the polo shirt was wearing baggy clothes, too, Nick realized.

"How new are you?" Nick asked, looking around at them. "Who changed you?"

Somehow, that ended up being the right question.

Or maybe the wrong one.

They all froze.

They stared at him, frozen, their scarlet eyes lost in confusion as they fought to make sense of Nick's question.

Or maybe they were trying to answer it.

Maybe as much for themselves as for him.

"Who did you work for?" Nick asked next. "Before you were turned into vampires? Who were you before the change?"

The vampires exchanged looks, the confusion in their eyes turning harder, possibly even colder. Nick watched them look at one another, and wondered if they were trying to remember what had happened to them, or if they were suddenly remembering they hadn't always been like this. That maybe they'd been pretty different before, and not too long ago.

That maybe the country club set wouldn't be eating children.

Sirens grew audible in the night air.

Nick turned with the rest of them, realizing they came from the front of the house.

He looked back at the lawn, where the vampires had been...

...but they had vanished.

They had left so quickly, the teenaged girl still stood there.

As Nick watched, her legs abruptly gave out.

She sank to her knees on the grass, clutching her neck, panting.

She whimpered, gazing plaintively up at Nick, her eyes still pleading for help. When he didn't move, didn't take a step in her direction, her head and eyes turned away from him. She looked around where she knelt, as if trying to make sense of where she was.

Her wide, dark eyes stopped when they found the bodies of the two adults lying face-down on the grass.

Her stare flickered between them in shock.

Her expression slowly crumpled as Nick watched.

She sucked in a breath, exhaling it out in a low sob.

Then she saw the little girl, and let out a strangled shriek.

Nick could only stand there, numb, as she crawled over the blood-spattered grass to what had to be her little sister. Nick noticed only then that the seven-year-old girl had also been left behind when the vampires fled. Now the younger child lay on her back in the family backyard, her eyes glazed from venom and shock, her purple, polka-dotted shirt covered in her own blood, and possibly the blood of her parents.

Nick stood there, watching them.

He honestly wasn't sure if he should approach them, given what he was.

Just then, he heard the door slam open behind him.

"POLICE!" A voice yelled. "WE'RE ACCESSING THE HOUSE! WE RECEIVED A CALL FROM AN OFFICER REQUIRING BACKUP!"

Footsteps echoed in the entryway, then filled the high-ceilinged house.

"Back here!" Nick yelled. "I called it in! I'm in the backyard!"

Snapped out of his paralysis by the arrival of the other cops, Nick summoned the SFPD's artificial lifeform again.

Bruce's cheerful face appeared and danced in the corner of Nick's headset screen.

"Everything okay, Nick? I sent the backup you requested—"

"Did you send the paramedics, Bruce?"

"I'm not authorized to do that until you've made visual contact with—"

"I've got visual contact," Nick growled. "You can see them via my headset, and through the backyard surveillance attached to the Das property. We've got two badly wounded kids, one roughly seventeen years of age, the other probably seven or eight. At least one is suffering from serious blood-loss, shock, probably other injuries associated with a vampire attack. Two adults are down... at least unconscious, but probably dead. I have to assume it's Mr. Viraj Das and his wife. I haven't yet checked their vitals..."

Three officers burst through the open glass door behind him, guns drawn.

They aimed those guns at Nick.

"Hands up!" the first one demanded, his face flushed bright red.

Nick raised his hands slowly, turning to stare at the officers standing there.

"Seriously?" he said. "I'm the one who called you guys."

"Just keep your hands up, bloodsucker," the young officer spat. "Until we've assessed the nature of the scene, don't make a damned move!"

Nick exhaled, motioning towards the lawn.

He did it with his hands still in the air.

"There are at least four vics. I just called your A.I., Bruce, and told him to send paramedics. The two kids are alive, but the younger one appears to be in severe shock, with probable vampire venom poisoning and severe blood loss. I didn't want to scare the kids more, so I haven't checked vitals on the parents. I'm pretty sure they're both dead."

The three cops exchanged looks.

Two of them immediately lowered their guns.

The first one, the one with the red face, didn't.

"Who the fuck are you?" he said. "I don't know you."

"Midnight. Out of NYPD. Homicide Division. Ident tag 9381T-112. I was helping out my precinct on a case back in New York. My boss asked me to conduct a few interviews while I was here—"

"Who did this?" the human cop demanded.

"I saw four vamps," Nick said. "Possibly newborns. They were feeding on the two kids when I got here. The parents were already down—"

"Why the fuck didn't you stop them?" the flushed asshole demanded.

Nick gave him a flat-eyed look. "I'm not carrying. I'm one vampire. And I'm injured. What exactly did you expect me to do? Irritate them to death? I told them I was police. I ordered them to let the kids go. They probably would have beat the living shit out of me, but they split when they heard the sirens."

Pausing, watching the cops look at one another, Nick couldn't quite keep the irritation out of his voice.

"Can I lower my hands now? I've got the whole thing recorded. You can ask Bruce about how I accessed the place... and any record of my movements. I just sent him the transcripts so he would send the damned paramedics."

More sirens erupted on the street outside the house.

Nick hoped like hell they were the paramedics.

Then he realized something else.

Wynter.

Not a single one of these assholes had mentioned Wynter.

She hadn't followed them inside the house.

Immediately, terror rippled through his mind.

CHAPTER 19

IT'S A TRAP

NICK SHOVED PAST THE RED-FACED COP AND HIS GUN. IT ONLY occurred to him later that he was damned lucky he didn't get shot.

Or arrested on the spot.

As it was, he barely noticed the guy, or his gun.

He completely ignored the alarmed yells, the calls from two of the uniforms for him to stop, to stay where he was until they could assess the scene.

Nick ran into the house.

He didn't look back, or look at anything in the house itself as he ran towards the front entryway, and the organic metal front door.

He didn't pause as he yelled out her name.

"WYNTER? WHERE THE FUCK ARE YOU? ARE YOU IN HERE?"

Silence.

He turned on his headset, trying to reach her through the line.

He screamed at her with his mind, even knowing she couldn't hear him, that she couldn't have heard him without the venom, even if he'd fed on her recently.

WYNTER! PICK UP! PICK UP YOUR GODDAMNED PHONE!

He ran out the open front door of the Das house.

For a few seconds, maybe two, he just stood there, looking around frantically.

The security gate was wide open.

An ambulance stood there, lights flashing.

She would have run in.

She would have come inside the house, looking for him.

Unless they arrested her, or physically held her back, she would have run inside the house just like he'd run outside, looking for her.

Two black and white cop cars were parked on the other side of the ambulance, their lights making patterns on the nearby houses, mixing with the lights from the ambulance. Nick saw a few neighbors standing on front porches, murmuring to one another as they watched the goings on at house of Viraj Das and his family.

No one sat in the back of either of the two black and whites.

They hadn't cuffed her and shoved her back there to get her out of the way.

Two paramedics were opening the back doors of the ambulance, pulling out medical kit bags while the lights rotated on the top of the long ambulance.

"WYNTER!" Nick yelled.

The two paramedics looked up, their eyes startled.

Another uniform cop, who Nick hadn't noticed until just then, standing in the front yard, also looked up at Nick.

Nick ignored all of them.

He ran down the stairs, so fast he nearly slammed into the cop, and the paramedics now coming through the open gate towards the house.

Nick barely looked at either of them, but he did grab the cop briefly by the arm.

"Did you see a woman out here?" he growled. "Outside the gate, when you first arrived? Dark hair? With blue and gold colored streaks? Blue-green eyes. Early thirties. She was wearing a white dress, light sandals—"

"Oh." The guy's eyes, which had widened in fear at whatever they'd first seen in Nick's face, now looked concerned. "Real pretty, right? Wearing a white dress?"

"Yes," Nick snapped. "Where the fuck did she go? Did you take her somewhere?"

"Take her somewhere? No. She left with that guy."

Nick felt a cold line of fire run down his back.

"What guy?"

"Well, you know. She got into a car with that man."

"What fucking man?"

The cop blinked, staring at Nick like he'd just slapped him across the face.

"Buddy, hey. Calm down. I don't fucking know what man. Just a man. Brown hair. I didn't see his face. He was wearing a black coat. It seemed like she knew him. She was arguing with him. I saw her yelling at him as he helped her into the car."

"Helped her into the car?" Nick snapped. "Or fucking kidnapped her? Just how much was he 'helping' her get in, asshole?"

The guy blanched.

Nick's jaw hardened further.

"What kind of car? What did he put her in?"

"I honestly don't know, man... sorry. It looked expensive, whatever it was."

One of the paramedics, the female, must have been listening to them.

"It was an antique," she said, calling down the stairs to Nick. "It looked like a restored corvette. One of the really old ones. It looked like they'd made it street-legal by modifying it for the solar grid, probably changing out the whole chassis, but the basic style was old-school. Definitely pre-war. It looked like something you'd see at the annual 'Historic San Francisco' parade... along with the other gas-powered cars."

Nick was already past them.

He burst out onto the street, looking in both directions.

He looked at some of the people standing on their stoops.

He considered asking one of them if they'd seen anything, questioning any of the neighbors watching from their windows, then decided that would take too long.

He followed her scent, instead, running down the sidewalk until he hit the corner of Steiner and Pacific.

The scent grew confused there.

Again, Nick gritted his teeth, half out of his mind with frustration from not being able to use any of his sensory organs properly. He could definitely smell vampires, though, which made his head throb with an intensity he almost couldn't see past.

He stared up and down the street, but they'd obviously left with her.

In the background, Nick's headset pulsed.

He'd told it to try to connect with Wynter's.

He'd left it on, left it ringing.

He'd more or less forgotten he left it like that...

...when the line suddenly connected.

Nick froze.

He stood there, paralyzed, in the middle of the street, as he heard someone on the other end abruptly pick up. He heard them breathing.

He heard her heart beating in her chest.

"Nick?"

"*Di'lanlente a' guete...*" He swore unthinkingly in seer. "Where the fuck are you, Wynter? *Gaos* fucking in heaven. Where *are* you?"

"I don't know. I can't see anything."

"Are you all right? Who has you? Where *the fuck* are you, Wynter?"

"Nick. I'm all right. I'm with..."

She sucked in a breath, like something or someone stopped

her from finishing that sentence. Nick listened to her breath hard through the line, fighting not to scream.

"Tell them…" He choked on the words. "Tell them I'll do it. Whatever it is they want, tell them I'll do it, Wynter. Tell them, baby… please…"

After a bare pause she went on, her voice taut.

"He wants to talk to you."

"I'll talk to him. Where?"

"He says he won't hurt me if you come talk to him, Nick."

"Okay. I'll talk to him. I'll talk to him for as long as he wants. Where, Wynter? Where does he want me to go?"

"He says not to tell the police. No one in the NYPD. No one here in San Francisco. None of Farlucci's people. He says not to contact anyone in the White Death. He says he'll know, Nick. He'll know if you contact someone. Same with Archangel. He says he'll know."

"Okay." Nick held up a hand, even though no one was there. "Tell him okay, baby. I won't call anyone. No one."

"He wants you to come alone, Nick. Just you."

From her voice, she had to force out every word.

He could hear her anger, her fury at being made to speak.

He could also hear the warning woven into every one of her words. She might as well be screaming in Nick's ear, DON'T BELIEVE HIM, NICK. IT'S A TRAP. IT'S A TRAP!

Yeah. No shit, baby.

No shit.

"Where?" he said. "Tell me where to go, Wynter. Where do I meet you? I'll go wherever he wants. I'll come alone. Unarmed. Just me. Right now."

There was a silence.

Her voice rose again.

It sounded even more taut and angry than before.

"He says the old Legion of Honor museum. Up by the water. Where the park is up there. There's a trail along the coast—"

"I know it. I know the Legion of Honor. Where? Inside? Or—"

"He says he'll tell you where to go when you get there. He says we'll wait for you there, and tell you where to go once you're inside."

"Okay. Okay, baby."

"He says we're there now. I can't see, Nick—"

Pain slammed into his chest.

"It's okay." He swallowed. "It's okay, Wynter."

"He wants you to come now, Nick."

"Okay. I'm going now. I'm leaving *right now*, Wynter. Tell him not to hurt you. Tell him there's no reason for him to hurt you. Whatever it is, I'll help him—"

But that was as far as he got.

The connection abruptly cut out.

The network line they'd been on, where he'd heard his wife's voice, fell dead.

Nick stood there, in the middle of the street, panting, even though he didn't need air.

For a bare handful of seconds, he couldn't make himself move.

CHAPTER 20

ACROPOLIS

NICK HAD ABSOLUTELY NO INTENTION OF WAITING FOR A TROLLEY.

He didn't plan to wait for any more expensive form of transport, either, like a private car he might have ordered, or even a motorcycle.

He stole a car.

Well, a truck, really.

First, he went back to the police car to look for weapons.

He found one of the hand-held devices they jokingly called "all-opens" in a compartment on the shotgun side of the vehicle. He used his ident and thumbprint to open the lock, then used the same to grab the hand-held.

He had to hope it would take them a few hours to notice it was missing, especially given all the chaos around the Das house. No one noticed him as he accessed the vehicle. No one looked at him at all, even as he went through glove compartments, looking for anything else he might be able to use.

He found a small taser, and used his ident code to unlock that from the steering wheel as well. He tried to do the same with the extra gun all police vehicles carried under the passenger side seat, but because he wasn't cleared for firearms in San Francisco, the lock wouldn't open.

He stuck the taser in his boot.

He found a knife in the glove compartment, something personal that must have belonged to one of the cops, and stuck that in his other boot.

Neither weapon was ideal for use against four newborn vampires.

But it was something.

Gripping the all-open in his hand, Nick climbed out of the second police car, and made his way up the block at a fast, military-paced jog.

The first car he found was a Porsche, outfitted with a liquid gas engine.

He stared at it.

Tempting as fuck, but it was probably a half-million dollar vehicle.

If the cops followed him to where he was going, he might get Wynter killed.

He moved on, looking for the next car.

A few blocks further down the street, Nick found the caterer's truck.

From the sound of drunken laughter and glasses clinking, the strains of music coming from the backyard and the splash of people jumping into the pool, they were having a party. The enormous house took up the entire corner lot; it was even bigger than the house that had recently belonged to Viraj Das.

But the catering truck was deserted.

No one was outside in the front part of the house at all.

Nick used the all-open to force the locks.

Climbing onto the front seat, he used the device again to start the truck's ignition.

Peering out the window a last time up at the house, he made sure no one was staring at him out the window, wondering what the fuck he was doing. Then, reasonably sure the cops wouldn't be right on his ass he made his way to meet the people who'd kidnapped his wife, Nick put the car into gear and gently eased it off the curb.

Once he'd made it a few blocks, he stomped on the gas.

The thing wasn't much of a mover.

The truck's engine struggled to go faster as he took it down Pacific Avenue to Scott Street. There Nick hung a left and another right onto Jackson. Once he got on Jackson and didn't see any traffic, he floored it, hoping the van had more juice once he gave it room to breathe, maybe even enough to build up some momentum.

Unfortunately, it didn't.

That fact might have saved him a ticket, but it had Nick cursing and egging the car forward in a snarling voice as it chugged dutifully up Jackson, past the edges of Pacific Heights and Presidio Heights, and into the Richmond District.

He made another few turns to get onto California, and then he was aiming the car more or less in a straight line for Land's End, where the Legion of Honor Museum was located.

He made a few more turns at the end, to get onto Clement Street.

Then he found himself surrounded by the darkness of trees and lawn in the park.

He didn't see any streetlights.

One barrier guarded the lower part of the road.

Luckily, it wasn't anything permanent.

A series of metal, star-shaped balls had been placed in a line across the road.

They were mostly dead metal, which made them heavy, but also meant the spiked balls didn't appear to be electrified, or even comprised of enough organic components to be connected to the city's main security grid.

That didn't mean drones might not be watching him, of course.

But there was nothing Nick could do about that.

He just had to hope like hell no one arrived fast enough to get him or Wynter killed.

Nick got out of the truck long enough to move two of the metal shapes out of the road. He moved them behind the others, so the difference might not be as noticeable from the road.

The barrier pieces reminded him of giant playing jacks from when he'd been a kid.

He remembered playing with those on the schoolyard when he'd been about the same age as the youngest Das girl. It all seemed so painfully primitive now. They'd bounced a colored rubber ball, then tried to snatch up as many of the star-like shapes before the ball hit the asphalt again. He even had a favorite set of jacks—iridescent blue with white sparkles.

He shoved the random thought aside, fighting to focus.

But he couldn't focus, really.

Not on what he'd face at the top of that hill.

Not on what he'd do if he couldn't save her.

But he couldn't think about that yet.

He had to assume the worst, but he honestly didn't know what the worst was.

Four newborn vamps, at the very least.

Along with whoever controlled them.

Once Nick made enough of a gap to squeeze the truck through, he climbed back into the front seat of the catering vehicle with the shitty, golf-cart engine and continued driving.

He floored the truck to make it up the hill, but he was beginning to think he could run faster than the damned thing.

If he hadn't been venom-depleted, he might have just parked the car and done that.

As it was, he grew conscious of how conspicuous the caterer's truck was up here. He found himself glancing at the virtual panel on the outside of the white-paneled truck, noting how it glowed, lighting up the dark line of trees on the empty road. The virtual dog running around in a chef's hat, eating hot dogs and frolicking happily on a rotating pepperoni pizza, reflected blue and white light on everything as the truck passed.

He pushed it out of his mind, focused on getting to the top.

He did get the damned thing to the top eventually, and pulled the truck into one of the dozens of open slots in the old parking lot below the museum.

There were no other cars in the lot.

Nick saw no other people, no vampires, no humans.

No Wynter.

Immediately, he opened a network channel.

He tried to reach her headset again.

When no one picked up, he set it to try again every fifteen seconds.

He also sent her a brief text.

I'm here. Tell me where to go, wife.

Cutting the engine, he set the "all-open" device on the truck's dashboard. Resting his arms briefly on the steering wheel, he peered out the window, staring up the slope at the stone ruins at the top of the hill.

As he gazed up at what had once been one of his favorite places to bring dates, back when he'd been human, he glanced at the line of texts that came up in his headset while he waited for Wynter to answer him.

Morley wrote him.

Morley. Morley. Morley.

Eight messages from Morley.

He was tempted to open them up, read what the detective had been trying so frantically to send him, but he knew Morley would be notified once he did, since the human detective had logged them as official police transcripts.

Given the number of messages he'd left already, Morley would likely call Nick immediately if he did that.

Nick needed to keep the line open.

He needed to stay focused on this, on where he was.

Whatever Morley had to tell him, it could wait.

Nick exhaled, refocusing on the view outside his windshield.

He hadn't realized the museum itself was no longer standing.

What little remained, reminded him of when he'd gone to Greece, a few million years ago, and he and his friends had hiked up to look at the ruins of the Acropolis in Athens.

He remembered some old pillars, a few walls.

The Legion of Honor Museum looked like that now.

It was a strange thought, to compare those two things.

Nick made out the El Cid statue to his right, down the hill from the museum itself.

El Cid was still standing. It looked like he'd taken some fire, though. Part of the bronze, life-sized, man-and-horse statue appeared to be damaged, and the whole thing looked slightly tilted, like it had been knocked off-kilter with its base by one of the blasts.

Some of the bronze even looked melted, and charred along the statue's face and the side of its head. As Nick focused on it, he saw that the tilt of the man and horse came from part of the base being cracked. The whole thing was blackened along that same side.

El Cid still held his flag in the air, though, and his horse still pranced... even if one of the statue's arms didn't look quite right, and the horse's tail was gone.

Nick's eyes shifted to the old museum itself.

Pillars, half of them broken off, formed a rectangular frame for the old courtyard, but most of those courtyard stones were missing or broken. One of the two side buildings, the one on the left, still had two of its four walls, with the outside wall looking surprisingly intact, despite the inner, courtyard wall being mostly rubble.

The building itself was gutted... which wasn't really a surprise.

Nick saw nothing but weeds and dirt through the openings in the crumbling edifice.

The building that had been to the right of the courtyard was completely razed. Most of the pillars on that side were cracked and broken, too, and Nick saw a lot more smoke and fire damage on that side of the hill.

All the priceless art, gone.

Even the Rodin statue appeared to be gone.

Everything but El Cid.

A carved stone arch still led into the courtyard, and Nick thought he saw part of the back dome still intact from the taller part of the building at the far end. That segment had once comprised the main lobby of the museum, as well as one of its wings.

It was also where the indoor and outdoor café had once stood, along with the museum's gift shop and a number of the larger exhibits.

He'd really liked that café.

It was weird to him, that they'd left it like this.

Hanging up the line he'd opened, he punched in Wynter's network address a second time, not waiting for the A.I. to do it.

It buzzed again, pulsing in his ear.

Again, no one picked up.

He typed in another text.

Wynter... I'm here. I'm in the white van with the cartoon dog on it. In the parking lot, looking up at the museum. Have that fucker call me. Please. Please.

He hit send.

Switching to live contact, he hung up the pulsing line.

He immediately re-entered her network address.

Again, he let it ring.

He was tempted to check his boots for the taser and the knife, but he was conscious there might be eyes on him. He didn't want to give them any reason to think he might be armed.

"Goddamn it, Wynter—"

Something metallic rapped on the driver's side window.

Nick jumped.

Then, more slowly, he turned.

He found himself staring into a pair of familiar brown eyes.

Nick cursed under his breath, doing it in seer, almost without realizing it.

It was Alan Rickson.

He was looking at goddamned Alan Rickson.

Only his brown eyes were no longer warm.

They stared at Nick through the clear window, cold as two burnt stones.

Rickson reached up again. Again, he tapped the piece of metal sharply against the semi-organic glass a second time.

That's when Nick realized what Rickson was using to get his attention.

It was a gun.

CHAPTER 21

F*CKING MORON

Nick walked up the hill towards the ruins of the Legion of Honor Museum. He held his hands up in the air on either side of his shoulders, conscious of the breaths of Alan Rickson behind him, conscious of the gun the human aimed at his back.

But it wasn't really the gun that caused Nick to be on his best behavior.

It was the four vampires waiting for them at the top of the hill.

It was the fact they had Wynter with them.

Well, according to Rickson they did, anyway.

Nick knew he might already be too late, regardless of what Rickson said.

Even if Rickson was telling the truth, which Nick couldn't be certain he was, Wynter's safety was only guaranteed if Rickson could actually *control* the four newborns he was using to hold Nick's wife. Rickson claimed he could.

The human assured Nick he commanded them absolutely.

He'd said it confidently, arrogantly, like his ability to mind-whisper the four newborns was a given, an unassailable fact.

Nick remembered being a newborn.

Granted, according to Brick, Nick was a particularly "difficult" newborn.

Still, as Nick thought about the four budding psychopaths he'd met briefly in Das' backyard, who he'd interrupted in the process of eating two children, after the four of them collectively murdered their parents in front of them…

Yeah.

Nick had his doubts.

He really had his doubts Rickson could control them as well as he claimed.

He was trying not to think about that right now, though.

He walked steadily up the uneven hill, his eyes trained straight ahead, looking for movement, looking for his wife. He grimaced, fighting not to lose his shit about the fact that he couldn't smell Wynter yet, that he *still* struggled to smell her, even though Rickson continued to assure him of how "close" they were.

He had to hope that was at least because she'd sprayed human pheromones all over herself.

It wouldn't keep those newborns off, not forever, but it might be the only thing to save her life long enough for Nick to get there.

He had to hope she'd done it.

He had to hope she'd thought to do it before they went out that night.

Apart from that, he fought not to think about her yet.

He fought not to run dark scenarios in his mind.

His cop brain had already figured out a few things, though.

It hadn't been Viraj Das who roped Gordon Murami into the bullshit company making fake vampire venom.

No, it had been his own husband.

Almost like he heard Nick's thoughts, Rickson muttered from behind him.

"They told me it would work," he said. "They *assured* me it would work. Even Boorman believed it."

"You're a fucking idiot," Nick informed him.

"You should have heard Antonio. He really thought we'd hit the jackpot. He thought all of us would be set up for life…"

"You're a fucking *idiot*," Nick said, a touch louder.

Alan Rickson barely seemed to hear him.

Still talking to himself, he pitched his voice deeper, imitating a strong, Italian accent with exaggerated, lilting tones.

"You'll get rich, Alan. You be the king of the Bay. This'll make you a shoo-in for Mayor in a few years. Then governor after that. Maybe head of the World Court! Or the Human Racial Authority! You can pick your next governorship, maybe. Chicago… Miami… even New York. You come to Rome! Visit me! We'll be richer than dragons!"

Alan made a disgusted sound, shaking his head.

"You got your own husband killed," Nick retorted. "You destroyed your own family."

Alan heard that.

He may have been talking to himself, but those word of Nick's, he heard.

His voice sharpened, even as he prodded Nick in the back with the gun.

"You don't know what you're talking about," he hissed. "Running for office was *Gordon's* idea. He was all-in… all the way. The whole family was. When I told you we shared everything, I wasn't lying! He *wanted* to go to New York! He *wanted* to be there for the initial tests in Zurich and Moscow!"

"Yet Gordon's the one who's dead," Nick pointed out. "You're the one holding the gun to my back. And now you're going to fuck up *my* life? Destroy *my* family? Because once isn't enough for you, I guess?"

The human shook his head, his voice turning harsh.

"You shouldn't have come to my house, Nick," he said, voice cold. "You definitely shouldn't have brought your wife. You should have just fought your fight at the arena under Union Square… then gone right back to New York."

215

"That was the fucking plan," Nick retorted. "I'm not the one who bashed me in the head in my fucking hotel room, and stole my damned venom, *Alan.*"

There was a silence.

Nick glanced over his shoulder when it stretched, still holding his hands in the air.

Rickson gave him a puzzled look, like he was trying to decide what to say back.

In the end, he said nothing.

Instead, he raised the gun to aim it at Nick's face.

Nick considered pursuing that silence, to try and find out whatever the human had been about to tell him. Then he decided it didn't matter.

"Why Das, Alan?" Nick asked. "Why the fuck did you send your newborns after him?"

Thinking about what he'd found in that backyard in Pacific Heights, Nick grimaced.

When he next spoke, his voice filled with disgust.

"They killed both of them," he said. "Did they tell you that? You left those kids orphans. Of course, that wasn't really the plan, was it? They would have killed the kids too, if they'd just had a bit more time. They were feeding on both of them when I got there, Alan. They'd nearly drained the little girl dry. Seven years old, and they were—"

"Shut up!" Rickson snarled. "That was *your* fault, Nick! Yours! If you hadn't come to my house, hitting me with all those damned questions... if you'd *called* first, and given me a chance to figure out what I was going to say. Or at least given me time to get a lawyer to advise me—"

"Really?" Nick grunted. "That's what you're going with?"

"Fuck off!" The human jabbed him again with the gun, hard in the back. "You made everything *worse,* Nick. It was terrible already. What happened in New York was *horrible.* It was fucking horrible, but it was an *accident.* A horrible, terrible accident, that cost me just about everything... but it was an *accident,* Nick."

"An accident?" Nick turned his head, glaring at him. "Seriously?"

"They were drunk," Rickson said. "I don't know whose idea it was. The vamps Ubelis brought in, they got rid of the surveillance tapes inside the hotel room—"

"Jesus." Nick felt a kind of dawning horror as he realized he understood. "They drank it. Didn't they? Or shot it up? No one turned them. They took their own damned poison serum."

"They'd been looking at tests for days! Weeks! They were drunk. They thought the damned thing worked! The vamp scientists told them it *worked!*"

Nick felt sick.

He could almost see it.

Those five idiot humans, drinking vodka together, crowing about how rich they were going to be. Crowing about how much smarter they were than everyone else. Staring at those jars of magic "not-vampire" elixir and imagining being young and strong and hot forever.

The temptation to sample the product had been just too much.

"Who killed them?" Nick asked, that nausea reaching his voice. "Was it the vampires Ubelis hired? Did they get them out of the way?"

"They started killing people!" Rickson burst out.

Nick let out a morbid laugh.

He couldn't help it.

"Well... yeah," he said. "They were fucking *vampires,* Alan."

"They were exhibiting 'pack' behavior, our vampire analyst said. Gordon was leading them. He was fucking *leading* them. He was their 'alpha' or whatever. And he was fucking *everyone.* He fucked all the people he murdered... the other four vampires. Strangers he picked up in bars and fed on. He fucked *Bleekman.* Gordon never had sex with a woman in his life!"

"He wasn't *alive* anymore, Alan."

"Bullshit! You're alive! You're even married!"

"When I first got turned, I wasn't," Nick said darkly.

"I don't think you understand—" Rickson began angrily.

Nick let out an involuntary laugh.

His voice grew even colder.

"Oh, I understand," Nick said. "Vampires don't give a shit about your sexual identity, Alan. Or about your marriage. Or your kids. He probably would have drank blood off all four of you. He might have fucked all four of you, too… right before he snapped your necks… depending on what kind of newborn he was, and how fucked up he was from being turned. He'd want to kill himself for it later, of course… once he remembered himself again… but then, if he was the most aggressive of the five, he'd probably take the longest to come back to himself, and maybe he'd never come back at all, after that. Some don't."

Alan Rickson didn't seem to hear any of Nick's words.

Maybe he just didn't understand them.

Maybe he didn't want to understand them.

He kept speaking louder, more insistently.

"You really don't get it," Rickson said, shaking his head. "You really don't. This wasn't *normal.* They didn't just feed a little bit, here and there… they turned into *monsters."*

He glared at Nick, like he didn't think Nick had any idea what he meant.

Like Nick hadn't been the worst monster himself, once upon a time.

"It was a damned nightmare," Rickson snapped. "I'm telling you, it wasn't anything like it is with most vampires. Gordon and the others… they were like wild animals. They killed *everybody!* They killed people *every day.* They fucked and killed and left messes everywhere. For *weeks.* We had to pay people to cover it up, to try to keep it out of the news. To try and keep it from blowing up into a huge problem with the other vamps."

Nick just stared at him, incredulous.

When he didn't react, Alan scowled.

The human stared off to the side, his jaw hard.

"It was impossible," he muttered. "It was just an *impossible* situation. The bank was getting nervous. The vampires were getting nervous."

Rickson turned, glaring at Nick.

"The vampires kept warning us that the White Death were going to step in... and then we'd really be fucked. According to our consultants, they would either recruit them or kill them. Or possibly recruit *some* and kill the rest. Whichever it was, the vamp techs warned us they would interrogate all five of them first. Then they'd come looking for us. They'd find out about the synthetic venom project and either shut us down or kill all of *us*, too—"

"You're a goddamned *idiot*, Alan," Nick spat, unable to suppress his anger. "How could all of you be this colossally fucking stupid?"

"They told us it worked!"

"Who told you that? The vampires who were scamming all that money off the banks?" Nick didn't hide his scorn. "And who *was* Boorman, really? Because he sure as hell wasn't any kind of 'genetic engineer,' or 'vampire scientist.' If he drank the venom along with the rest of those idiots, he's no more of a scientist than I am."

Alan glared at him.

Nick didn't think he'd answer,

But, exhaling angrily, Rickson did.

"He was a salesman, they told me later," he said. "Boorman."

Nick burst out in another humorless laugh. "Jesus."

"He worked for the vampire group that organized the initial project out of Russia," Rickson warned. "They told me later that the scientists were all supplied from there."

"Idiots," Nick muttered, shaking his head. "Fucking morons, all of you."

"I'm telling you, the science looked *good*, Nick."

"No, Alan. It didn't look good. It was shit. It was pure junk."

"We couldn't have known that! How could we have known that?"

Nick gritted his teeth.

When he spoke next, his voice grew even colder.

"So who gave the order to have the five of them killed?" Nick asked. "Was it you, Alan? Ubelis Bank? The vampires out of Russia? Who made the final call?"

Rickson didn't answer.

He began muttering to himself, half under his breath.

He stumbled on the uneven ground as they entered the ripped-up courtyard. He still aimed the gun at the back of Nick's head.

"No one was even *looking* at me," Rickson muttered. "No one thought I was involved in this in *any way.* No one even *questioned* me about any of it. I got condolences. Flowers. Notes. No visits from cops. No speculation in the news, apart from people noting I'd gotten a bit of an uptick in my polling, due to the sympathy vote."

Nick gave him an incredulous look, his hands still up in the air.

Rickson didn't seem to notice.

"Then *you* had to show up," the human muttered angrily. *"You* had to show up on my door with your damned wife and start asking your million and one questions. You couldn't just let the investigation stay in New York. You had to come out here, pull *me* into it. You just had to turn everything into a fucking *disaster*—"

"I guess you're right, Alan," Nick said dryly. "I guess you're just blameless. Clearly, your part in all this makes you look as innocent as a baby duck. After all, it's Gordon's own fault he got pulled into this shitty venom scam, right? It's Antonio's fault you gave it to Gordon. It's *my* fault you sent those vampires after Das. It's everyone *else's* fault you put out a hit order on your own husband. Clearly, you didn't do *anything* wrong in any of it, Alan—"

"Shut the fuck up!" Rickson spat, hitting him in the back with the gun. "Shut your goddamned mouth!"

"Why?" Nick growled. "Clearly you plan to kill me and my wife, regardless of what I do. It's not like you brought me up here just to bear witness to your shitty confession. You certainly aren't the type to own up to your responsibility and turn yourself in."

"IT'S NOT MY FAULT!" Alan burst out. "I DIDN'T DO THIS! I'M RUNNING FOR OFFICE, FOR CHRIST'S SAKE!"

Nick blinked, staring at him.

Then he let out another disbelieving laugh.

"You really think that's still happening, Alan?"

When Nick turned his head, Alan Rickson stared at him.

The human's eyes reflected a kind of angry confusion, his mouth pursed.

"That's over, Alan," Nick said, cold. "It's *over*, do you hear me?"

"So you say," the human sneered.

"You really think they're not going to figure it out now?" Nick asked incredulously. "My boss was already onto you, Alan. It wasn't *me* who decided to look you up and talk to you over here. It was him. I came here to fight. My boss is the one who wanted me to stay in town a while longer, ask some questions about the case."

Nick paused, studying the human's face.

His voice grew a touch harsher.

"I've already sent him the entire transcript of our interview. It's done, Alan. They already have it. You really think they won't put two and two together? Especially if me and my wife mysteriously disappear?"

Pausing another beat, Nick added,

"All they have to do is dig into your b.s. story about Suntrode being the ones to sponsor Gordon to work with Ubelis. That's a great big ole red flag right there. A damned stupid lie, Alan, if you don't mind my saying. They'll try to verify that, of course, especially with Das dead, and they'll find out Suntrode has no friggin' idea what they're talking about. They'll find the *real* players behind your bogus project. Then they'll find *you,* Alan. And once they realize you were lying about that, they'll start to wonder what *else* you were lying about. And it won't take them long after that to see your fingerprints *all over* this…"

Nick let out another cynical snort.

"And that's just the cops. Wait until the media gets ahold of this, Alan. Not to mention the Human Racial Authority. If me or Wynter disappears, your problems multiply. A whole new investigation starts up here. Celebrity boxer and his schoolteacher wife, dead or missing while visiting San Francisco? Oh, and they just *happened* to be investigating a high-profile murder for the NYPD? Oh, and they were there, at the house, when Viraj Das was murdered? The media will be all *over that shit,* Alan. That's like Christmas morning for them…"

Nick let out another disbelieving laugh.

"It's over, Alan. It's fucking *over.* Do you really not see that?"

Rickson shoved at the small of Nick's back, viciously that time.

Nick was about to say something else, when he glimpsed movement ahead.

He turned his head, sharp…

…and realized they were finally there.

CHAPTER 22

FINAL REQUESTS

N<small>ICK LOCKED EYES WITH</small> W<small>YNTER.</small>

He felt such a rush of intense feeling, he gritted his teeth.

It was that or he was going to grab Alan Rickson around the neck and snap the bone between his hands.

He felt his fangs grow as he stared at his wife.

Her blue-green eyes held his, strangely calm.

Something about the look there brought up an even more intense swell of love.

It brought up other things, too.

Heat, desire, a fierce protectiveness that made his muscles clench all over.

"You okay, honey?" he asked.

They had a gag in her mouth. Even so, she nodded, that colder, more predatory look still in her eyes.

Nick felt a wash of red begin to tint his vision.

He felt the heat of that swirl of blood, even before he saw it.

His eyes darted around, taking in the four newborn vamps around her. None of them were touching her at the moment, but he could see them looking at her. He could see the hunger in those stares. Still, he relaxed slightly, looking at them.

Gaos. He'd forgotten they were newborns.

Well, he'd forgotten one component of them being newborns, at least.

Being newborns meant they were more vicious, yes.

It also meant they didn't know shit.

They had no idea what Wynter was.

Even if they *had* known what she was, in terms of her specific racial classification, they had no idea what seer blood meant to them, as vampires. They had no idea just how fucking good she would taste, how mind-fuckingly, addictively good any seer blood tasted to a vampire's tongue and mouth... particularly a seer with as many seer gifts as Wynter.

Nick was damned if they'd ever know that.

And thank the gods, she had covered herself in human pheromones.

He could smell it now. Like always, it made his nose wrinkle.

She wouldn't even smell particularly tasty to them.

"Where did these ones come from, Alan?" Nick's voice sounded calm, cold, borderline detached as he spoke to the man standing behind him with a gun. He motioned with his jaw towards the four newborns. "More satisfied customers?"

As soon as he said it, he realized it was true.

That's exactly what they were.

Briefly, he felt nauseated.

"Jesus," he said. "You sold it. The venom. Even after you knew."

"I'm *protecting* them," Alan snapped. "I told them I'd keep the White Death from finding them, if they would help me clean up this mess."

"The White Death wouldn't be going near them if you hadn't turned them into fucking *vampires*, Alan," Nick said. "Jesus. Did you sell them on the same faked 'tests' that convinced your husband and the rest of them in New York?"

Alan didn't answer.

When Nick turned his head, staring at the human, Alan scowled.

"It's not like I had much choice!" he said, sharper. "Those other vamps disappeared back to Russia after what happened. They just... vanished! Ubelis pulled out. Not only that, they scrubbed themselves off every document. They basically erased the entire electronic trail of their involvement. Then they *threatened* me..."

Nick let out a dark chuckle.

Rickson scowled, his voice furious.

"Damned cowards. All of them. They thought the thing in New York was a warning. They were scared shitless of the White Death."

"Maybe they were right to be," Nick observed.

"I needed *someone* to help me! I wasn't going to hold the bag on this, not all alone. I wasn't going to take the fall for everyone else. I already lost my husband! I lost everything in New York. Isn't that enough? Do I have to pay for all of it, for the rest of my life?"

"Yes," Nick said coldly. "You do."

"Fuck you. I'm as much of a victim in this as anyone else!"

"Sure. That's why you sold your leftover miracle venom to a few of your rich pals. Probably for a few million a pop." Nick's voice remained empty. "I guess that's two birds with one stone though, right, Alan? Make a little bit of your investment back on the leftover venom. Cash in one last time. And hey! Get some useful henchmen in the bargain. All you had to do is lie to a few people about what that stuff would actually do to them."

"I didn't lie to them," he said coldly.

"Oh, I'm sure. I'm sure you told them the unedited, totally factual, unvarnished truth, Alan. Including what happened to your husband when *he* took the stuff."

Rickson didn't answer that.

He just jabbed at Nick's back, urging him forward a few more steps.

Nick moved obediently. He stepped closer to the burnt-out

husk of the main building of the Legion of Honor with its crumbling dome.

He stepped closer to his wife.

Staring at her blue-green eyes, the delicate bones of her face, he fought past the intensity of his own emotions.

He tried to decide the best way to do this.

Ideally, he could use a distraction.

Something that would work on the vampires, as well as Rickson.

"Why did you even bring me up here?" Nick growled. "What is the point of this?"

"I need you to do something for me," Rickson said.

"What?"

"If you do what I ask," Rickson said. "Then you and your wife will die quickly, at least. Otherwise, I've been told by these vampires…"

He motioned around at the four newborn vamps.

"…that they can make this an extremely unpleasant experience for both of you. Especially for your wife. They can also make it last for weeks. Possibly even months. One of them seems quite taken with your wife, Nick. He even commented on the possibility of turning her… making her his companion on a much more permanent basis."

Nick let out a low grunt.

He looked over at the big male, and knew it had to be him.

Glancing at Wynter, he winked at his wife.

"Tell him good luck with that," he muttered.

Through the blindfold, Wynter smiled.

Rickson looked between Wynter and Nick, as if trying to figure out why they were both so calm. That, or maybe he was just waiting for Nick to focus back on him.

When he didn't, the human exhaled in irritation.

"Well?"

"Well, what?" Nick's head and eyes swiveled back to look at

the human. "I haven't heard a question yet, Alan. Just a lot of shitty threats about raping my wife."

Rickson let out an irritated sigh.

He seemed to hesitate another minute.

Then he stepped out from behind where Nick stood.

He walked around to the front of him, and pointed the gun directly at Nick's face. For a few seconds, he just stood there, looking at him.

Nick spent most of that time looking at the gun.

He noted the model, the make.

He noted the security mechanisms in place.

It was an older gun, and not a particularly good one. It definitely wasn't something most wealthy gun aficionados would buy.

Nick guessed Alan bought it recently, and probably out of the back of someone's car.

When his eyes returned to Alan's face, he saw the wary look in the human's eyes. It occurred to Nick that the human was bracing himself. His whole body looked tense, like he was waiting for Nick to make some kind of move.

Nick wondered if the human expected him to try and run for it.

Seeing the way Alan's eyes kept darting to the road, and back to the catering truck, Nick realized that's exactly what Rickson thought.

"I'm not going to abandon my wife, Alan," he told him mildly. "You can lower the fucking gun."

Alan smiled humorlessly. "Sure. Of course you won't run. Why would you run? It's not as if I didn't just tell you I plan to kill you."

Nick rolled his eyes. "Yeah. I bet you were a peach of a husband, all right."

He grunted, lowering his hands and resting them on his hips.

"Alan, I'm not abandoning my wife. I would never leave her.

For any reason. If you truly *got* that, you would already know you aren't the threat that's keeping me here."

He motioned towards the newborns with his jaw.

"…They are."

Alan frowned.

From his facial expression, he still didn't believe him.

When Nick only stood there, the lithe human rearranged his shoulders. Moving his feet around until he found a position and distance he liked, he pursed his lips.

The gun never stopped pointing at Nick's face.

"I want you to talk to the White Death for me," Alan said.

There was a silence.

Then a hard laugh burst out of Nick's lips.

"What?"

"You heard me. I know you used to run with them. Everyone knows it. I read it in like twenty different online magazines. I even saw it mentioned on the news. It's all over your press materials. And you wear their tattoo…" he added, motioning with the gun towards Nick's back. "The two angel wings. I've seen it. I've seen your fights."

Rickson paused, waiting.

Maybe he was waiting for Nick to deny it.

Nick didn't.

When the silence stretched, Alan frowned. "I'm told no one can wear that tattoo unless they're high up in the organization. Is that true?"

Nick stared at him.

A smile played at his lips, in spite of himself.

"What would you like me to say to them for you, Alan?" he asked. "Is there a particular message you would like me to convey to my brothers and sisters, cousin?"

He couldn't quite keep the sarcasm out of his voice.

Then again, he didn't try very hard.

Alan frowned, like he wasn't quite sure what to make of Nick's attitude.

In the end, he waved the gun at him.

"What the fuck do you think?" Rickson snapped. "I want you to tell them to leave me alone. I want you to *tell* them I'm not in the fake-venom-selling business!"

"Just the real venom-selling business," Nick muttered.

Alan Rickson raised his voice.

"Tell them to back the fuck off! Tell them I'm *clean* now! That I'm completely out of all of that! Tell them that it was a mistake. Tell them they can just let this go!"

Nick chuckled, in spite of himself.

He couldn't help it.

It was all just so utterly ridiculous.

"Are you done?" he asked. "Is there anything else?"

"Will you do it?" Alan demanded.

Nick turned his head, staring at him coldly.

"No."

Alan blinked.

Clearly that wasn't the answer he was expecting.

"No? Why the fuck not?" Alan's voice rose. "You think it's an empty threat? You think I won't do it? I'll let them do it, Nick! I'll let them do *whatever they want* with her! Don't think I won't! They'll hurt her! They'll hurt her a lot!"

Nick clicked at him softly, seer style, shaking his head.

He considered answering the threats to Wynter, then didn't.

Instead, he met Rickson's gaze, eyes flat.

"What makes you think the White Death would listen to me, Alan?"

"I told you why!" he snapped. "You were one of them! They know you! I need you to tell them to leave me alone! I need you to tell them—"

Another, silkier voice rose.

It cut Rickson off.

The drawling, metal-cold, insidious, lulling, boundary-less voice drew a liquid finger up Nick's spine.

Its owner nearly whispered, but every other being in the clearing turned their head.

All but one.

"Why don't you tell me yourself, brother?" Brick asked softly.

It was exactly what Nick needed.

A distraction.

CHAPTER 23

MANNERS

ALAN TURNED HIS HEAD. SO DID THE FOUR NEWBORNS.

So did Wynter.

Out of all of them, only Alan Rickson didn't seem to understand what he was seeing. The handsome, brown-eyed human gaped, uncomprehending, at the auburn-haired vampire king standing in the rubble of marble and granite.

Nick didn't bother to turn.

He had other things on his mind.

He struck without warning, moving fast.

Not as fast as normal, even now.

But with his wife's life in the balance, it was damned well fast enough.

He took the gun off Rickson before the human knew what happened.

He did it without making a sound.

Then, before the newborns fully comprehended what had happened, before any one of them had looked back at Nick from where Nick's sire had distracted them...

...Nick squeezed off four rounds with deadly precision.

Each one of them hit their targets.

Four headshots. One after the other.

It wouldn't kill them, but Nick didn't need it to.

He was already running before the last one fell.

Shoving Rickson aside, he pelted across the concrete and stone rubble, climbing up to what remained of the marble floor where Wynter stood. She just stood there, waiting for him, like some kind of centuries-old human sacrifice, ready to be burned on a pyre.

He reached her in seconds, but it still felt like it took him way too damned long.

Wrapping his arm around her, he ripped the gag off her mouth and over her head with his other hand. He did it carefully, precisely, so that he wouldn't hurt her, while still getting it off her as quickly as he possibly could.

He kissed her mouth, forgetting his extended fangs as he yanked her against him.

She kissed him back, and he deepened the kiss, crushing her against him in his arms, burying his hand in her long hair. He clenched the same hand into a fist and broke off the kiss, worried he might hurt her, just out of sheer relief.

Still holding her tightly, he wondered why she wasn't holding him back, then looked down and realized her wrists and ankles were bound.

"Fuck. Sorry."

He bent down at once, reaching into his right boot.

He yanked out the knife he'd stolen from the cop car, and used it to cut through the plastic ties holding her ankles together. The bands parted easily under the sharpened blade, but Nick remained crouched there briefly, looking at her bruised skin.

He caressed the mark there gently, frowning at the deep gouges that bit into her skin.

Rising swiftly to his feet, he cut through the bindings on her wrists.

He looked her in the eyes then, holding her hands.

"You might want to go to the truck, Wynter," he told her seriously. "I don't think you'll want to be here for this part."

She met his gaze. He saw the fleeting question there, right before her gaze lowered, and she looked down at the four vampires crumpled at her feet.

Her head and eyes shifted sideways then, and Nick saw her looking at Alan Rickson.

"He has children," she said. "They lost a father already."

"It's out of my hands," he said.

"Nick—"

"Honey." Nick shook his head. "It's out of my hands."

He turned his head, gazing down the hill meaningfully.

He let her see his eyes as they flickered over the field, helping her to pick out the vampires that stood there.

After he'd shown her the first dozen or so of Brick's people stationed all around the parking lot, the area of the old fountain, the statue of El Cid, not to mention in different parts of the ruins of the Legion of Honor... she sighed.

"Okay," she said. "Okay. I see."

"Okay?"

"Are the keys in the truck?"

"It doesn't need keys. There's a kind of universal key on the dash. It should be enough to start it up. To run the heater." He gave her a more meaningful look. "To drive it back to the hotel."

Hesitating, he added,

"Although you might not want to drive it *to* the hotel. You might want to park it somewhere dark. Then walk a bit. Then call a taxi. If you know what I mean."

"Let me guess..." she murmured.

"I stole it," he confessed. "Borrowed it, I guess you could say."

She nodded calmly.

She looked resigned now.

She also looked exhausted.

Even so, she squeezed his fingers, giving the vampires on the rubble around them a slightly regretful look before she looked back at Nick.

"You can't come with me?" she asked. "Now, I mean?"

233

He glanced at Brick, who was watching their interaction with undisguised interest.

Nick looked back at her. "No," he said. "I can't, honey. I'm sorry."

She nodded again, but didn't let go of his hands.

He gripped her tighter.

"Go on, honey," he murmured. "Take a shower... or better yet, sit in the hot tub. Nude. Order a shit-ton of room service..." He thought about that. "...but put on a robe before you answer the door."

She laughed, almost like she couldn't help herself.

He saw her wiping her eyes, though.

He squeezed her hands again. "I'm so sorry," he said.

She shook her head. "It wasn't your fault." Then, thinking about her words, she grunted. "Well. Leaving me out on the street on the other side of that fence was kind of your fault."

"I know." Pain flickered through his chest. "I know. I'm sorry."

She nodded.

She wiped her eyes again, then took a deep breath, letting it out slowly. He watched her pull herself back together, bringing that softer vulnerability he loved so much back behind a tougher veneer. He saw the precise instant when she got herself under control.

She nodded a final time, and he saw her mouth firm.

"Okay," she said. "Don't be long."

She let go of his hands.

He had to fight not to grab for her, and pull her back to him. She spent a minute adjusting the dress she wore, and resettling her feet in her sandals, before she began to climb down from the marble floor into the main courtyard.

Nick watched her go.

She walked right by Brick on her way back to the field below the ruins.

Nick's sire gave her a sweeping bow, smiling broadly.

"My dear Ms. James. I am so sorry I was not able to be here sooner."

"Hello, Your Highness. That's all right. And thank you."

"Please... Brick! Call me Brick, my lovely daughter. And of course you needn't thank me. You *are* always and *will ever be* a part of my closest family, my dear."

"Thank you, Brick," she said. Hesitating a bare breath, she bowed her head in return. "...And please don't keep my husband for too long."

Brick chuckled in delight. "Of course, my dear. Of course."

His crystal eyes darted up to Nick, right before he winked.

After she'd passed by his sire, Wynter glanced over her shoulder, quirking an eyebrow in Nick's direction.

She didn't look at him for long, and she never stopped walking, her long legs making long, swishing strides in the white dress.

The contrast of the moon and dark grass, the white dress and her long black hair, made her look like an image from an old romance novel.

Or perhaps from something more akin to a gothic horror.

It was the last time she looked back.

Even so, Nick watched her the whole way down the hill, the whole way past the reflecting pool and the statue of El Cid, and the whole time she walked over the faded lines of the ancient parking lot. He watched the other vampires bow to her as she passed, as if she really were the wife of one of their generals.

The thought made him more than a little uneasy.

Still, he felt vaguely reassured when he saw each of them greet her politely, with an open deference that made it clear they would not touch her.

Wynter was just as polite to them.

She might have been a little more bewildered.

She might have been a little less warm.

But she was unerringly polite.

Only after she climbed inside the catering truck and shut the door behind her, did Nick feel himself start to relax. He waited until the engine of the truck clicked on, the electric motor emitting a soothing, if unimpressive hum.

She didn't idle there long.

The trucks lights flicked on, and she drove in a tight circle, heading for the exit.

The dancing, VR dog frolicked brightly around the side of the van.

When the truck disappeared around the first curve, heading down to Clement Street, and back towards downtown San Francisco, Nick felt himself relaxing for real.

His eyes shifted then, turning to where Brick stood in front of Alan Rickson.

Brick seemed to have been waiting for him to turn.

It struck Nick that his sire had been standing there patiently, waiting for Nick to be watching him before he did what came next.

The instant Nick focused on his sire and the middle-aged human, the vampire leapt.

With no preamble, no flowery speeches, no pretense whatsoever that he might listen to the man plead for his life, or for the lives of his children, or for anything else…

…Brick snapped his neck.

He released him, the instant it was done.

Alan Rickson collapsed like a broken doll, inert within the museum's rubble.

Brick didn't even do him the courtesy of eating him.

CHAPTER 24

A REAL ANSWER

"Come. Have a drink with me, my brother. Before you head back to your wife." The older vampire's eyes flashed red in the dim light of the moon. "...I insist. There are things we must discuss."

Internally, Nick sighed.

Still, he didn't disagree with his sire's words.

There were things to discuss.

Quite a few things.

"All right," he said.

"It can be a more... conventional drink, brother," Brick assured him. "I know you are exclusive these days, with your eating."

"I said all right, Brick. It's fine. I'll go."

A series of sounds drew his eyes to the right.

He heard the thick ring of metal on metal, followed by a low, snarling hiss.

He glanced over just as one of Brick's men beheaded the last of the four newborns. It was one of the females, the same one that had been clutching and petting the seven-year-old daughter of Viraj Das. She must have come to from the bullet Nick put in her skull, right before the big vampire with the white wing tats on his hands drew his sword.

The sword ended that low, threatening hiss.

It also signified the end of their business here.

Nick grimaced a little as the female's head made a sickening, squelching thud on the stone before rolling onto the grass.

He looked back at Brick.

"Where did you have in mind?" he asked.

THEY WENT TO AN OLD BAR ON BROADWAY, ONE THAT HAD BEEN there since the time before the war.

Nick glanced up the wooden walls, noting the ship-like shape of the bar's interior, the comfortable leather booths, the polished bar that might have once been part of an actual fishing boat from the bay.

Despite his current company, he felt himself relax even more.

Brick must have chosen this place for that reason.

This was Nick's kind of dive.

He ordered a beer, two vodka shots, a shot of tequila, and a shot of whisky.

He knew all of it would run through his system quickly, likely in under an hour, but he hoped he could drink it fast enough to be a little drunk for at least part of that hour.

He and Brick slumped into one of the warm, red-brown booths.

Seemingly as soon as they were situated, the waitress brought over the drinks, quirking an eyebrow humorously at Nick as she lined up his four shots.

She placed his beer last, and closest to his hand.

"Enjoy." She smirked at him in a friendly way.

Flouncing off, she smiled at him again over her shoulder.

It just made him wish he was back in the hotel.

Drinking this with Wynter.

"Females really do like you," Brick observed. "I have often noticed this."

Nick rolled his eyes.

It didn't stop him, or even slow him down, in the motion of downing his first shot.

He started with one of the vodkas.

He promptly moved to the tequila.

Then the whisky.

Then the other vodka.

Only then did he lean back, closing his eyes briefly and tugging his beer mug closer to his fingers.

"How are you feeling, my child," Brick asked. "After your assault?"

Nick cleared his throat, opening his eyes and taking a few swallows of beer to wash down the last mingling tastes of hard alcohol.

"Not great," Nick said, blunt. "It's definitely one of the *less*-pleasant experiences I've had in the past few hundred years."

Brick chuckled a little, watching his eyes. "What did your fellow homicide detectives say about all of this?" the older vampire said next. "I presume you listened to their messages on the way here. Did you not?"

Nick nodded, lowering the beer from where he'd been taking another long drink.

He did listen to his messages. Most of them.

Like he'd suspected, even before he got into the car with Brick, a number of the ones he got from Jordan and Morley were attempts to warn him about Rickson.

They'd discovered the middle-aged prosecutor went to college with Antonio Formi.

Not only that, the two of them remained extremely tight over the years.

Gordon and Alan's kids even called him "Uncle Tonio."

Their respective families met up in Europe together to ride boats on the Seine, to eat dinner at outdoor cafés, to attend

239

concerts in Versailles. They'd met in New York to go Christmas shopping a few years running, London, Paris, Istanbul, Miami to go touring... even the Swiss Alps, and the Northeastern Protected Area to go skiing in the winter.

They'd spent holidays together in San Francisco at least once a year.

Morley also contacted someone at Suntrode, just like Nick predicted he would.

Suntrode had no record of arranging any kind of private contract work for Gordon Murami to conduct a "special project" in new product research. The person Morley spoke to also seemed highly skeptical that Viraj Das knew anything about that, either.

As far as anyone at Suntrode knew, Gordon Murami quit his job at Suntrode to pursue a "new opportunity," something like six months ago.

It was too bad they hadn't put all the pieces together a little quicker.

Still, all's well that ended well.

Or something like that.

Nick took another long draught of beer.

He tried not to think about Viraj Das, or his wife, or his two orphaned kids.

Or the kids of Alan Rickson and Gordon Murami.

Setting down the mug, he wiped his mouth.

He closed his eyes, but it didn't help.

"Did you learn anything new, in all these messages?" Brick queried.

Nick opened his eyes.

Thinking, he frowned.

"I asked him what it was I was supposed to see," he said, taking another drink of beer. "On the bodies. Morley seemed certain I'd see something there... something the investigation in New York wasn't actively pursuing. Something he thought might give me some ideas in terms of suspects. He claimed he had no idea what it meant, himself."

Brick quirked an eyebrow. "Oh? And did he finally tell you what it was?"

"No bite marks." Nick made exaggerated biting motions with his teeth, smiling wryly. "Morley didn't see any bite marks, so he was already wondering what the hell was going on. One of the coroners mentioned it in his notes, apparently, but the initial investigation kind of blew it off as a detail, since it was known the five bodies had been changed."

Nick shrugged.

"Morley's too smart for his own good sometimes."

"You think he knew they administered the venom to themselves deliberately?" Brick asked.

Nick shook his head. "No. Well... I don't know. I just meant, I think he knew that was a pretty big fucking clue. How they got turned."

He glanced up, smiling when the same waitress returned, bringing him another round of the same five drinks.

She started laying them out in front of him in the same formation.

"I like this," Nick admitted, looking from the drinks up to her. "But I didn't order it."

"I know." The woman smirked at him, like she had before. Then she turned her head, motioning over in the direction of the bar. "He did. That adorable little elf on the other end of the ship's prow. I think he has a bit of a crush, Mr. Tanaka." She winked at him again. "...Not that most of us don't. Good luck on the fight when they reschedule."

He smiled back, lifting the first shot in a salute. "Thanks."

"Anytime, sweetie."

Nick raised his shot glass higher, making a toast to the man on the other end of the bar.

He smiled at the small human with the curly, bleached blond hair.

Simon, the kid who picked him up off the floor of his hotel suite about a week earlier, smiled back at him shyly, raising his hand in a returning wave.

He was sitting with a group of friends, all of them roughly his age.

Nick saw them all staring between him and Simon, like they hadn't quite believed Simon when he told them he knew Nick Tanaka, The White Wolf, famous fighter in the underground vampire circuit.

From their faces, he might have told them he was buddies with Jack the Ripper.

Or maybe a human-eating tiger.

Chuckling a little at the thought, Nick downed the first shot of vodka.

When he glanced at his sire, the other vampire was watching him shrewdly, a dense scrutiny in his cracked-crystal eyes.

"I want to go back and fuck my wife," Nick told him bluntly, now a little buzzed. "Not to be crude. But it is what it is."

Brick smiled wanly. "Okay, brother."

"Did you have something in particular you wanted to ask me, Brick?"

The older vampire just sat there for a few seconds, unmoving.

His pale face contrasted with the reddish-brown leather, just as his auburn hair blended in with it. Nick watched his sire's long-fingered hands as they mindlessly stroked the top of the table. The vampire sighed then, an affected sigh, like he might do with a human.

"I suppose I am wondering one thing," Brick said carefully.

Nick downed his second shot, watching his sire toy with him.

When Brick let out a second dramatic sigh, Nick almost laughed.

He didn't laugh, though.

"What is it you're wondering, father?" he asked.

"I am wondering when it is I can ask a favor of you," Brick said, his voice studiously casual. "...After all of these favors I find myself doing for you and your lovely wife of late." He glanced up at Nick, his crystal eyes probing. "When can we speak about this, Naoko? I have indulged this extended vacation of yours, working for the humans. I have said nothing at all about it. I have put no pressure on you—"

Nick let out an involuntary laugh.

Then he threw back his head, downing the tequila.

The kid bought a better brand than Nick had for himself.

Nice kid.

Brick ignored his laugh.

"I would like you back with me," Brick said, his voice a touch harder. "I am tired of dancing with you, brother. I sometimes think your wife understands what I want better than you do yourself. That, or she is simply more honest about it."

Nick downed the second vodka, and now he really was buzzed.

His head swam for a second, and he gripped the top of the table.

Once it steadied, he looked his sire in the eye.

"You think I owe you for tonight?" he said.

Brick blinked.

It was the closest to surprise Nick had seen in his sire's eyes for quite some time.

"Do you have a different interpretation of events, Naoko?" Brick asked, his voice deceptively light. "While I do not mind rescuing my children out of scrapes, I do appreciate a *little* gratitude for my efforts... at least every now and then."

Nick nodded, but not in agreement.

Leaning over the table, he placed his arms on the wood, looking at his sire from only a handful of inches away.

"Okay," Nick said casually. "Fair enough. And believe me... I *am* grateful."

He paused.

As he sat there, Brick's mouth slowly pinched.

"But?" the vampire king prompted. "I am sensing a qualification to this gratitude."

"You probably are," Nick conceded, nodding agreeably. "I guess I'm just trying to square the whole thing with why you had your goons jump me in my hotel room, Brick... and extract all of my venom... thus probably making my 'rescue' necessary in the first place?"

His voice put a question mark in the end, but that question never reached his eyes.

He watched his sire react to his words.

Then, slowly, Nick leaned back, making his voice casual.

"Morley and Jordan thought Alan was behind that, incidentally," he said, shrugging as he picked up his second mug of beer. "They speculated that Alan knew I worked for the NYPD, and didn't want me in town to ask questions about what happened to his mate."

Nick paused, taking a long drink of the beer.

He plunked the mug down on the table when he finished swallowing, sloshing a bit of the sticky liquid over his fingers.

He didn't try to wipe them off.

"But see, there's a few funny things about that, Brick," Nick said. "Alan Rickson seemed genuinely surprised when I first showed up at his house... but he didn't seem at all worried, not until we started asking specific questions about the five vics in Manhattan. I think he wasn't really worried about me at all, frankly... probably because he thought I was a dumb fighter, and he thought of himself as some kind of cunning super-genius. I'm sure he believed he could easily convince me that he was absolutely innocent, and that he had nothing at all to do with what happened to his husband in New York."

Nick paused, then shrugged, still studying Brick's wary eyes.

"See, I've noticed people do that with me... even more so, since I started fighting. Wynter calls it my 'play dumb puppy' face. Miriam Black used to call it my 'Columbo thing'... like that old detective on t.v., the one who always acted like a scatterbrain so people would underestimate him and say too much..."

Brick's mouth hardened.

"Are you saying I am foolish enough to think you stupid, Naoko?" he hissed softly.

Nick laughed.

He shook his head, still smiling.

"You? No. I would never accuse you of that, Brick. Never in a million years." His eyes and voice lost their humor. "But Alan Rickson? Definitely. I don't think he realized I had a brain at all, not until he'd already told me far, far too much. Then he panicked. Which is why he set his pet vampires on Das... and then on Wynter."

Pausing, Nick added,

"Which is why I also don't think there's any way in hell he pulled that job in the hotel. Those were professionals, Brick. In and out. Nothing on surveillance. No traces left behind. No clue they were there at all, apart from me and my splitting headache on the floor. They didn't hurt me... apart from the venom... and they could have. Easily. They were out of there before my room service guy over there, Simon..."

Nick paused to wave at the little human over at the bar, and Simon flushed bright red, right before he waved back at him, smiling cheerfully.

"...got to be the poor sucker who found me passed out on the floor. Right after he pushed in a cart with the assortment of blood bags I'd ordered after my fight that night."

There was a silence.

For the first few seconds of that silence, Brick only looked at him.

Then his crystal eyes shifted away.

He motioned for the waitress as she walked by, and she approached their table, smiling at him cheerfully. "Did you want something, sir?"

"A gin martini," the vampire said. "Dirty. Six olives. And your freshest O-negative."

"Of course, sir. Right away."

With Brick, she was businesslike, deferential... borderline afraid.

Like Nick evoked responses, his sire evoked certain responses, too.

Energy was energy.

"Why, Brick?" Nick asked.

His sire smiled wanly. "Is that what you wish to know? Why?"

"It's the obvious question, isn't it?"

"Are you really going to treat me as the fool now, brother?" Brick raised an eyebrow slowly, staring Nick in the face. "After you just now so eloquently assured me you would never ever do such a thing?"

When Nick frowned, Brick tut-tutted under his breath.

"Come now. You have a theory about this, brother. You would never have come to me if you didn't." He paused, then continued more pointedly. "I would like to hear it."

Nick's frown deepened.

Still, his sire wasn't wrong.

Exhaling in irritation mixed with a kind of surrender, Nick shrugged.

"Well. Obviously you wanted me out of San Francisco."

"Obviously," the vampire king agreed.

"Obviously, it wasn't about the fight, or you would have done it while I was still in New York. So clearly, you were okay with me coming here, with the understanding I would be fighting in a ring for a few days, then going home to New York and my wife."

Pausing, Nick added,

"In fact, I strongly suspect you're the reason my wife didn't come out here with me in the first place. A little added motivation for me to spend as short a time here as possible. And easily arranged with your new best pal, Lara St. Maarten, CEO of Archangel and my wife's new employer."

246

Brick quirked an eyebrow, a smile toying at his lips.

"A fair assumption," he commented.

The vampire king leaned back in his leather booth seat, making room for the waitress as she laid out a cocktail napkin on the damp table, right before carefully setting down Brick's martini. She put down a round blood-warmer next, and even more carefully placed the glass of O-negative on top of it, centering it in the middle of the heat coil.

"Is there anything else you need, sir?"

"No. This is most acceptable. Thank you, cousin."

She flushed, obviously flattered, even with her fear.

"You're very welcome. Let me know if you need anything at all." That time, Nick was the afterthought as she glanced at him second. "...Either of you."

Nick smirked a little himself that time, but only nodded a thanks.

When she left, he looked back at his sire.

"I don't really get the impression you minded me helping Morley with the murder case," he added. "Or helping you flush out the last of that fake-venom group operating out of Europe, either. Not to mention San Francisco... and Russia."

"And New York," Brick added.

He raised a finger, swallowing a mouthful of the O-negative before lowering his glass. "They had looked into opening a distribution center in Miami, as well. Although we still have the most work to do with our brothers and sisters in Russia, it's true," he added with a smile.

Nick didn't return the smile.

He hesitated, staring at his sire.

His jaw clenched as he continued to stare.

"Ask it, Nick," Brick said, his voice flat. "Just ask. It is clear you want to. You have gotten this far... you may as well ask."

Nick swallowed.

He was a vampire, so he didn't need to swallow.

He swallowed anyway.

"This isn't our world," he said, blunt.

Brick quirked an eyebrow at him.

"That didn't sound like a question, my love."

"Yet, I'm asking," Nick growled. "It's not our world. Miri and Black didn't leave Earth." He clenched his jaw, staring at his sire. "We did. Didn't we?"

Brick stared at him, his crystal eyes unmoving.

"Why would you say that, my love?" he asked, taking another sip of the blood.

Nick felt his jaw slowly clench harder.

"Because I'm pretty sure there was a *different* Nick Tanaka who lived here, on this version of Earth," Nick answered next. "One who had a wife named Claire... and four kids... and who died as a human, surrounded by a human family who loved him. And I'm pretty sure his descendants are still living in a house on Potrero Hill in *this* version of Earth... a house that looks exactly like my parents' house but isn't my parents' house, and never was my parents' house. Especially since the house my parents lived in ceased to exist in *our* version of Earth a few hundred years ago..."

Nick could have said more.

He could have told him about the vampire at the arena after his first fight.

He could have told him about the kid in the house on Potrero hill, the weird memory flashes, the sense that this was his city but not, the strange, surreal way everything felt since he got here. He didn't say any of those things, though.

Instead he let his words trail, at a loss.

Silence fell, once he did.

Something about saying it out loud scared the shit out of him.

Something about saying it out loud made it real.

But nothing made it real like the look in Brick's eyes when Nick finally made himself meet his sire's gaze.

He saw the truth there.

He saw it, seconds before his sire actually spoke.

In the end, the vampire king said only one word.

But really, there was only one word that needed to be said.

"Yes," Brick pronounced simply.

Lifting his glass of O-negative, he drank the rest of it down to the last drop.

Nick only stared at him, watching that long throat move in thick swallows.

Utterly silent.

Wondering what in the hell he was supposed to do now.

WANT MORE NICK & WYNTER?
Grab the FREE bonus epilogue!

Just click the link or the graphic below to get your FREE bonus story!

Link: http://bit.ly/VDM06-Ep

BLACK IN WHITE
Quentin Black Mystery #1

Link: http://bit.ly/BlackInWhite

"My name is Black. Quentin Black."

Gifted with an uncanny sense about people, psychologist Miri
Fox works as a profiler for the San Francisco police. When her
best friend, homicide detective Nick Tanaka, thinks he's finally
nailed the serial murderer known as the "Wedding Killer," she
agrees to check him out, using her gift to discover the truth.

But the suspect, Quentin Black, isn't anything like Miri expects.

He claims to be hunting the killer too, and the longer Miri talks
to him, the more determined she becomes to uncover his secrets.

When he confronts her about the nature of her peculiar "insight," Miri gets pulled into Black's bizarre world, and embroiled in a game of cat and mouse with a deadly killer--who might just be Black himself.

Worse, she finds herself irresistibly drawn to Black, a complication she doesn't need with a best friend who's a homicide cop and a boyfriend in intelligence.

Can Miriam see a way out or is her future covered in Black?

THE QUENTIN BLACK MYSTERY SERIES encompasses a number of dark, gritty paranormal mystery arcs with science fiction elements, starring brilliant and mysterious Quentin Black and forensic psychologist Miriam Fox. For fans of realistic paranormal mysteries with romantic elements, the series spans continents and dimensions as Black solves crimes, takes on other races and tries to keep his and Miri's true identities secret to keep them both alive.

See below for sample pages!

Or go to the link below for more information:
http://bit.ly/BlackInWhite

NEW SERIALS!

Check out my brand new serial fiction! Now available on KINDLE VELLA and on Patreon!

Check out Patreon here:
https://www.patreon.com/jcandrijeski

 Radish

Or go here for Radish + Kindle Vella:
https://www.jcandrijeski.com/serials

FREE DOWNLOAD!

Grab a copy of KIREV'S DOOR, the exciting backstory of the main character from my "Quentin Black" series, when he's still a young slave on "his" version of Earth. Plus seven other stories, many of which you can't get anywhere else!!

★★★★★

This box set is TOTALLY EXCLUSIVE to those who sign up for my VIP mailing list, "The Light Brigade!"

For your FREE COPY go to:

https://www.jcandrijeski.com/mailing-list

REVIEWS ARE AUTHOR HUGS

Hi there!
Now that you've finished reading my book,
PLEASE CONSIDER LEAVING A REVIEW!
A short review is fine and so very appreciated.
Word of mouth is truly essential for any author to succeed!

Leave a Review Here:
https://bit.ly/VDM-6

SAMPLE PAGES

BLACK IN WHITE
(QUENTIN BLACK MYSTERY #1)

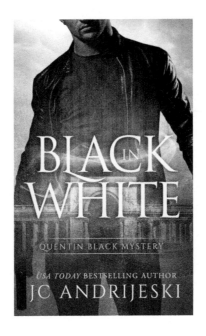

PROLOGUE
PALACE

FIFTEEN-YEAR-OLD Janine Rico was having a good night.

Scratch that.

She was having a *great* night.

An epically awesome night, by pretty much any standard.

First of all, getting alcohol was easy, for a change. She and her pals Hannah and Keeley managed to shoulder-tap some epically challenged, can-I-come-party-with-you-kids loser on their very first try, outside a seedy liquor store on Fillmore. The owner, an older Indian man, didn't care—so loser boy emerged five minutes later with one of the big bottles of peppermint schnapps and another of cheap rum. They ditched him in the park minutes later, running off with two guys from their school and laughing their asses off.

That was like, hours ago now.

The boys had gone home.

They'd been wandering the city most of the night since, determined to make the most of Keeley's mom being out of town and letting them stay in her condo in the Marina District. They'd stopped at a few parks to pass the bottles around and talk and snap pictures with their smart phones, watching the orange-tinted fog billow in odd, smoke-like exhales across the wet grass.

They'd already discussed their plans for the next day...which mostly involved sleeping in, along with ordering pizza and movies with Keeley's mom's credit card.

An epic weekend, all in all. Awesomely flawless.

Janine was tired now, though. The cold wind cut her too, even through the down jacket she wore over her hoodie sweatshirt and multicolored knit tights.

It was Keeley's idea to stop at the Palace of Fine Arts before they headed back.

"Nooooo," Janine whined, flopping her arms dramatically. "I'm ready to pass out. I'm cold. I have to pee...this is stupid!"

"Come on," Keeley cajoled. "It's totally cool! Look...it's all lit up!"

"It's lit up every night," Janine grumbled.

Hannah hooked Janine's arm, but sided with Keeley. "We can take pictures...send them to Kristi in Tahoe and make her *crazy* jealous!"

Hannah always wanted to dig at Kristi. Maybe because Kristi's family was rich, or maybe because Hannah was jealous that Kristi and Janine were best friends.

Either way, Janine couldn't fight both of them.

Her eyes shifted to the orange-lit, fifty-foot-tall, Roman-esque columns. They stood on the other side of a man-made lake covered in sleeping ducks and swans, making a disjointed crescent like ancient ruins from an old amphitheater. The fountain in the lake was turned off, so the columns reflected a near-perfect mirror on the glass surface of the water.

As they tromped over slippery grass, Janine found herself thinking it did look pretty cool, with the robe-draped stone ladies resting their arms on top of each column, showing their stone backs to the world. Broken by deep black shadows, the stone faces looked otherworldly. Willow trees hung over the lake, rustling over the water as the wind lifted their pale leaves.

"All right," she mumbled, rolling her eyes to let them know they owed her.

Hannah broke out the last of the peppermint schnapps, handing around the bottle by the neck. Shivering and pulling her down jacket tighter against the wind, Janine took a long drink, choking a bit. The warmth of the burn was welcome.

She thought about school on Monday, and telling the other kids about their night.

Hannah was right. This was *so* going to blow Kristi's mind.

Cheered at the thought, Janine grinned, taking another slug of the schnapps and shuddering when it wanted to come back up her throat.

"I think I'm done," she said, handing the bottle to Keeley and wiping her mouth.

"I soooo want to get married here!" Keeley said, after taking her own drink.

"Me too!" Hannah seconded.

The three of them wandered the asphalt path between orange-lit columns. The path led to the rotunda, but would also spit them out through the row of columns on the other side, and back to the lawn that would eventually let them off at the edge of the Marina District.

Maybe this wasn't such a bad short cut after all.

The columns looked way bigger and taller up close, like something really and truly old. Janine gawked up with her two friends, despite the dozens of times she'd walked here with her parents or during school trips or whatever.

Pulling out her smart phone, she took a few pictures, first just of the columns themselves, then of Keeley and Hannah as they posed, hanging on the base of pillars and stone urn.

"We should send these to Kristi *now!*" Hannah squealed, laughing with her arm slung around Keeley's neck. "She will be *sooo* pissed!"

"No, her mom checks her phone, like, every day," Janine warned. "She would totally bust us if she saw what time we'd sent these."

Hannah's expression sobered.

Before she could answer, they all came to an abrupt stop.

Keeley saw it first.

She smacked Janine, who came to a dead stop, right before Janine grabbed Hannah, gripping her friend's peacoat jacket in a tightly-clenched fist.

Hannah froze.

Before them, a woman wearing a white, flowing dress lay in a strangely elegant pose on the ground. Something about the way her legs and arms were positioned struck Janine as broken-looking, despite the precision...like a store mannequin that had been accidentally knocked over and lay facing the wrong direction.

The woman's legs were almost in a running or leaping pose. Her arms curved up over her head, the wrists and fingers positioned inward like a ballerina's. Her chin and face tilted up, towards the lake, as if to look between her delicately positioned hands.

Whatever caused the position, it didn't look right.

The woman's face didn't look right, either.

It belonged to a porcelain doll. Someone had slathered so much make-up on her cheeks and eyes that they appeared bruised.

Those details, however, Janine remembered only later.

In those few seconds, all she could see was the blood.

The woman's dress from waist to bust-line was soaked a dark red that looked purple in the orange light under the dome. That same splash of red covered her all the way to her thighs, past where the dress bunched up and flared out like the dress of a princess in fairytale.

It was a wedding dress.

The teenagers just stood there, all three of them breathing hard now, like they'd been running. They stared at the woman under the Palace of Fine Arts rotunda as if the sight put them in a trance. Janine found herself unable to look away.

Then she realized they weren't alone. Next to the woman in white, a man crouched, staring down at her.

Janine must have seen him there.

She must have been staring right at him, along with the woman. Even so, his form seemed to jump out at her all at once.

Her first, irrational thought was: *He must be the groom.*

Then Janine saw his hands reach for the mid-section of the woman on the ground.

He was touching her.

His face remained in shadow. Black hair hung down over his eyes. He straightened in a single, fluid motion and like the woman in white, blood streaked his skin like glistening paint, all the way past his elbows to the edges of his black T-shirt.

His face and neck wore dark and shining splotches of the same.

He turned his head, staring at the three girls.

For the first time, the angles of his face caught the light, displaying high cheekbones and a distinct lack of expression in the sunset-colored flood lamps aimed at the dome. Those almond-shaped eyes looked oddly yellow—almost gold—under that glow of the rotunda.

Janine saw those feral-looking eyes focus on Hannah, then Keeley.

Right before they aimed directly at her.

Her trance finally broke.

A loud, familiar-sounding voice let out a piercing scream. The scream echoed inside the hollow chamber of the dome, replicating there.

It occurred to Janine only later that the scream came from her.

That was *her* screaming, Janine Rico.

In the same instant, a voice rose in her mind.

This one didn't sound like her at all.

Run away, little girl, the voice whispered. *Run away now, little one, all the way home, before the big bad wolf decides to eat you, too...*

Janine didn't have to be told twice.

1 / SUSPECT

"YOU'VE GOT TO GET a load of this guy, Miriam," Nick told me that morning, leaning against the jamb of my office door and grinning. "You really do. He's a *serious* piece of work...like..." He made a motion by the side of his head with his fingers, expanding them out sharply, like his own brain just exploded. "...Total head job. Right up your alley."

I scowled.

It was seven in the morning.

I hadn't even managed to finish my first cup of coffee yet.

Inspector Naoko "Nick" Tanaka hadn't bothered with a hello first, when he showed up at the door of my inner office. He was also there an hour before reception opened, not like that ever stopped him. I knew Gomey was out there too, as in Gomez Ramirez, my so-called administrative assistant and personal pain in my ass. And yeah, I knew Nick was a pushy bastard who never knocked, never asked permission, but it still bugged me that Gomey hadn't even *tried* to stop him. He could have warned me at least.

I combed my fingers through my long black hair and sighed, looking up at Nick with what I hoped was a flat-eyed stare. I hadn't even put on make-up yet, telling myself I'd do it in the office bathroom before my first client. I could pull off the no make-up thing better than most, I knew—thanks to inheriting my mom's Native American skin tone and good bone structure and dark eyelashes—but I still felt a little naked without it. I'd left my hair down too, and for some reason, that always made me feel a bit too visibly female at work.

Truthfully, I felt unprepared to deal with anyone this early, even Nick, who I'd known forever. I hadn't donned my professional armor yet.

Nick took his weight off the doorjamb, all five-foot-eleven of him, most of it solid muscle.

He looked tired, I couldn't help noticing.

I assessed his overall mental state out of rote, more occupational hazard than because I meant to do it. Tired, and more stressed out than usual, even if he was doing his usual and hiding it under a grin and his own professional armor, that of the swaggering, b.s.-talking cop. I knew that armor was partly calculated. I also knew it worked, in that people who didn't know him constantly underestimated him.

Nick knew I saw through it of course, but he couldn't help himself.

He lingered in my doorway for a few seconds more before entering all the way.

I don't know if he'd been waiting for an invitation or just letting me get used to the fact he was there. Nick, being a homicide cop, wasn't dumb about psychology either.

Technically, that was my bailiwick, though.

I'm not a forensic psychologist by training, but somehow I ended up one—a *de facto* one at least—and most of that was Nick's fault, too. Technically I'm a clinical and research psychologist, and honestly, I tried my damnedest to stick to the research side of that as much as humanly possible.

Nick and I had history, though.

He'd even introduced me to my current boyfriend (now fiancé, I reminded myself)…Ian. Ian was another old military buddy of Nick's. They met in Iraq, though—not Afghanistan like me and Nick. I'd gone in later than Nick, being over a decade younger.

Since Ian was British and worked in intelligence, not the regular armed forces, he and I never crossed paths over there. We met after Ian moved to San Francisco over a year ago and Nick took us all out for drinks, thinking me and Ian might hit it off.

Well, that was Nick's story, anyway.

Ian told me that the drinks had been his idea. He claimed he'd pushed Nick for an introduction after seeing a picture of me on Nick's mantle in his crappy apartment in South San Francisco.

Either way, Nick and I had history.

And Nick might be a cop now, but he still thought like a guy in a firefight.

I watched Nick do his cop-walk into my personal space, wearing a rumpled black suit with a dark blue shirt underneath. Only then did I notice the splattering of stains on the front of his suit, visible under the heavier motorcycle jacket he wore over it.

I frowned, trying to identify the exact stains.

They didn't look like coffee. Even so, the more conscious part of my mind refused to acknowledge the "blood" categorization that popped into my head.

So yeah, Nick was tired, wound up, and he had blood on him.

He put his hands on his hips, which rumpled both jackets enough that I saw the handle of his Glock poke out from where he had it in a shoulder holster on his right side. I noticed he'd cut his midnight-black hair shorter than usual on the back and sides, but left it longer in front.

Even exhausted, he still looked good, did Nick Tanaka. Even at this ungodly hour.

Unfortunately, he knew it.

So did the women he burned through on a monthly or sometimes weekly basis.

Not me, though.

I'd become part of Nick's inner circle, one of his go-to people when he was working a case, like an oddly-shaped tool in his tool box that he pulled out when he found the right-sized bolt that needed unscrewing.

I'd already known something was going on at the station.

Whatever it was, it had a lot of people excited. I'd heard smatterings on my way into the office, mostly via low-voiced conversations while I stood in line for my daily dose of high-octane coffee from The Royale Blend, the gourmet coffee shop that lived in the storefront directly below my office. Since my office is located just a few blocks from the Northern District police station, I share the same coffee shop with a lot of the cops that work out of there.

Well, the cops willing to fork over four bucks for a decent cup of coffee.

Still, even though I knew something was up, I was surprised to see Nick here already.

Usually he didn't need me this early.

"Seriously," Nick said, grinning at me as he assessed me with his dark brown eyes. "I can't wait to get your diagnosis, doc." He gave his head a theatrical shake. The smile didn't entirely mask the tenser look I glimpsed underneath. "This guy… wow. You're going to get a kick out of him, Miri. Assuming you can get him to talk to you at all."

I arched an eyebrow, giving him my best clinical stare.

"You think he's mentally unfit?" I said. "On what diagnosis?"

As per usual, he totally blew past my sarcasm.

"On the diagnosis that I think he's a total nutcase," Nick said, grinning at me. He pulled a toothpick out the back row of his white teeth, a habit I'd told him more than once was disgusting. I grimaced now as he tossed the frayed piece of wood into my trash can. "…That's my expert opinion, doc. No charge. But I still want you to talk to him. If I could nail this guy without him dropping down into an insanity plea, I'd sleep better at night."

Given that I was still nursing my first cup of coffee, I wasn't sharp enough yet to get anything but annoyed at the glint of denser meaning in his dark eyes.

Then again, I've always hated cagey, hinting crap.

It even annoyed me coming from Nick.

Despite the tiredness I could see around his eyes and the blood on his shirt and suit jacket, Nick looked amped up and almost on edge, even for him. I knew Nick ran every day before work. He left his apartment like clockwork at four a.m.—unless he happened to be working, like today. He also surfed, at least on the mornings he didn't get called in, and was a member of the same martial arts club as me.

Unlike me, Nick also lifted weights, went mountain biking, played basketball.

He was one of *those* cops.

He also lived almost entirely for his job. Nick was in his early forties at least, but he'd never been married, which probably helped with the near-singular focus. He was just one of those intense, burn-the-candle-at-both-ends kind of guys.

Driven, I guess would be the non-clinical word.

I continued to cradle my coffee cup for a few seconds more, not moving in the half-broken down, leather office chair I still hadn't managed to get Gomey to either fix or declare dead and replace. Glancing around at the papers strewn across my desk and the filled-to-overflowing in-box with its beat up manila and dark green folders, I could only sigh.

My one and only office plant looked like it was screaming silently at me, possibly in its death throes since it had been so long since I'd remembered to water it.

I knew Gomey hadn't been doing that, either.

"Why?" I said finally, when all Nick did was grin at me. "What's his deal?"

"Oh, don't let me spoil it…"

"Seriously?" I said. "What are we, twelve?"

"Trust me," Nick said. "You'll want to talk to this one in

267

person, Miri. I don't want to say anything until you see him. I don't want to… bias anything."

Realizing he wasn't going to let me off the hook, and further, that he was actually *waiting* for me, expecting me to just drop everything I hadn't yet started for the day and follow him to whatever piss-smelling interrogation room where they were holding this clown, I sighed again.

"You can't give me a few minutes?" I said.

"No."

"I have an appointment coming in at nine, Nick."

Frowning, Nick looked at his watch, as if a ticking bomb were counting down somewhere in another part of the building.

"Any chance you could cancel it?" he said apologetically, shifting his feet. "We're pretty sure he's the guy on the thing last week. That mess at Grace Cathedral."

I glanced up sharper at that.

He meant the wedding guy.

Once more glimpsing the more serious look behind the humor in Nick's eyes, I nodded my defeat and rose to standing from behind the broken chair.

Sadly, I guess there's a reason Nick counts on me.

I'm a sucker.

There wasn't a lot of pre-work on this one.

Well, not yet.

No one wanted to debrief me on much in the way of details, presumably because Nick told them not to. So I didn't get handed the usual cobbled-together file of scribbled notes and photos and whatever else from the preliminary interrogations, or much in the way of details of what they'd found at the actual scene.

Nick gave me the bare bones story only.

Three fifteen-year-old girls stumbled upon the suspect at the scene of the crime. According to them, he'd been covered in blood. He also looked like he'd just finished—or maybe remained deep in the process of—doing "something" to a woman's dead body. Their testimony was pretty vague on details, according to Nick.

He admitted to me that he couldn't really get a sense if they'd seen *anything* concrete, apart from the suspect himself... as well as the victim, a white dress, a lot of make-up and a lot of blood... all of which were damning enough, under the circumstances.

Well, that and what had been done to the victim herself.

I only got the bare bones on that, too, and didn't ask for more. Truthfully, I've never gotten used to seeing that kind of thing, not even in pictures.

The three girls ran like hell once the suspect spotted them.

Even so, more than an hour passed before they called in what they'd seen, although they freely admitted they all had smart phones with them at the time. The latter had been confirmed by the presence of photos they'd taken on the walkway leading up to the Palace before they reached the dome where the body had been displayed.

From what Nick told me, the delay on calling had more to do with the girls' fears of getting caught by their parents than fear of the suspect himself, who hadn't bothered to chase them. Something about being out all night and drunk while crashing at the home of an out-of-town parent. Nick said they admitted to arguing amongst themselves about what to do after they arrived back at a Marina residence.

They finally called it in around five o'clock.

A black and white had already picked up the suspect by then, as it turned out.

They saw him crossing Marina Boulevard towards the promenade, presumably to reach the coast. Bad luck on his part, Nick said with a wry grin. He figured the guy had been heading for the yacht harbor north of the Palace of Fine Arts, either to hop a boat or to wash off the blood, or maybe both. If he'd succeeded in either, they might never have got him.

As it was, they pulled guns on him to get him to comply.

From what I could tell, they pretty much lifted this guy off the street and parked him in an interrogation room while they called the coroner and forensics to the scene of the murder. I knew someone must have talked to him, and likely cleaned him up—probably Nick and whatever officer arrived first on the scene.

But they couldn't have gone through the whole range of the usual song and dance, either.

Which meant Nick was bending the rules a little, bringing me in now.

I knew Nick had a tendency to pull me in when he had a gut feeling, so I figured that must be the case with this guy, too. Despite the overwhelming evidence, at least in terms of the Palace of Fine Arts murder, Nick probably wanted me to help him crawl into the guy's head, maybe so he could get a sense of his connection to the Grace Cathedral killings, or maybe to build evidence against an insanity plea, like he said.

Maybe he liked him for other, possibly-related crimes.

They'd do the DNA testing thing and everything else, of course, but Nick tended to be thorough. He probably wanted me to confirm or deny his working profile on the guy before he started running up blind alleys.

I peered through the one-way glass of the interrogation room, sipping my now lukewarm coffee and trying to assess the scene before me objectively.

"So you like this guy for the Grace Cathedral murders?" I said, as much to myself as Nick, who stood right at my arm.

"I like this guy for Jimmy Hoffa," Nick said, glancing at his partner, Glen Frakes, who snorted from the other side of him. "I like him for the Zodiac killings… and the death of my Aunt Lanai in Tokyo, God rest her soul."

Rolling my eyes, I nodded, getting the gist.

I continued to look through the one-way glass, trying to get a sense of what I might be in for when I went in there.

The guy just sat there, not moving.

I don't think I'd ever seen anyone sit so still in an interrogation room before. His eyes didn't dart to either the door or the cameras, which just about everyone looked at, seemingly without being able to help themselves.

No one liked being watched.

No one liked being trapped inside a featureless room, either.

This guy wasn't trying to be clever, either, staring at us through the one-way glass, which a lot of them did to show us they *knew* they were being watched.

Nick's suspect didn't seem to care.

I got nothing. A blank wall.

That didn't happen to me very often, truthfully.

Maybe thirty, thirty-five years old.

Muscular. Obviously in good shape, but not bulky like Nick with his weight-lifting and kung fu and judo and whatever else. This guy had the lean musculature of a runner or a fighter, not an ounce of excess flesh on him anywhere. I'd seen criminals and even addicts with that kind of body type of course, but I wasn't getting any of the other signs of career criminal or addiction or living on the street on Nick's new favorite perp.

His eyes were clear, as was his skin, which was on the tanned side, but still light enough to be ethnically ambiguous. He looked healthy. He was handsome, actually, if in a feral kind of way. He had black hair, high cheekbones, a well-formed mouth, and some of the lightest, strangest-colored eyes I'd ever seen… so light they looked gold, and strangely flecked.

Those eyes reminded me of a tiger. Or maybe a mountain lion. Or maybe an *actual* lion… although I couldn't remember what color eyes either of those had in real life.

Even those oddly riveting eyes weren't the most noticeable thing about Nick's new friend. Not at that precise moment, anyway.

No, the most noticeable thing about him *now* was that he was covered in blood.

Unlike with Nick, I couldn't even pretend to not know what it was.

A good portion of his visible bare skin wore a mostly-dry layer of reddish-brown smears and spots. It covered his hands and arms from his fingertips up to his rock-hard biceps, just below the cuffs of the stretchy black T-shirt he wore, which also accentuated the size of his chest. More smears and splatters of the same covered his neck and one side of his face. I could see it on the rings he wore, where his wrists were cuffed together and resting on the metal table.

I also saw blood smearing the face of his military-style watch.

I wasn't an expert of course, but even if Nick hadn't already told me how they'd found him on the street, I would have known just by looking at him. It was definitely blood.

He'd practically been bathing in it, this guy.

It explained how Nick came to have it on his own shirt, too.

The suspect's clothes, which included that form-fitting black T-shirt, black pants and black leather shoes, the last of which I could just see under the table, absorbed most of the color and texture of what decorated his bare skin. I'd already been assured by Nick and Glen that blood covered a good portion of his clothes, too, visible or not.

I was kind of surprised they hadn't stripped him yet, to pull evidence.

They'd even left his shoes, rings and watch, which was unusual when they had a suspect cuffed like this and chained to the floor.

As if he'd read my mind, Nick said, "We've got forensics coming up here in an hour. They're at the scene now. We thought we'd give you a look first… while we wait."

I gave Nick a skeptical stare.

That time, he had the grace to blush.

"Okay," he said, holding up his hands in a gesture of surrender. "*I* wanted you to look at him, Miriam. He won't talk to us. I thought you might be able to give me some suggestions. Before we go all Guantanamo on his ass."

Frowning, I pursed my lips.

Then I looked back at Nick's blood-covered suspect.

That time, I tried to push aside the emotional impact of the blood and assess the man himself. I still couldn't get anything off him in the usual way. Even so, his war-paint aside, he had something about him, this guy. I couldn't put my finger on what it was, not in those first few seconds, but I found it difficult to look away from his face. He looked surprisingly calm, and those odd-colored eyes shone with intelligence.

If anything, he looked alert.

Not quite waiting, but expectant... even as he seemed to be using the time in some more complex mental exercise I couldn't see. That sharpness he wore had a calculating quality, as if he were otherwise occupied in some further reach of his mind.

I also distinctly got military.

Only after I'd been looking at him for a few seconds more did I realize that the alertness told me more about his demeanor than the calm he wore over it. Something about that calm of his was deceptive, in fact. Behind it, he looked high-strung.

Like, *really* high-strung.

Like he was remaining where he sat through sheer force of will.

I reassessed my "not a drug addict" summation briefly, but then went back to my original conclusion a few seconds later. What I was seeing didn't come from drugs. He looked like he wanted to be elsewhere, without looking the slightest bit afraid, or nervous, or even angry. He didn't look smug, either, like most psychopaths I'd seen.

Instead, he seemed to view his being here as a colossal waste of his time.

Once I'd seen that, I couldn't un-see it. Further, it occurred to me that he didn't even seem to be hiding his impatience particularly well.

I might have noticed it before if I hadn't been trying so hard to read him in other ways.

"What's his name?" I said.

Again, Nick and Glen exchanged a look.

"What?" I said. "What's the joke now?"

"If you can get a name out of that guy, I'll buy you dinner," Nick said. Grinning, he gave me a teasing once-over. "Of course, I'd do that for free, doc. Just name the day."

Glen snorted again, folding his thick arms over his chest.

Raising my left hand to Nick in what had recently become a running joke with us, I tapped my engagement ring with my thumb.

Nick grinned, feigning disappointment, then motioned with his head towards the man sitting in the other room. My eyes followed his stare back to the guy with the flecked, gold-colored eyes, even as Nick's voice grew more openly cop-like.

"He won't give us a name. No ID on him. His prints aren't in the system."

"Mystery guy, huh?" I said.

I said it casually, even with a lilt of humor. Still, I was puzzled. Television aside, that almost never happened, not anymore.

You couldn't get anywhere anymore without some kind of ID.

"We're running facial rec on him now," Nick said, almost like he heard me. "We'll give him to Interpol if we don't find him here. He's got to have at least an alias… somewhere."

"No military record?" I said.

"Nothing on the books."

I nodded, only half-hearing him as I frowned at the suspect.

Nothing. He really was a blank wall.

That was pretty rare for me, like I said.

Not unheard of, but yeah… rare.

"What makes you think he'll talk to *me?*" I said finally, looking back at Nick.

Nick just smiled, shifting his weight on his feet.

"He probably won't," Glen volunteered from Nick's other side.

"But Nicky here seems to think you walk on water, doc, so he wanted to give it a shot."

Shrugging, even as I gave Nick an annoyed look, I tossed my paper cup of coffee in the plastic-lined bin under the desk and made a somewhat overdone motion towards the other room.

"Well?" I said. "We might as well kill time until forensics shows up, right? I canceled my morning's slate for this dog and pony show."

I added that last part with more bite, giving Nick a harder stare.

Grinning at me, Glen, who was a good five inches taller than Nick and built like a linebacker, or maybe some kind of throwback to his Viking roots, nodded. Motioning for me to follow, he aimed his feet for the door so he could let me inside the interrogation room.

As I walked past him, though, Nick caught hold of my upper arm.

"Don't fool around with this guy," he warned.

The smile vanished from Nick's face, leaving my friend, the guy I knew behind his schtick.

I remembered that look from Afghanistan, too.

"...I mean it, Miri. He's probably a serial killer. At the very least, he likes dead bodies a little too much. We'll be right outside that door. If you want out, get out. Right away. Don't play tough for the cop crowd. Hear me?"

Normally I would have chewed him out for the whole damsel-needing-protection crap, which I thought we were well past, given everything we'd been through together. Normally I also would have thrown in a few cutting reminders about just how many murderers, rapists, child molesters and other pillars of society I'd interviewed for him already.

Something about the way he said it diffused my anger though.

"I hear you," I said, giving him a mock salute.

As I did, I glanced at the guy on the other side of the one-way glass.

The suspect just sat there, a faint frown touching the edges of his dark lips.

For the first time however, he was staring at the one-way mirror.

It looked like he was staring directly at me.

Seeing the speckle of blood to the right of where that sharp mouth ended, I felt my pulse rise, in spite of myself.

Nick might just be right about this guy.

He usually was.

Pushing the thought out of my mind, I looked away from the glass, following Glen out into the corridor. As I did, I let my face slide into a blank, professional mask and hoped that this time it would protect me.

2 / FIRST INTERVIEW

HE LOOKED ME OVER when I walked in.

Unlike a lot of people I'd interviewed in this room, suspects and witnesses alike, he didn't hide his appraisal. He also didn't do anything to try and get me on his side—like smile, or make his body language more accommodating or submissive.

He didn't try to intimidate me either, at least not that I noticed.

Again, the predominant emotion I saw in his assessment remained impatience.

He seemed, more than anything, to assume I was here to waste his time, too.

At the same time, I got the sense there was more there—more in relation to me specifically, I mean. Nothing sexual, at least I didn't think so.

What that "more" was exactly, I had absolutely no theories at that point.

Maybe I simply wasn't what—or who—he'd expected.

Maybe my appearance threw him.

I'm used to that, to a degree. I'm tall for a woman, almost five-nine.

My mom was Native American, like I said, and from one of

the plains tribes that actually had some real height on them. I'm not sure what our dad was, since I'd been young when our parents died and hadn't stayed in touch with any of his family, but he was tall too. I'd gotten hints of his bone structure, along with my mom's. I also got his light-hazel eyes, which people tell me are striking on me but were positively *riveting* on my father.

My mom joked once she could have fallen in love with my father from his eyes alone.

The rest of me was my mother, according to my aunts. Straight black hair, full mouth, my sense of humor, even my curves, which were slightly less curvy from the martial arts classes, but not fully absent either.

In other words, even under all of my professional armor, I'm definitely female.

I can't exactly hide it, even in suits and with my hair tied tightly back.

For my part, I didn't bother to smile at him either, or do any of the usual heavy-handed shrink things to try and convince him I was "on his side" or even particularly friendly towards him. Right off, I got the feeling that those kinds of tactics wouldn't work on this guy.

He would see right through them.

Worse, trying it would probably cause him to dismiss me, too.

So yeah, I approached him assuming he was a psychopath.

Of course, the technical term these days, at least according to the latest Diagnostic and Statistical Manual of Mental Disorders, (or "DSM" as we shrink-types called it) is "Anti-Social Personality Disorder" or ASPD. Those of us who work in forensic psych know a lot of the specific signs that go with this diagnosis—as well as ways to pick out the truly dangerous ones—but generally, there's a longer sussing-out period involved.

The most dangerous types were harder to spot.

Often highly intelligent, deeply manipulative, glibly charming, uninterested in other people and totally unwilling to acknowledge the individual rights of anyone apart from themselves, the more dangerous individuals with anti-social personality disorder were masters at evading detection by psychs who couldn't see past the veneer.

Narcissistic bordering on grandiose. Inflated sense of their own entitlement. Zero compunction about manipulating others. Generally lacking the capacity for love. Generally lacking the ability to feel shame or remorse. They either experienced only shallow emotions or feigned emotion altogether. They had a constant need for stimulation…

Well, you get the idea.

Truthfully, I doubted this guy would talk to me any more than he would talk to the cops.

Well, unless he decided I could help him in some way, or perhaps entertain him… since "short attention span" was often a big issue for the average psychopath. Or perhaps he would treat me differently because he wanted a female audience instead of a male one; I was reasonably certain that only male cops had been tried on him so far.

Either way, I strongly suspected I wouldn't win him over by trying to play him for a fool, at least not right out of the gate.

I seated myself in the metal folding chair across the table from him.

I did my own quick once-over of the room, even though I'd been in here a few dozen times already—reminding myself of the location of the cameras, looking at the four corners out of habit. My eyes glanced down to where the suspect's ankles had been cuffed, not only to one another but to metal rings in the floor. His wrist cuffs were also chained to his waist, as well as to those same rings in the floor.

Glen already assured me that the range of the chains wouldn't allow him to reach me as long as I stayed in the chair.

Still, he'd warned me not to get any closer.

I didn't need to be told twice. The guy looked a lot bigger from in here.

He also looked significantly more muscular.

Leaning back in the hard, metal seat, I watched those gold, cat-like eyes flicker over me. They didn't pause anywhere for long, much less conduct one of those lecherous, lingering appraisals some convicts did in an attempt to unsettle me.

I sensed a methodicalness to his stare, instead.

That unnerved me a little, truthfully, maybe because it surprised me.

Even for a psychopath, that kind of focus was rare. Usually other people just weren't that interesting to them.

Then again, captivity may have changed that for him, too.

My eyes took in his appearance for the second time that day, lingering on the strangely high cheekbones still colored with smears of dried blood. I saw flakes of that blood on the surface of the table too, from where it had been rubbed off by his metal cuffs.

Wincing, I glanced up to find him staring at me once more, his gold eyes bordering on thoughtful as they took in my face.

When he didn't break the silence after a few seconds more, I leaned back more deliberately, crossing my legs in the dark-blue pantsuit I wore.

"So," I said, sighing. "You don't want to talk to anyone."

I didn't bother to state it as a question.

The man's eyes flickered back to my face, specifically to my eyes.

After a pause, I saw a faint smile tease the edges of his lips.

"I doubt my words would be very convincing," he said.

I must have jumped a little in my chair, but he pretended not to notice.

"...Covered in blood," he continued, motioning with one cuffed hand, likely as much as he could, given the restraints. Still, something in the odd grace of the gesture struck me, causing me to follow it with my eyes. "...Picked up near the scene of the crime. And you have witnesses, too, I suspect? Or did those three little girls decide it wasn't worth getting in trouble with their parents by calling the police in the wee hours of dawn?"

His words surprised me.

More, the longer he spoke.

Not only because he said them, but because they came out with a clipped, sharp accuracy and cadence. They wore the barest trace of an accent too, although it was one I couldn't identify. His manner of speech certainly implied a greater than average amount of education.

"In any case," the man said, leaning back so that the chains clanked at his ankles and on the table. "...I imagine I lack credibility, wouldn't you say, doc?"

I heard murmurings of surprise through my earpiece, too.

Apparently, I'd already gotten more out of him than any of them had.

I smoothed my expression without trying to hide my own surprise. Instead, I watched him openly, letting him see me do it.

"Doc," I said.

At his widening smile, I returned it, adding a touch of wry humor and raising an eyebrow.

"You think I am a doctor?"

"Aren't you?" he said at once. "Military, too, I suspect. Once upon a time. I saw you checking the corners. You've carried a gun... haven't you, doc? Maybe you even carry one now." He glanced around him ruefully. "Not in here, of course."

I shifted in my chair, not answering him.

"Aren't you a doctor?" he prompted.

"Depends on who you ask," I said drily, sighing a little.

Without taking my eyes off his, I leaned to the side somewhat, resting my arm on the back of the folding chair.

"Psychiatrist then," he said, adjusting his posture as well, a perhaps intentional replication of the old psychology trick of imitating the poses of those you want to confide in you. "Or psychologist... only a real one, with a PhD. So perhaps it was a criminal psych ward where you honed your paranoia, not the military. You could be a social worker too, I suppose... although I have my doubts. You have too much of a clinical air about you, not enough of that needy, do-gooder type of saccharin that the softer arts tend to attract." His smile sharpened. "I would say dentist, but under the circumstances…"

Again that eloquent gesture of his fingers, this time indicating the room.

"…I am thinking that is not likely."

"I'm a psychologist," I told him easily. "Right in one."

"So you are here to assess me, then?" he said. "Or are they hoping the presence of an attractive female would send me frothing and panting? Get me to show my true colors? Shall I start screaming 'Die Bitch!' to satisfy those watching through the glass?"

I smiled again, unintentionally that time.

"If you want," I told him, muting the smile. "Do you want me to die?"

"Not particularly," he said.

"Really? Why not?" I said.

"I think you're the first person I've seen here with an IQ above that of a balding ape. Although that one inspector… he's got a *bit* of that base, instinctive kind of intellect. Only a bit, mind you. You know who I mean. Joe Handsome."

"It's Nick, actually," I said, smiling in spite of myself.

"Ah, he's a friend of yours, then?"

"Not a special friend, if that's what you mean."

"I didn't, but it's interesting information to have. Clearly the topic has come up between you, or you wouldn't have bothered to qualify it."

I shook my head, unimpressed with this last, and letting him see that, too.

"Really?" I said. "You're going there?"

"Going where?"

"Discredit the female by making some disparaging reference to her sexuality? Dismiss her as an equal by highlighting her value or lack thereof as a sexual object?"

"I profoundly apologize," he said, giving me a startled look.

The surprise I could see in those almond eyes may have been mocking me, but it looked genuine. "My comments certainly weren't meant to be disparaging. I have no intention of resorting to such cheap tricks, doctor, simply to feel I've 'outwitted' you. Sadly, my ego won't permit it."

Pausing, he added, "Would it help you to know I get sex on a regular basis too? I don't know that it would demean me in your eyes or if it would come off as bragging... in any case, I did not bring up your own sexuality as anything other than a personal curiosity."

I tilted my head, still smiling, but letting my puzzlement show.

"Why are you talking to me at all?" I asked finally.

"Why shouldn't I talk to you?" he said. "I've already told you that you're the first person to walk in here that I thought might be worth my attempting to communicate."

"Because I'm female?" I said.

"Because you seem to be less of a fool than the rest of them," he corrected me at once.

"But you said Nick had a mind?"

"I said he had a mind *of sorts.* Not the same thing at all. Although, given the nature of his intellect, he has undoubtedly chosen the right profession for himself."

I smiled again. "I'm sure that will be quite a relief for him."

I heard laughter in the earpiece that time, right before Nick spoke up.

"See if he'll tell you his name," he said to me.

"Certainly, if you really want to know," the suspect said, before I could voice the question aloud. "My name is Black. Quentin Black. Middle initial, R."

I stared at him, still recovering from the fact that he'd seemingly heard Nick give me an instruction through the earpiece.

Clearly, he wanted me to know he'd heard it, too.

"You heard that?" I said to him.

"Good ear, yes?" he said. Smiling, he gave me a more cryptic, yet borderline predatory look. "Less good with you, however. Significantly less good."

He paused, studying my face with eyes full of meaning.

I almost got the sense he was waiting for me to reply—or maybe just to react.

When I didn't, he leaned back in the chair, making another of those graceful, flowing gestures with his hand.

"I find that... fascinating, doc. Quite intriguing. Perhaps that is crossing a boundary with you again, however? To mention that?"

I paused on his words, then decided to dismiss them.

"Is that a real name?" I said. "Quentin Black. That doesn't sound real. It sounds fake."

"Real is all subjective, is it not?"

"So it's *not* real, then?"

"Depends on what you mean."

"Is it your *legal* name?"

"Again, depends on what you mean."

"I mean, could you look it up in a database and actually get a hit somewhere?"

"How would I know that?" he said, making an innocent gesture with his hands, again within the limits of the metal cuffs.

Realizing I wasn't going to get any more from him on that line of questioning, I changed direction. "What does the 'R' stand for?" I said.

"Rayne."

"Quentin Rayne Black?" I repeated back to him, still not hiding my disbelief.

"Would you believe me if I said my parents had a sense of whimsy?" he asked me.

"No," I said.

"Would you believe that I do, then?"

I snorted a laugh, in spite of myself. I heard it echoed through the earpiece, although I heard a few curses coming from that direction, too.

I shook my head at the suspect himself, but less in a "no" that time.

"Yes," I conceded finally. "So it *is* a made-up name, then?"

The man calling himself Quentin Black only returned my smile. His eyes once again looked shrewd, less thoughtful and more openly calculating.

Even so, his weird comment about "listening" came back to me.

Truthfully, he was looking at me as if he were listening very hard.

The thought made me slightly nervous.

Especially since I'd been doing the same to him from inside the observation booth.

Seeing the intelligence there, I found myself regrouping mentally as the silence stretched, reminding myself who and what I was dealing with. The fact that he'd nearly made me forget that in our back and forth of the last few moments was unnerving on its own.

I found myself looking him over deliberately, for the second time since I'd left the glass-enclosed booth behind the one-way mirror. I fought to reconcile his physical presence with the words I'd heard come out of that well-formed mouth. The two things, his physicality and his manner of speaking, didn't really fit at all, at least not from my previous experience in these kinds of interviews.

The all-black clothing, the dense, rock-like muscles I could see under that blood-soaked shirt, the expensive leather shoes, the expensive watch, the ethnically-ambiguous but somehow feral-looking face... nothing about him really fit, from his made-up name to his wryly humorous quipping with me.

I found myself staring at that strange, somehow *animal*-evoking face with its abnormally high cheekbones and almond eyes, and wondered who in the hell this guy really was.

"Where are you from, Quentin?" I asked, voicing at least part of my puzzlement.

He shook his head though, that smile back to playing with the edges of his lips.

"You don't want to tell me that?" I said.

"No," he said. "...Clearly, I don't."

"What do you do for a living?" I said, trying again. "Do you have a job of some kind, Quentin? Some area of expertise you'd like to share?"

That time, he rolled his eyes openly.

Before I could respond to his obvious disdain, he let out an audible and impatient sigh.

"You're not going to resort to shrink games on *me* now, are you, doc?" he said, giving me another of those more penetrating stares. "...Not so soon in our new friendship? I haven't intimidated you already, have I?" At my silence, his voice grew bored. "The constant repetition of my given name. The clinical yet polite peppering of questions in an attempt to quietly undermine my sense of autonomy here..."

"Fine." I held up both of my palms in a gesture of surrender. "What do you want to talk about, Mr. Black? Do you want to tell me what you were doing at the Palace of Fine Arts earlier this morning?"

"Not here," he said cryptically, smiling at me again.

I frowned, glancing around the gunmetal gray room.

"Somewhere else, then?" I said.

"Yes," he said. "For all of your questions, doc. Including the ones I wouldn't answer before."

I gave him another puzzled smile. "I hate to tell you, Mr. Black, but you're not likely to be anyplace that is significantly different from this room anytime soon. Not in terms of a non-institutional setting... if that's what you're driving at."

"It must certainly appear that way to you, yes," he said, raising his chained wrists for emphasis and glancing around the room with those gold eyes. "...But perhaps you are mistaken in that, doc. Perhaps you'll find that we can speak in a much more

286

comfortable setting, just the two of us… and in not too long a time."

I narrowed my gaze at him.

It didn't sound like a threat, at least not coming from him. But the words themselves could definitely have been construed as one.

I gave him a wry smile. "You think so, huh?"

I do, a voice said clearly in my mind. *I do think so, doc.*

I jumped, violently.

Truthfully, I almost lost my balance in the chair.

"Miri?" Nick asked in my ear. *"Miri? Are you okay?"*

For a long-feeling few seconds I only stared at Black, breathing harder.

I could feel as much as see him watching me react. He smiled, lifting the bare corners of that sculpted mouth. Then he shrugged, his expression smoothing.

"Perhaps you'll accept a raincheck on that particular discussion, doc?" he said. "…After I've finished my business here?"

It unnerved me, hearing him use the nickname yet again. I knew it wasn't exactly an original thing to call someone in my line of work, but it still struck me as deliberate.

I fought the other thing out of my mind, sure I must have imagined it.

Even so, the smile on my face grew strained.

"Okay," I said. "You pick the topic, then. For today I mean… pre-raincheck."

Quentin Black smiled, leaning back deliberately in the bolted, metal chair.

"No," he said, after assessing me again with those strangely animal eyes. "No, I think we're done for now, doc. It was my *very* great pleasure to meet you, however."

I pursed my lips. "You don't want to talk to me anymore?" I said.

I want to talk to you so badly I can fucking taste it, that same voice said in my mind, making me jump again, but less violently that time. My breath stopped, locking in my chest as the voice rose even more clearly. *But not here, doc. Not here. Patience. And believe me when I say I am speaking to myself in this, even more than I am to you...*

I could only sit there, breathing, staring at him.

Those gold eyes never wavered.

When I didn't move after a few more seconds, or speak, he smiled.

Do they know what you are, doc? Does that handsome cop in the next room have any idea why it is that you are so very, very good at your job? Or how you managed to keep him alive that time in Afghanistan...?

My chest clenched more.

It hurt now, like a fist had reached inside me, squeezing my heart.

The voice fell silent.

The man in front of me looked at me, his expression close to expectant. Then he gazed pointedly down at my engagement ring.

Does anyone know about you, doc? Anyone at all?

My throat closed as he raised his eyes back to mine.

Those gold flecked irises studied my face, watching my reaction.

I can't hear you, the voice said next, flickering with a tinge of frustration. *I cannot hear you at all... but I know from your face that you hear me, doc. That shield of yours is damned strong. I confess, it's positively turning me on at this point. It also makes me very curious. Were you ever ranked, sister? If so, I would love to know at what level...*

Another smile ghosted his lips, even as a curl of heat slid through my lower abdomen, one that didn't feel like it originated from me, at least not entirely.

It made my face flush hot, even as my thighs clenched together in reflex.

I'll show you mine, if you show me yours... the voice said, softer.

My throat tightened, choking me with a caught swallow.

Still, he didn't say anything aloud.

We'll talk more later, doc, I heard in my mind, softer still. *I have so many, many questions. So many things I'd like to discuss. But I really do not wish to do any of that here. Not with them watching us. They are wondering at this silence as it is. You must try to speak to me again, doc, before your handsome cop decides there is a problem. Before he and his meat-headed partner make an issue of it...*

I blinked again, my heart now slamming against my ribs.

But he wasn't looking at me now.

As I watched, Quentin Rayne Black lapsed back into the bored, stone-faced man I'd glimpsed through the window before I'd entered the room.

I'd finally managed to clear my throat.

Clenching my hands together in my lap, conscious of how clammy they felt, I kept my voice carefully polite.

"Do you want to tell me about the body in the park, Mr. Black?" I said.

Nothing. Silence.

"Mr. Black?" I said, hearing the slight tremble in my voice. "Did you kill that woman? Did you pose her in that wedding dress?"

He didn't look up from where he stared down between his cuffed hands.

I tried again, asking the same thing a few different ways.

But nothing I said in those next fifteen or so minutes appeared to reach him. I tried being friendly, annoying, disdainful, mocking. I belittled his intellect... even threw out a few offers to deal, along with some not-so-veiled threats. Nothing.

I got nothing.

In fact, I doubt I penetrated the veneer of that thoughtful, somehow puzzle-solving stare he aimed at the empty surface of the metal table.

Clearly, I'd been dismissed.

WANT TO READ MORE?
Continue the rest of the novel by following the link below*:*
BLACK IN WHITE
(Quentin Black Mystery #1)

Link: http://bit.ly/BlackInWhite

BOOKS IN THE VAMPIRE DETECTIVE MIDNIGHT SERIES
(RECOMMENDED READING ORDER)

VAMPIRE DETECTIVE MIDNIGHT (Book #1)
EYES OF ICE (Book #2)
THE PRESCIENT (Book #3)
FANG & METAL (Book #4)
THE WHITE DEATH (Book #5)
A VAMPIRE'S CURSE (Book #6)

BOOKS IN THE QUENTIN BLACK MYSTERY SERIES
(RECOMMENDED READING ORDER)

BLACK IN WHITE (Book #1)
Kirev's Door (Book #0.5)
BLACK AS NIGHT (Book #2)
Black Christmas (Book #2.5)
BLACK ON BLACK (Book #3)
Black Supper (Book #3.5)
BLACK IS BACK (Book #4)
BLACK AND BLUE (Book #5)
Black Blood (Book #5.5)
BLACK OF MOOD (Book #6)
BLACK TO DUST (Book #7)
IN BLACK WE TRUST (Book #8)
BLACK THE SUN (Book #9)
TO BLACK WITH LOVE (Book #10)
BLACK DREAMS (Book #11)
BLACK OF HEARTS (Book #12)
BLACK HAWAII (Book #13)
BLACK OF WING (Book #14)
BLACK IS MAGIC (Book #15)

BLACK CURTAIN (Book #16)

Books in the Light & Shadow Series - COMPLETE
(Recommended Reading Order)

LIGHTBRINGER (Book #1)
WHITE DRAGON (Book #2)
DARK GODS (Book #3)
LORD OF LIGHT (Book #4)

Books in the Gods on Earth Series - COMPLETE
(Recommended Reading Order)

THOR (Book #1)
LOKI (Book #2)
TYR (Book #3)

Books in the Alien Apocalypse Series - COMPLETE
(Recommended Reading Order)

THE CULLING (Part I)
THE ROYALS (Part II)
THE NEW ORDER (Part III)
THE REBELLION (Part IV)
THE RINGS FIGHTER

THANK YOU NOTE

I just wanted to take a moment here to thank some of my amazing readers and supporters. Huge appreciation, long distance hugs and light-filled thanks to the following people:

Shannon Tusler
Robert Tusler
Sarah Hall
Elizabeth Meadows
Rebekkah Brainerd
77Daisy

I can't tell you how much I appreciate you!

JC Andrijeski is a *USA Today* and *Wall Street Journal* bestselling author of urban fantasy, paranormal romance, mysteries, and apocalyptic science fiction, often with a sexy and metaphysical bent.

JC has a background in journalism, history and politics, and has a tendency to traipse around the globe, eat odd foods, and read whatever she can get her hands on. She grew up in the Bay Area of California, but has lived abroad in Europe, Australia and Asia, and from coast to coast in the continental United States.

She currently lives and writes full time in Los Angeles.

For more information, go to: https://jcandrijeski.com

facebook.com/JCAndrijeski
twitter.com/jcandrijeski
instagram.com/jcandrijeski
bookbub.com/authors/jc-andrijeski
amazon.com/JC-Andrijeski/e/B004MFTAP0

Printed in Great Britain
by Amazon